OUTAGE

Also by Tony Frank

THE LESSER OF EVILS
THE ALTAI

Prologue

The plan's simplicity drove its success. The joint CIA/Mossad team, skeletal by the exigencies of operational secrecy, had initially favored the tried and tested human approach, the use of a mole to deliver the worm via thumb drive. The method had proven spectacularly successful in Operation Babylon in 1981, when a Mossad operative had surreptitiously deployed the homing beacon that enabled Israeli F-16s to so efficiently decimate Iraq's Osirak nuclear reactor. Only 2009 was not 1981, and Iran wasn't Iraq. Indeed, Iran had learned from Operation Babylon critical lessons about securing its nuclear facilities, and not just from aerial attack. The intelligence the Mossad garnered about security protocols at Iran's facilities suggested they were practically impenetrable by spies, with the likelihood unacceptably low that an attempt would result in anything other than the body of a colleague dangling from gallows in a public square in Tehran. But the intelligence also uncovered Iran's secret procurement of embargoed industrial automation and control equipment from Siemens AG, Europe's largest engineering company, headquartered, serendipitously, in Germany. So by way of necessary innovation, the spies infiltrated the supply chain.

By the time Siemens computers were shipped to Iran and put into service in the country's nuclear program, they had already been infected with the virus that came to be widely known as Stuxnet. Brilliantly engineered, it was the cyber equivalent of an expert marksman sniper. By targeting the Siemens Step7 software used to reprogram PLCs, programmable logic controllers that controlled the uranium-enrichment centrifuges, Stuxnet could make centrifuges spin so fast they tore themselves apart while simultaneously sending false signals to the Iranian technicians monitoring the process that all was hunky-dory. The Iranians eventually caught on, but not before one fifth of their centrifuges had been destroyed, setting their program back a few years and denting their morale. But the intersection of dignity and humiliation can breed an irrepressible desire for revenge, so even though in the end it was the relatively simple approach of supply chain infiltration that trumped the Iranians, it wasn't really the end. In fact, it was just the beginning

Chapter One

Friday, April 10th, 2015 brought Northern Virginia weather that could not have been better suited for a round of golf. The sun gleamed in a resplendent sky, tempering the mid-morning chill. An absolute stillness dominated the air, allowing onboard computers controlling airplanes landing at Washington Dulles Airport to forgo any compensation for crosswind. It was one of those airplanes, a United Airlines Boeing 777 two miles north of where its wheels would smoke at touchdown, that caused Nick Lorimer to kill his backswing, step back and wait for the deafening roar to pass. As the din of the engines faded, Lorimer retook his practice swings and shuffled back into position at the third tee. He aligned his driver with the ball and swung the club back over his body, only to abort again, this time distracted by another, less familiar sound. A peculiar buzzing came from the trees lining the fairway, as if a large swarm of bees had taken flight. He and his brother jerked their heads to the left in unison.

"What the fuck is that?" Lorimer murmured.

His brother adjusted his visor against the sun's glare. "Sounds like—"

A drone appeared above the trees, its presence as mesmerizing as it was intrusive.

"This is ridiculous! We don't need drones flying around—"

"Wait—what's that below it?"

The sun glinted off a long, thin steel rod suspended vertically below the drone as it approached the overhead power lines that ran parallel to the fairway.

"Watch out for those—"

The brothers watched in stunned disbelief as the rod spanned the power lines, erupting with a dazzling power flash that sprayed showers of arcs and sparks. Within seconds it was over, the stillness now starker than before.

They were in two minds, stay on the tee or run across to see what had become of the drone, which had seemingly vaporized, when a figure suddenly emerged from behind the trees, a slender man sporting a goatee, wearing a green GMU hoodie sweater and denim jeans rooted in black sneakers. Tufts of curly black hair were slicked back behind his ears, held in place by a baseball cap. A pair of reflective-lens Ray-Ban Aviators concealed his eyes. Cradling a remote controller attached to a lanyard looped around his neck, he resembled a sinister sicario caressing a detonator.

"Hey!" Nick Lorimer shouted.

The man took off his sunglasses and stared at the golfers. He held his ground, seemingly unmoved by the fact they had seen him. When they took their first steps toward him he bolted away across the grass to the road on the other side of the trees. They gave chase, but could only watch as he jumped into the driver's seat of a blue Toyota FJ Cruiser and screeched off, leaving behind the acrid stench of burning rubber.

"Mother*fucker!*" Lorimer yelled.

The man behind the wheel glanced at his rearview mirror as he accelerated away. That was close, but it had gone according to plan. Heartbeat in overdrive, he merged with the southbound traffic toward Chantilly. Two minutes later he took the exit for Dulles Airport, scanning the surroundings for any sign of police. He drove to the parking lot of the Marriott, took the first open spot he found and killed the engine. He stepped out and glanced around the parking lot. Everything looked normal. He slung his backpack over his shoulder and strode purposefully toward the hotel entrance.

Five miles northwest of Dulles Airport, in what is officially referred to as the census-designated place—as opposed to city, town or village—of Ashburn, Loudon County, Dana McLaughlan pulled into the campus of eRock Datacenters, unaware that of all the days to arrive at work late due to an early teeth cleaning appointment, she had picked a most inauspicious one. Barely six months into her employment at eRock, she was now grappling on a daily basis with the irrepressible sense that she'd erred by retiring from the Secret Service. Corporate life lacked the visceral gratification of the life-on-the-line aspects of some of her assignments as an agent. Even the purely investigative aspects of Service life were a thrill compared to the mind-numbing mundaneness of the corporate nine-to-five routine.

Her decision had been driven by dollars. Government pay wasn't the worse—at forty-one years old she had enough savings to sustain herself for a year without income, but that was it. When the headhunter had called and dangled not only a salary increase, but also stock options, eRock's status as a privately held company that would likely go public in the non-too-distant future had swayed her. Now it had become clear she had quit a life that she loved, but one that would never give her financial security, for a position that held the promise of a windfall, but was, alas, a bore. She had spent the first month reviewing and revamping the company's security policies and procedures, the second month implementing her tweaks. After that, it seemed like her job description was simply "wait for something to happen." As she parked her car, she was unaware that the wait was over.

She locked the car and slowed her walk as she approached the entrance to the administration building, beholding her reflection in the entry vestibule's glass façade with a critical eye. At six feet tall, with the right curves in the right places softening a slightly underweight frame, she might have graced the covers of glamour magazines. She liked to think of her hair as autumnal, nuances of brown that glowed in today's sun, a mélange of subtle hues. She favored a chignon, back or side, but today she had left it loose and free, and she thought its flow became her. Her features—large, inquisitive blue eyes, smoothly rounded cheekbones, sculpted nose and ample lips naturally skewed into a lopsided smile—presented a sardonic demeanor that could intimidate or enchant depending on whether her inner Leo was in on-point lioness or playful kitten mode. The bluish translucence of the glass created an effect she found compelling, worthy of her first Instagram moment. Two months ago she had set up an account at the relentless urging of her fifteen-year-old niece, Allie, her biggest weakness in life, but she had yet to post a picture, which only gave Allie more cause to needle her. Now, tempted, she held up her phone to snap a selfie. Before she could take it she was startled as the door burst open and Chris Banks, her boss and eRock's Chief Uptime Officer, exploded out of the building, galloping past her like a man possessed. Dana was momentarily chagrined by the realization he might have seen her acting like a self-engrossed narcissistic airhead.

True to his title, Banks was responsible for the uptime of eRock's ten datacenters, six of which were here in the company's northern Virginia campus, the other four in Silicon Valley. Six months ago Banks had personally interviewed and hired Dana for the position of Director of Security, yet despite making eye contact as he tore past her, he neither waved nor otherwise acknowledged her. That meant this was not a security incident. Dana watched him run past the adjacent building, VA1, to the one beyond it, VA2. Gathering her wits, she hurried after him, keen to find out what the issue was. The security guards reported to her, and they would likely know. Their station was in the lobby, before the mantrap. Dana held her access badge to the scanner at the front door, heard the mag lock release, and entered the building. She immediately noticed that only the battery-powered egress lights were on, which meant one thing.

"Dominion Power is down," one of the guards behind a pane of bulletproof glass confirmed.

"Generators?" Dana asked.

The ex-navy man shook his head. "They started, then tripped out."

"The other buildings?"

"All on generator."

"So the problem is just VA2?"

"Yes Ma'am."

Still remarkably fit and trim at forty-one, Dana brought to eRock a unique set of skills courtesy of her twenty years with the Secret Service, competencies that included physical and digital security. But she had only limited knowledge of mission-critical datacenter infrastructure, the electrical and mechanical systems that powered and cooled the server rooms. So in situations like this, it was best to leave things in the hands of the engineering experts. She knew they would be under tremendous stress because they were now in a race against time.

The paradigm-shifting revolutions of human history, starting with the Cognitive Revolution, then the agricultural, scientific and industrial variants, all led to the Technology Revolution and the information age norm of computers on every desk and in every pocket. As the desire to access, process and store information mushroomed, so too did the need for round-the-clock availability of the systems—hardware and software—that enable instant

7

fulfillment of that desire. Those systems are concentrated in datacenters, buildings designed and constructed to provide a hardened, stable and secure environment for information and communications technology infrastructure. Some companies, the likes of Apple, Microsoft, Google and Facebook, own and operate proprietary datacenters that house only their gear. Others, like eRock, provide multi-tenant datacenters in which numerous corporate and governmental clients deploy their IT equipment. The single most important metric is uptime, which depends on uninterrupted delivery of the electricity that powers customer equipment, and the heat removal systems that keep that equipment cool. Dana was aware of the time lag between an unplanned loss of utility power and the availability of onsite generators, normally up to twenty seconds, during which massive banks of batteries keep the servers humming. She was also aware that if the generators failed, the batteries could power the IT loads for up to fifteen minutes, giving engineers a window of time to pinpoint and fix the problem with the generators. If they didn't do so before the batteries completely discharged, the result would be disastrous, the datacenter world's nightmare scenario: outage. The IT gear— customer servers, routers and storage devices—would all crash, severely disrupting customer operations for days or weeks, depending on how long restoration efforts took. The largest customer in VA2 was by far Bank of America. The financial losses would be huge. There would be hell to pay and untold damage to eRock's reputation.

This was the first time since she had joined eRock that one of the company's datacenters was on the ropes, so it was with an unprecedented sense of impotence that she accepted there was nothing she could do to help. She crossed her fingers and wished Chris Banks and his team of engineers Godspeed.

Nobody at the airport Marriott paid any attention to the man wearing Ray-Bans and baseball cap as he walked passed the lobby bar and made his way toward the elevator, just another passenger on his way in or out of Dulles. He didn't stop at the reception desk because he didn't need to. He had checked in earlier that morning and already had his key. Once in his room, he dropped his backpack on the bed and went to work on himself in the bathroom.

He spread out several open pages of a newspaper on the counter. Using facial hair scissors, he snipped his goatee as closely as he could while taking care not to cut himself, especially around the mole on the left side of his chin. Then he moved to the washbasin, applied shaving cream and finished the job with a razor. With a pang of irritation, he realized that the only spot he couldn't shave cleanly was around the mole. He'd had the goatee for six years, and he remembered how hard it was to stanch the flow of blood whenever he nicked the mole, but in planning for today it was one little detail he had failed to remember. He hoped it was the only one. He made a mental note to stop and buy a battery-operated shaver to erase the remaining little island of stubble.

He stared at himself in the mirror. He didn't like the way he looked without the goatee. His thick black eyebrows all but met, and the goatee balanced them out. Without it they became more prominent and he looked like a wimp. But this was no time for vanity. If everything went according to plan he would be out of the country in four days, maximum five, and then he could grow it back.

All *would* go according to plan, because God, *Khoda,* was with him. This was all meant to be. Coming to America, graduate school, it had all been preparation for now, and he was ready. He

9

just needed to banish fear, which is why it was imperative to push on without delay. As he gathered his belongings he likened himself to a great white shark, a perfect killing machine that would die if it stopped moving.

He folded the newspaper with his facial hair inside it and squished it into a tight ball. He removed the plastic liner from the trashcan and put the crumpled newspaper inside it. He wiped down the countertop and the washbasin with a wet hand towel that also went into the plastic liner, as did the two pieces of the room card key after he sliced it with the scissors. The magnetic strip contained information about the holder, including credit card information that, in the wrong hands, could be gleaned. He stuffed the liner with its contents into his backpack. He left the room and hung the DO NOT DISTURB sign on the outside door handle. He turned right and walked down the corridor, away from the lobby. After taking the stairs to the ground floor he exited the building through a side door to the west parking lot. The silver Volkswagen Jetta he had rented a few hours ago was where he had parked it. One roller suitcase containing his remaining worldly possessions was already in the trunk. He relaxed as he pulled out of the parking lot. If the police were already looking for him—and they would be sooner or later—they were looking for a Toyota, not a VW. A few minutes later he merged onto 28 southbound toward Centerville. From here he would take 66 east and connect with 286 to Newington, where he would link up with 95 for the straight run south through Richmond and out of the Commonwealth of Virginia. He estimated that, barring traffic snags, he would cross the state line into North Carolina in four hours.

He thought back to the incredible flash he'd witnessed when he shorted out the power lines, quite literally a blast. By now the effect will have been felt at eRock, and panic will have set in. He could just imagine his ex-colleagues scrambling in vain to save the situation. They were mostly good guys, and he wished them no harm, but he couldn't say the same for the assholes in HR, or that Dana bitch that had so coldly escorted him off the property like he was some encroaching mongrel. Americans have a poor understanding of the concept of personal dignity. He would have loved to watch them squirm, but his mantra had to be discipline. Causing an outage at eRock using the drone attack on the power lines was merely a prelude, phase one of his plan. Location and timing had been intentional. He had waited for the golfers to be where they were so they would see his face and later identify him as the perpetrator. The FBI would lead the chase, because of the impact of the outage at eRock on Bank of America. In time their investigation would uncover who—and what—he was, all a necessary and integral part of his plan. Now he had to stay ahead of them so he could avoid capture and get out of the country on his own terms.

He sighed deeply, not out of fear, but uncertainty. What he planned to do had no antecedent in the history of the United States. Not even Pearl Harbor and 9/11, because the effects of those attacks were so limited in comparison. And the mind-blowing thing about it all was he didn't need a navy, no armada, no aircraft carriers, no planes and no bombs. His weapon was on the passenger seat next to him, tucked securely into the laptop compartment of his backpack. But thanks to the advent of the Internet, the damage it could wreak was staggering.

He checked both side mirrors and the rearview mirror. Satisfied that he was anonymous on the road, he set the cruise control to the speed limit and allowed himself a barely perceptible nod.

***

Back in the admin building, Dana retreated to her office and dropped her purse on the credenza, above which hung a pastel plaque with the word *Ananda*. The name of one of Buddha's disciples, and the Sanskrit word for 'bliss,' it was an overt nod to her predilection for Buddhism, although none of her colleagues at eRock had asked, and she hadn't said. She lifted the top off a glass jar of nuts—almonds, pecans and roasted chickpeas, part of her daily staple—and popped a few into her mouth. She chewed on them and stared out the window at the big picture of a campus comprising five datacenters running on generator power and one in imminent danger of crash. A sickening thought suddenly occurred to her. The stricken datacenter was VA2. Only yesterday eRock had terminated the employment of one of its facilities engineers, Mike Massey. Dana herself had handled the distasteful business of collecting his keys, access badge, company cell phone and laptop, and escorting him off the campus. Massey had been stationed in VA2.

Coincidence?

As a special agent of the United States Secret Service, Dana had hunted down cell phone cloning rings, identified and nabbed computer hackers and worked on protective details entrusted with safeguarding the President of the United States, as well as foreign heads of state visiting New York City during United Nations General Assembly sessions. By nature and training she defaulted against chalking anything down to coincidence. But this situation challenged her instincts because it was tied to a failure of Dominion Power's local grid. Surely Massey couldn't have had anything to do with that?

Dana was still at her desk, her disquiet festering, when a colleague from Human Resources stuck his head around the door and dourly announced that VA2 had just crashed.

Chapter Two

It took less than an hour for Dominion Power to restore electricity to homes and businesses affected by the outage resulting from the drone attack on the overhead lines in Ashburn. With the exception of building VA2, the incident was transparent to the customers of all datacenters on eRock's campus because their standby systems automatically transferred building loads to the generators and seamlessly retransferred back to the utility after it was restored. But for VA2 it was worst-case scenario, and the aftermath was as bad as Chris Banks feared. His immediate reaction was three-fold.

First, he had to minimize the duration of the downtime. He instructed his staff to rent portable generators of ample size and quantity to carry the VA2 load in its entirety, no matter the cost. Within minutes he was informed that two large semi-trucks would arrive at VA2 within three hours, and an electrical contractor would be on hand to make the temporary cabling connections between the portable generators in the trailers and the VA2 power system. Second, Banks placed a call to the Washington, D.C. consulting engineering firm that had designed the datacenter's power system. Two senior electrical engineers were immediately dispatched to Ashburn, their mission to determine root cause of the backup power system's failure, and what steps were necessary to remediate it. Knowing that his third task would be the toughest, Banks braced himself and joined the eRock team now immersed in customer-facing damage control.

A preliminary official incident report was hastily composed and sent to Banks for review before being shared with customers. He knew it was weak, at this stage unavoidably so, because it provided a detailed timeline of what had happened, but offered no insights as to why. Regardless, customers were already baying for an official report, so Banks authorized its circulation with the caveat that it was a work in progress, updates to follow.

As he prepared to face the inevitable barrage of customer ire, Chris Banks thought back to an episode that had etched itself in his consciousness from the early days of the datacenter industry. It was back in 1999 when, as a consulting engineer with a firm that specialized in the mission-critical facilities of that time—hospitals—he had led the team assigned to the firm's first datacenter project. During a design review meeting with the client, a startup website hosting company, he had remarked that the multiple levels of redundant critical system components—standby generators, uninterruptible power supply modules and the like—that the client was asking for way exceeded normal design practice for hospitals. The client's VP of Construction had leaned forward in his chair and, addressing Chris openly along the length of the conference table in all seriousness, had said, "Son, with hospitals, what's at stake is life and death. With datacenters it's money."

As expected, it was the largest customer in VA2, Bank of America, which first commanded the attention of eRock's high-level crisis management tag team, CEO Steve Smith and his direct subordinate, Chris Banks. The disruption to the bank's operations was so large it was still being assessed. Servers that suffer an unplanned shutdown cannot just be restarted when their power supplies are rejuvenated. An unplanned crash plays havoc with the applications that run on the servers, and getting everything restored and running in an orderly fashion can take days, and hundreds, if not thousands, of man-hours. So Bank of America's Chief Information Officer, Mark Abbott, was himself under immense pressure and thus apoplectic when his voice boomed out over the speakerphone in Steve Smith's office.

"I want you guys to know, this is a game changer," Abbott seethed. "It was my decision to collocate with you and you've let me down. If I survive this, I can't tell you that our relationship will."

"Understood, Mark," Steve Smith said. He was practiced in the art of staying cool, always acting in control and never arguing with a client. "There's no denying this was mission failure for us, and I pledge to you we will spare no cost or effort to get to the bottom of what happened and do whatever is necessary to ensure it never happens again."

"You're telling me you don't know root cause?"

It was the limits of Smith's engineering expertise, not a desire to pass the buck, that made him hand over the baton. "I've got Chris Banks here with me, and I'm going to hand it over to him," he said.

Banks stepped into the firing line. "Chris here, Mark. I can only echo what Steve said. You have my word I will not rest until we know what caused this failure and fix it."

"What do you know now?" Abbott demanded.

Banks swallowed hard. Experience had taught him that in times of crisis, sticking with truth and transparency was always best. "The generators started but dropped out every time they tried to transfer," he said. "The problem is not campus-wide. VA2 is the only building affected. Temporary gensets are being delivered on semis as we speak. In a couple of hours we'll have them onsite and connected and they'll stay that way until we've identified and fixed the problem. I have a team of subject matter experts en route for root cause analysis. I estimate that by this time tomorrow we will know what caused this and how to make it right."

Abbott grunted out loud, his exasperation intentionally audible. "What happened to your redundant generators?"

17

"They were in play, but every time the system tried to switch the load to generators they all dropped out."

Abbott's anger trumped his professionalism. "Sounds like a fucked up system," he snapped.

Steve Smith winked at Chris Banks, a stay-calm gesture.

The flak continued for twenty minutes. Given the circumstances, Smith and Banks knew better than to try to parry the vitriol, so they maintained their acceptance of responsibility and let Abbott tire of repeating himself.

It was 3:30 p.m. when the investigative team's efforts bore fruit. The details uncovered led to a startling but inescapable conclusion. What Chris Banks had expected to be a technical glitch that caused the outage now appeared to be something altogether more ominous. Gallingly, the signs pointed to an act of sabotage. No evidence yet as to the perpetrator's identity, but with all the monitoring and control systems in place, Banks believed that was only a matter of time.

When he met again with Steve Smith, Banks took his time to give his CEO a detailed explanation of what he'd learned. He slipped a hand-drawn sketch onto Smith's desk and pointed at it. "The circuit breakers on the output of generators are provided with adjustable time delays so they can ride out the inrush current of downstream transformers without tripping and disconnecting the load. The factory sets time delay on generator circuit breakers at three seconds. We checked the time delay settings on all the generator breakers. Three seconds at all of the other buildings. At VA2, zero seconds."

Smith blinked impassively.

"With zero time delay, the generator breakers will trip out every time due to the inrush current to the transformers. That's why the VA2 generators couldn't come online."

Steve Smith was not an accidental CEO, and he immediately zeroed in on the critical question: "How is it we have zero time delay?"

Banks swallowed hard, a display of nerves he wished he could learn to suppress. "The last maintenance on the generators was a month ago," he said. "The vendor logs show the technician checked them and confirmed they were at three seconds."

Smith let his impatience show. "So how are they at zero now?" he demanded.

"There's no magic involved, Steve. Someone reset them to zero."

Smith sat still as a statue. "Why would anyone do that?"

Banks started to shake his head.

Smith narrowed his eyes and said menacingly: "More importantly, who would do that?"

Banks' expression hardened. "We don't know. But I've got Dana looking at all the video archived over the last month. We have three cameras in the generator room. If anyone went anywhere near the output breakers we'll have it on video. If we have video of someone going to all of them…Gotcha!"

***

WELCOME TO NORTH CAROLINA
NATION'S MOST MILITARY FRIENDLY STATE

The sign by the side of the I-95 freeway brought a sneer to the face of the silver VW's driver. Since he was at the state line, he was just an hour away from Rocky Mount, his destination for the day. He pulled into the Visitor Center. He adjusted his baseball cap low over his hairline, covered his head with the hood of his GMU

19

sweatshirt, and kept his Ray-Bans on while he used the restroom. Getting out of Virginia was a milestone of sorts, but he couldn't let his guard down.

He sat in the car and googled the nation's most military friendly state to find out what made it so. He learned that more than 400,000 jobs in North Carolina are tied to defense firms and military installations, which included the Army's Fort Bragg, the Marines' Camp Lejeune, Cherry Point and New River Air Station, the Pope and Seymour Johnson Air Force Bases, as well as several Coast Guard stations. He also learned that the North Carolina Bankers Association had underwritten the state's welcome signs. That brought a smile to his face. He thought of the bank that was his immediate destination in the city of Rocky Mount, just one hour south of the state line.

The cash in his pocket was not enough to sustain him over the coming weeks on the run, and what he planned to do was far too important to be foiled by a shortage of money. The solution he had devised for that particular challenge was something very few people would think possible, and fewer yet would dream of trying. He had seen a demonstration of it on YouTube, and he'd read reports of a Russian hacker who had pulled it off successfully. If it didn't work, he would have to borrow money from his uncle. At 28 years of age, that was a humiliation he didn't care to contemplate. He was on his way to see his uncle to warn him to leave the country, not to lean on him.

He had arrived in America in September 2011, on an F1 student visa, to attend graduate engineering school at George Mason University. Three months later he had attended a Black Hat information security conference in Arlington, where he first became exposed to network vulnerabilities, the tools used to exploit them, and the defenses deployed to thwart the tools. The ease with which he absorbed every last detail reflected his incandescent desire to master the material. The following July he travelled to Las Vegas and attended DefCon, one of the oldest and largest hacker conventions, where he maintained a low a profile while learning as much as was on offer. He came out of his shell only as necessary to acquire the tools he sought, of which three were instrumental to the task at hand today.

First, WarVox, a free tool that uses the Internet to automatically scan and dial a list of telephone numbers, usually all the numbers in a local area code, to find computers or modems that can act as entry points into electronic networks, thereby achieving in a matter of hours what would take weeks or months if performed manually. Second, Dillinger, an exploitive tool named after a notorious American depression-era bank robber, which can access automatic teller machines connected to the Internet, and glean and transmit to its user key information: machine settings like passwords and receipt data, including the names of the businesses that own the ATMs, and, in many cases, the physical address of a machine. Finally, Scrooge, malicious software that conceals itself between the software and hardware that together make an ATM function according to pre-set commands. In skilled hands, the three tools can produce astonishing results. He had applied himself obsessively to trial and error, and, within a few months, his hands had become skilled.

Over time he had built a database of modems in different exchanges, focusing on area codes just beyond the borders of Virginia. Dillinger coughed up device locations, street addresses which, courtesy of Google Maps, he could correlate with businesses. He had mapped out which ATMs he could reach remotely via TCP/IP, the communication language of the Internet, and discovered to his delight that what he'd learned from the conferences and the hacker blogosphere was true. Some ATM manufacturers delivered machines to their customers with the remote monitoring feature enabled by default, even if the customers never intended to use the feature. Moreover, the same feature included a vulnerability that allowed all authentications on the ATM to be bypassed without anyone knowing. So once Dillinger had penetrated an ATM, Scrooge could be installed on it and could perform an upgrade to the machine's software that included a new set of commands and effects. All from a remote location, over the Internet.

He had found what he was looking for in Rocky Mount, at the Sunset Avenue branch of a small, three-branch local institution, Old North Bank. With all the pieces in place, the firmware upgrade he had initiated over the Internet from his apartment in Herndon the previous evening had taken less than a minute from start to finish. Now he was an hour away from Rocky Mount, and from finding out if his handiwork would strike, if not gold, then the desired green. Success would relieve him of financial worries in the immediate future, but it would have another effect. It would validate his understanding and command of the malware tools at his disposal, and confirm his ability to pull off the big one.

Now that he was out of Virginia, he succumbed to a need to know if his plan to sabotage eRock had worked. He speed-dialed a number from his phone's contacts list.

"Security," a voice he recognized said.

"Bank of America IT. Any update on the power outage?"

"I'm sorry, Sir, you'll need to call your account manager for that."

He smiled and hung up. The security guard at VA2 had not said, "What power outage?"

God was on his side.

He thought about what he'd left behind. The apartment and the sparse furniture it contained were rented. The appliances—refrigerator, oven, washer, dryer—had all come with the apartment and were creature comforts of no importance now. He owned the television, but that was an easy sacrifice because he no longer had any use for it. He harbored a tinge of regret about abandoning the Toyota, for its go-anywhere-do-anything look and feel had grown on him. Plus, it was the first car he had ever owned—but then ownership was not the right term to apply to a leased vehicle. It would be found and repossessed by the dealer, but so what? The only thing that mattered was safe in the backpack on the passenger seat beside him. His laptop was the game-changer, information access, processing and storage device, communication portal to the universe, and—above all—weapon. Not just weapon, *weapon of mass destruction.*

He took a deep breath and swept his hands over his face in the manner of someone who had just come out of deep meditation. The prickly stubble around the mole on his chin was an irritant. He straightened his posture and cranked the engine. At the first opening in the freeway traffic, he pushed on toward Rocky Mount.

***

When Chris Banks gave Dana McLaughlan her marching orders, she did not react right away. She stayed at her desk for a few minutes after he left her office, as was her habit when faced with a potentially laborious task.

Of all she had retained from high school, the most meaningful lesson was learned during the first mathematics class, and it had more to do with human behavior than with crunching numbers. A true story about the German mathematician Johann Carl Friedrich

23

Gauss had stuck with her and informed her own behavior at crunch times like this. While in elementary school at the tender age of seven, Gauss was in a class assigned by the teacher to find the sum of the numbers from 1 to 100. The other students, all of them older than Gauss, started adding numbers using pencil and paper, all taking the same, obvious approach. Only Gauss sat back and looked at the ceiling for half a minute before blurting out the correct answer, 5050. The teacher, who had proposed the question as busy work for the class, couldn't believe her ears. Gauss had noticed a simple pattern:

$$1 + 100 = 101$$
$$2 + 99 = 101$$
$$3 + 98 = 101$$

All the way to $50 + 51 = 101$. So he reasoned that the answer was 101×50. Dana was fascinated by a seven-year-old boy's ability to take a step back and think, with a clear, unfettered mind, while everyone around him rushed headlong into the same tedious approach. It was her first introduction to the power of Zen.

Every challenge was an opportunity. By the time she reached the security office at VA2 she had a strategy clearly defined in her mind. The security cameras were motion-operated, meaning they only started recording when there was movement in the space they monitored. The generator room was accessed by vendors every three months, during maintenance operations, and by eRock engineers twice a day during their rounds of the facility. Video recordings of the latter normally amounted to a mere four minutes per day. Dana figured that by fast-forwarding at will through the digital archive, she could review all the footage from the past month in under an hour. And so it proved. There were numerous clips of facilities engineers entering the room, as she expected, but no record of suspicious behavior.

She could have stopped there and reported back to Banks the lack of foul play. But Dana decided to dig in another direction. She checked the camera logs to confirm they had been in a continuous state of readiness for the entire one-month window. And she discovered an anomaly. There was a half-hour period on the afternoon of Wednesday, April 8th, two days ago, when the cameras had been dysfunctional. Someone had turned them off for that length of time.

Placid on the outside, but her mind racing, Dana was pumped. She knew she was onto something. Her dissatisfaction at eRock stemmed from her belief that she was way overqualified for the work. You don't need twenty years with the Secret Service to master security policies and procedures in a corporate environment. Now, for the first time at eRock, she felt she was bringing the full weight of her intellectual brawn to bear on a matter of critical importance.

Dana next checked employee access logs and found that two facilities engineers had been on duty on the afternoon of April 8th. Her pulse quickened as she navigated to one final log. Her excitement welled up when she compared the personnel access log at the two doors to the generator room with the timing of the deactivation of the cameras. There it was, stark and immutable: Mike Massey had entered the generator room a few minutes after the cameras had been turned off, and they had been reactivated a few minutes after he had exited. And the record showed that his movement in and out of the room was not part of his normal tours of the building, which took place only at the beginning of each shift. What sealed it was the fact that April 8th was Massey's last full day at eRock. Human Resources had questioned him that afternoon about his expired work visa. The very next morning his employment had been terminated and Dana had sensed he was seething as she had escorted him off the property.

This was awesome. Steve Smith and Chris Banks, the two people above her in eRock's corporate hierarchy, would be floored. What a way for her to prove her worth to the company!

The sun had not yet set when Steve Smith completed his perusal of the folder on his desk and looked up at Chris and Dana. "Great work," he intoned dryly.

Dana's pride was palpable, yet she sensed something in Smith's eyes, something unsettling.

"That said," Smith continued, "I want an independent security consultant in here right away to audit all of our security processes and procedures."

Dana's high evaporated. "Why would—?"

"Because Massey's tampering with the breaker delay settings may be the root cause of the generators failure, but the underlying root cause is the hole in our security operations that allows our security cameras to be disabled without us knowing about it. How can that happen? I would expect there would be an alarm or some trouble signal if a camera were deactivated. How can we go blind and not know about it?"

Dana was stung. Smith's tone had turned accusatory.

Banks quickly chose sides. "I'm with you, Steve," he said. He turned to address Dana. "That's a pretty gaping loophole."

"I want an audit underway immediately, so we can report to customers that we're already addressing the security angle," Smith added. "Goddammit! How is it even possible to deactivate the cameras?"

Dana could feel she was red-faced now. She shook her head lamely. "I'll look into it, but I do know that the security systems of all seven buildings are networked together," she said, hating how deflated she sounded. "Guards at one building can look at video from a camera in any other building in real time. That provides redundancy, but it also provides remote access points. He could have penetrated the network and gained control."

"Jesus!" Smith hissed. "I want to press charges against this asshole."

Dana nodded. "I know the sheriff," she said listlessly.

"So you go report it, I'll arrange for the security audit."

Dana suppressed the impulse to protest. Security was her domain, and her CEO was telling her that he, not she, would engage a security consultant. The sense that this incident was now trending as her fault sickened her. Mental clarity, intellectual bite, and spiritual Zen, her foundational pillars, deserted her.

Smith arched his eyebrows at her. "What the hell are you waiting for?"

She glanced at Chris Banks, who gave her a cold stare. She left the office feeling eviscerated.

Chapter Three

The Loudon County law enforcement force comprises over seven hundred deputies that answer to the sheriff, the only elected law enforcement official in Northern Virginia. The sheriff's office was in Chantilly, off the Lee Jackson Memorial Highway on the other side of Dulles Airport, a ten-minute drive from Ashburn in flowing traffic. Dana had visited once before, during her first week at eRock. She had made a point of meeting the sheriff in person lest she should ever need help with a security breach. A burly 57-year-old with a cherubic face and a bulging midriff, Sheriff Jason Hart had been warm when Dana had introduced herself. It wasn't every day he met an attractive, assertive lady that just happened to be a retired Secret Service agent. Now, when she called from her car in eRock's parking lot to ensure he was in the office and available, he said of course he remembered who she was, yes he was in his office, and he would be happy to meet with her as soon as she arrived.

Before leaving the eRock campus, Dana stopped by the VA2 security office again and printed out a color copy of Mike Massey's access badge photograph, along with the address on file for him in the eRock database. *Ugly son of a bitch,* she thought as she pulled his photograph off the printer.

In such nice weather she would normally have dropped the soft top on her Audi A4 cabriolet, but her sullen mood left her disinclined to consider engaging in this luxury. The top would stay up on the drive to Chantilly, the better to hide her state of shellshock.

She had anticipated accolades, but instead Steve Smith had impaled her with an accusation of incompetence, and Chris Banks had agreed. Didn't they know that all the security in the world would not necessarily stop a determined and resourceful attacker? How many presidents had been shot? How many heads of state had been assassinated? The notion that somehow a deficiency on her part was the root cause of today's shit was manifestly false and unfair. Maybe that goes with the territory at a place like eRock, and if so, it was unfamiliar terrain. She was aware of media reports about the domination of alpha males in high tech industry management, and now she believed it. Smith and Banks had shown their true colors, and they were bastards. As she left the campus she was fuming. The only way to steady her shaking hands was to tightly grip the steering wheel. She thought she might resign from eRock, but only when she could walk out with her head held high, when the bastards were beseeching her to stay after she delivered to them Mike Massey's scalp.

Dana shook her head and reflected on what a bad week it had been. Symmetrically bad, starting with the painful episode at her parent's house on Sunday, and now this shit at work as the week wound down, and she had been unfairly blamed for both. Could it get any worse tomorrow?

For years now the immediate family would get together for dinner at her parents' home in Hampstead, Maryland, on the first Sunday of every month. It was always a small, intimate affair, because there would only be six of them around the dining table: Dana's father, Darren, pastor of the St. John Roman Catholic Church in Westminster, her mother Meryl, her younger sister Kate with her husband Mark, who lived in Baltimore, and their daughter, Allie. The open secret was that Darren McLaughlan favored his younger daughter on several counts. He was appalled by Dana's outspoken skepticism—to put it mildly—regarding scripture, and he disapproved of Dana being still unmarried at forty-one. They had discussed, debated and argued about religion. As to being single, Dana always asserted that she would never get married for the sake of getting married. Then there was the beef that he had never openly vocalized, other than to his wife, because even contemplating it was agonizing enough—he worried his daughter might have behavioral tendencies God deemed an abomination.

Last Sunday, April 5th, with heads around his dinner table bowed and eyes closed, Darren McLaughlan had said grace, as he did before every meal, during which he asked the Lord to guide the justices of the Supreme Court, to grant them wisdom, and the courage to stand firm against those who would legalize the sin of gay marriage come June.

Meryl McLaughlan sneaked a peek at her older daughter. Kate nudged Dana's leg under the table, imploring her sister to let it be. But Dana couldn't help herself. When the *Amen* chorus abated, she spoke softly and respectfully: "The Constitution is the supreme law of the land, Daddy, not the Bible."

Her father fixed his gaze on her. "The Constitution may be the supreme law of the land, Child," he said, not quite as softly. "But the Bible is the supreme law of humanity."

"I might agree if it told us where Cain's wife came from."

It was an argument Dana had used before. From the Bible's opening pages, God created Adam and Eve, they produced Cain and Abel and Cain killed Abel, leaving three people in the world. Then Cain went east of Eden and married his wife. To Dana, the provenance of Cain's wife remains unexplained and unexplainable. It was a line of argument she and her father had gone down before and failed to resolve to their mutual satisfaction. But last Sunday her father's reference to the sin of gay marriage had put a chip on

Dana's shoulder, and she pushed it. He held up Genesis 19 and the destruction of Sodom as proof of God's proscription of homosexuality. Dana snapped and asked what he thought of Genesis 33 and 35, wherein Lot's two daughters drug him with wine and rape him. She then wondered aloud how it would sit with him if she and Kate did that to him.

There was an outcry, of course, Meryl and Kate telling Dana she was out of line. Stunned, her father told Dana he was going to pray for her and excused himself. They didn't see each other again because he didn't come back downstairs until after she had left.

Dana had driven back to Reston feeling eviscerated. She hated being on bad terms with her father, but she also hated that her mother and sister blamed her for the falling-out. His birthday was next Thursday, April 16th, and Dana was resigned to following her mother's advice and waiting till Thursday before coming back up to Hampstead for a rapprochement. In the meantime, she would have to endure the stress of estrangement from the one man she loved despite the two of them seeing life through different—and incompatible—prisms.

It had started twenty years ago, before their disagreements about religion and marital status, when he had objected to her choice of career. While a senior reading sociology at the University of Maryland's College of Behavioral and Social Sciences, she had watched—and been bewitched by—*To Live and Die in LA,* the movie that had set her heart and mind on a career in the U.S. Secret Service. Highly motivated, able-bodied, and buttressed by a 3.8 GPA that put her in the top five percent of her graduating class, she had mostly breezed through the application process. Barely clearing the minimum age of twenty-one, her vision perfect, she had passed a written examination and an Applicant Physical Abilities Test. After undergoing a complete background investigation, acing drug screening and polygraph exams, she had qualified for a Top Secret clearance, only to be stymied by one little glitch she hadn't considered would ever be problematic. During the medical examination she had been dismayed to learn that the *Stay Strong* tattoo on the outside of the little finger of her right hand violated the Secret Service's prohibition against employees sporting visible markings on their head, face, neck, hands and fingers. Staying true to the tattoo, she had endured, at her own expense, cryosurgery to have it removed. With that she was in, an achievement her father disparaged with a terse, "That's a man's world."

Extensive training led to proficiency in firearms marksmanship, use-of-force and control tactics, emergency medical techniques, financial crimes detection and physical/site/event protection. At only twenty-six years of age she excelled during her first undercover field assignment when she enabled the capture of a computer hacker ahead of stiff competition from the FBI and state and local law-enforcement agencies. Her reward had been a stint in the most coveted and prestigious of special agent assignments, Protective Operations.

No congratulations from Daddy.

She had eventually gravitated back to the investigative side of the Secret Service's mission, and applied herself to crimes involving financial, computer and telecommunications fraud, false identification documents and money laundering. The tattoo might have been erased from her finger all those years ago, but its words were still a mantra she repeated to herself when tested. Now, as she pulled up in front of the Loudon County Sheriff's office, Dana set aside the hurt of her relationship with her father and concentrated on the issue she hoped would be resolved before next Thursday, driven by one thought. No punk named Mike Massey was going to get the better of her.

Sheriff Jason Hart greeted Dana in his office with a firm handshake. He invited her to sit down and closed the door for privacy. After she declined his offer of coffee or a soda, he discerned from her straight-faced demeanor that this was something serious, and he let her speak uninterrupted until she had finished telling him what she knew of the incident at eRock.

"I think he's got a case to answer to," Dana concluded as she dropped Massey's photograph on the desk. "But I'm not sure it's a crime you can bring him in for questioning about."

As Hart listened intently, he couldn't help thinking what a disarmingly beautiful woman Dana was, but he didn't show it because he was both a consummate professional and entirely comfortable with his place in the world. Framed photographs in his office spoke of a family-oriented man that gave selflessly of his time and being to his community. He picked up the photograph of Massey, studied it and said, "You're telling me you think he manipulated the generators so that they'd fail if there was a Dominion outage, knowing that would bring the datacenter down?"

Dana nodded. "Yes. We believe he knowingly messed with the circuit breakers on the generators so they wouldn't support the load when the utility went down."

"And the Dominion outage happened this morning."

"Ten-thirty-ish."

Hart peered down at the goateed face in the photograph, then looked back at Dana inquiringly. "You wouldn't happen to know if he drives a blue Toyota FJ Cruiser, would you?"

The question jolted her. "Yes! Why? How do you know?"

"We took a call from Dominion Power today. Golfers out at the club on Waxpool Road reported seeing a drone short out an overhead line. It was right around ten-thirty. They saw the guy flying the drone. Said had a goatee, just like your man here, and he fled in a blue Toyota FJ Cruiser."

Dana was stunned.

"And it wasn't no accident, Dana. He had attached a length of pipe, or something, under the drone, and it looked like he intentionally brought it down across two of the power lines. It produced quite a fireworks show, apparently."

"He purposely took down Dominion's line?"

Hart shrugged. "Why else would he attach a pipe to the drone?"

"The guy's an electrical engineer." Dana quipped.

"Well, there you go! He knew exactly what he was doing. The golfers called Dominion and waited till a crew showed up to investigate. They apparently salvaged the charred remains of the drone."

"Who has the remains of the drone?"

"Dominion."

Dana's mind was racing. "Have you spoken to the golfers?"

"No."

"Do we know their names? Can we talk to them, see if we can get a positive ID?"

"We didn't have anything for them to ID," Hart said. Then he tapped Massey's photograph. "Until now. Give me a minute." He rose, the photograph in his hand, walked around his desk, opened the office door and stepped out. Dana could hear him issuing instructions. When he returned he filled her in: "I've got the names and addresses of the golfers who reported the incident this morning. Let's go."

As they made their way out of the sheriff's office he kept talking. "A scan of Massey's photograph is being sent to all our vehicles. We're also getting the information on Massey's Toyota from the DMV database, and we'll put out an APB. Deputies are on their way to the home address you gave me for Massey. We'll get this guy."

"We want to prosecute him," Dana said. "Can we get the drone from Dominion? Or what's left of it."

"Hell yeah, we're going to prosecute him," Hart agreed. "Dominion reported that the outage affected customers in a thirty square mile area, including the Washington Redskins' training facility and the Kaiser Permanente Ashburn Medical Center. You bet we're going to prosecute." He issued one more set of instructions that sent deputies hustling to the Dominion Power office in Herndon.

Within twenty minutes Dana and Sheriff Hart were at the front door of Nick Lorimer's house in Sudley Springs. Lorimer took one look at the photograph Hart handed him and nodded. "Yep, that's him."

"Are you sure?" Hart said.

Lorimer didn't hesitate. "I was with my brother. When he flew the drone into the power lines we called out to him. The guy just stood there, took his shades off and stared at us, almost like he was asking us what we were going to do about it, challenging us, you know? Then he took off. We ran after him but he jumped in his car and was gone. No question it's him."

"So you'll be able to ID him if you saw him again," Hart said.

"Of course!"

"And it was a blue Toyota FJ?" Dana said.

"Sure was."

Dana and Hart exchanged a quick glance. "Thank you, Mr. Lorimer," Hart said. "We'll be back in touch if we need anything else."

***

As soon as he exited from I-95 onto Sunset Avenue in Rocky Mount, the man Dana knew as Mike Massey pulled the silver VW Jetta into a Burger King parking lot and searched on his iPhone 6 maps app for the nearest Walgreens. There was one on the way to the bank, and a few minutes later he found it. It was dark out now, and he considered that wearing his Ray-Bans and covering his head with the hood might make him look suspicious. He compromised by covering his eyes with the sunglasses, and limiting his head cover to just the baseball cap.

There were only a few customers inside, including two at the pharmacy counter with their backs to him, and nobody paid him any attention. He hurriedly loaded four gallons of water into his shopping cart. Next, from closer to the pharmacy, he picked up a pack of anti-bacterial hand wipes and box of cone-style facemasks, like those worn by cancer patients with low immunity. One size fits all, they covered from the top of the nose down to the bottom of the chin and cheek to cheek, so perfect for his needs. From the school supplies section he sourced a two-foot square white foam poster board, a pair of large scissors and a roll of duct tape. Finally, the last item on his mental checklist, a battery-powered Braun shaver. The package said two AA batteries were included, but he bought a separate Duracell four-pack just in case. He paid in cash and left the store thinking that had gone well, no eyebrows had been raised. Still, he was nervous. He figured it was natural, like an athlete before competition, and he willed himself to feed off the nerves, to use the adrenaline to stay sharp and heighten his awareness of the surroundings. He was hungry, and he decided to eat now, not after the heist. There was a McDonalds next to the Walgreens, so he wouldn't have to go out of his way.

He lifted the hood over his head, and from the drive-through lane ordered a burger, fries and milkshake. He ate in the parking lot, savoring the food, thinking McDonalds was one of the best things about America. He disposed of the packaging so it wouldn't stink up the car, cleaned his hands and mouth with one of the wipes, then used another one to wipe down the steering wheel, gear shift lever, and the other surfaces of the car's interior his hands would touch. He didn't need to use the restroom because he had done so at the Visitor Center, so there was no reason to further delay the inevitable.

He drove past the Old North Bank once to scope it out. The ATM was in one of three drive-through lanes, and the sight of it raised his anxiety a notch. He feared getting caught; the prospect of seeing the inside of an American jail was a hellish proposition, but he knew he was going to do this, for he had already rationalized it over and again. He needed the money. And he had to see if the many hours he had spent preparing for this moment would bear fruit. Taking down the Dominion power line had been simple enough; a short circuit between two phases would cause a large amount of fault current to flow, which in turn would cause upstream protective circuit interrupters to open, disrupting the power. Electrical engineering 101. But this was a different animal. This was something not taught at any university in the world.

He pulled into the parking lot of Sam's Club across the street from the bank, and noted a security guard making rounds in a golf cart. He parked in a spot the guard had just passed and reached for the Walgreens bag. He cut two 12 x 7 inch sections of the poster board with the scissors, then jumped out of the car and used the duct tape to affix them to the license plates. Back in the driver's seat he scanned the surroundings. It was almost 7 p.m., the bank was closed, the few parking spots in front of its quaint little building were empty, and there were no cars in the drive-through lanes. He took his MacBook Pro out of his backpack and turned it on, then activated his personal WI-FI hotspot on his phone. Once he verified he had Internet access, he logged on to the ATM across the street.

There was very little traffic on Sunset Avenue. His heart was pounding as he prepared to cross the line. He ripped open the pack of facemasks and put one on. He looked at himself in the mirror. With the mask and his shades covering his face, and the hood covering his head, he was truly incognito. There was one more little detail, an important one. He took his sweater off and turned it inside out. He put it on again and re-hooded his head. It wouldn't do for a video camera to pick up the GMU across his chest.

He waited for a good break in the traffic, then eased across the street and pulled up to the ATM. He opened his window as he approached, aware that now CCTV cameras would capture now his every move. He slid his seat back as far as it would go and lifted the laptop off the passenger seat onto his lap. Taking extreme care and typing slowly, he unerringly keyed in the Jackpot command.

Crunch time. His heart beat so fast he could feel the blood pressure in his ears and the sweat on his brow.

It took less than fifteen seconds for the bills to start pouring out, and the process was over in a gut-wrenching minute.

When he drove off, the only eyes that had registered him were the electronic ones. He steered back to the Walgreens parking lot and feverishly removed the foam strips he had taped to the license plates. He saw no police cars, heard no sirens. As he slid back onto Sunset Avenue there was nothing around him to indicate that anyone knew he was now richer to the tune of some twenty thousand dollars in cash.

He was on a soaring, natural high as he drove west on U.S. Route 64, destination Raleigh, fifty miles away. It had worked! It had fucking worked!

The hardest thing now was to chill, to stay grounded and take this heartening success in stride. This was huge. It was monumental, not least because of what it did for his confidence in his ability to bring America to its knees.

Technology was the great equalizer. All you need is curiosity, a will to learn, determination, and the right tools. It didn't hurt that some ATM manufacturers delivered machines with their remote monitoring features enabled, and that some of their customers were too fucking stupid to disable them.

He reached into the Walgreens bag for the shaver. He tore the packaging open and took it out, turned it on and ran it over and around his mole. He checked with his fingertips. Ah, finally, nice and smooth.

***

The sheriff's deputies that were dispatched to the tasks related to the Mike Massey case had already been out on patrol, so they reached their destinations quickly and were soon relaying information back to the Sheriff's Office. The news from Massey's apartment was not good. There were no lights on in the apartment, no response to the knocks on the door, and no sign of the blue Toyota FJ Cruiser in the designated parking space. The deputies were not yet armed with a search warrant, so getting inside would have to wait.

"I'm not surprised," Dana said. "I didn't think he would be sitting there waiting to be arrested. He knows he was seen. He's in hiding or on the run."

The Dominion field crew that first responded to the outage had indeed retrieved what remained of the drone, they handed it over to the deputy that called on them, and he in turn delivered it to the Sheriff's Office without delay. It was charred on one side, but Dana noted that the manufacturer's name and the unit's serial number were still legible on the underbelly. A quick Google search revealed that 3D Robotics was an American company headquartered in Berkeley, California.

It was just before four on the west coast when, at Dana's urging, Sheriff Hart called the corporate headquarters of 3D Robotics. He used his desk phone and activated the speaker so Dana could hear the conversation. He identified himself and was put through to the company's vice-president of operations. Hart explained the situation, spelled out the drone's serial number, and requested the names of the dealer who had sold it and the end user who had bought it. Dana sat across the desk from Hart, listening expectantly.

There was immediate pushback: "How do I know you're who you say you are?" the VP said.

Hart ran a finger along an eyebrow and sighed.

"Go to the Loudon County Sheriff's Office website," Dana interjected. "There's a photograph of the sheriff on the home page."

"OK..." Audible keyboard clicks came through the line. "Got it."

"Do you have FaceTime or Skype?" she said.

"FaceTime. And who are you, if I may ask?"

"I'm Dana McLaughlan, assisting Sheriff Hart in this investigation. Take down this number and FaceTime me." She gave him her number.

Hart was impressed. He gave Dana a thumb up. When her iPhone rang Dana accepted the call and handed the phone to Hart.

Now the two men could see each other, and the one on the west coast relented.

They heard more keyboard clicks. "That unit was sold by one of our resellers on Amazon. Our database shows the buyer didn't register it with us, so we'll have to go to the reseller for the buyer's name."

"Can you please do that for us?" Hart said.

"I'll call you right back."

True to his word, the 3DR man was back on the line with them in minutes. "Got that info for you. Buyer's name is Richard Sloane."

Dana frowned.

"You sure about that?" Hart said.

"Yes."

"What was the shipping address?" Dana said.

When she heard the recited address Dana turned pale. She hit the mute button on Hart's speakerphone. "That's us! eRock! That's VA2, where Massey worked!"

Hart unmuted the phone. "Do you have a delivery date?"

"April 1st."

"Thank you," Hart said. "You've been very helpful."

Hart hung up the phone and looked at Dana. "Is there a Richard Sloane at eRock?"

April 1st, she thought. *April Fool's Day.* "Not that I know of," she replied. "But I can find out."

She called the eRock Human Resources director's mobile phone and was told there was no one by that name employed by eRock.

"So who the hell is Richard Sloane?" Dana said with a scowl as she hung up. "Does Massey have an accomplice?"

"Could be," Hart said, studying Dana intently. There was something about her he had felt from when she walked in a couple of hours ago, something he hadn't quite put his finger on, until right now. She hadn't smiled. Not once, not when she came in or at any time since. Frowns and scowls, but not a smile. All steely determination and single-minded focus on Mike Massey. He decided he would have her on his team any time.

Hart's assistant buzzed him on the intercom and told him that someone from 3D Robotics was on line one, a man who said they had just talked. Hart took the call.

"Just one more thing I thought you might want to know," the voice on the speakerphone said. "Richard Sloane didn't order just the one drone."

Dana's eyebrows shot up.

"No?" Hart said.

"Uh-uh. He ordered two."

Chapter Four

The calculations in Sheriff Jason Hart's mind were simple. Based on what he knew as fact, the drone attack against the Dominion overhead line was not vandalism; it was a deliberate act of sabotage, albeit limited in scope, against the U.S. national grid. It had potentially caused material harm to at least one corporation, eRock, and by extension to its customers, and it had also impacted a medical center, potentially threatening the welfare, if not the lives, of patients. It had happened within the 521 square miles of his office's jurisdiction, but in the case of some of eRock's customers, the impact was felt across state boundaries. And, as he had just learned, the perpetrator was in possession of an additional drone—at least—that he could presumably use in another grid attack. Hart knew well that the county law enforcement agency he managed was not subordinate to the Federal Bureau of Investigation, but effectively a partner of the federal agency, and that he could leverage the latter's investigative resources in a joint effort to investigate cases and locate fugitives. So with no threat to his ego or authority, Hart had no hesitation about picking up the phone and calling the nearest FBI office, the resident agency just five miles down the road in Manassas. Not only was it closer than the Washington, D.C. field office, there was also the personal connection Hart had with the special-agent-in-charge in Manassas, Joe Mayle. The two men had worked together on several cases in years past.

Dana listened while Hart brought Mayle up to speed. It did not escape her that Hart did not put Mayle on the speakerphone, and she was not involved in the conversation, a little detail that drove home the reality of her position. She was technically an employee of a complainant in the case, not part of the law enforcement team investigating it. That meant that whatever access she would to have to details regarding developments would depend on Hart's willingness to share. Worse yet, now the FBI would be the lead agency handling the case, so she was another step removed, not only from information, but also from the decision-making. So Hart involving the FBI was good from the perspective of nailing Massey, but it would curtail Dana's involvement. That was not where she was used to being and not where she wanted to be, but she had to live with it.

When he concluded his call with Mayle, Hart placed another call, this to his wife, and told her he was leaving the office now. Dana sensed that message had really been for her ears. She stood up and slung her purse over her shoulder.

"I will keep you up to speed as I get updates," Hart said. "OK if I call you?"

"Please," Dana replied. She handed him a fresh business card. "Any time of the day or night, please call my cell phone. In the meantime, I'll go through Massey's file at eRock and see if there's anything of interest there."

"Alright. I'll just tie up a couple of loose ends before I head out. You can see yourself out?"

"Of course," she said. "Thanks for all your help."

Dana was troubled as she joined the evening rush hour traffic. She hated not being in control. She had started her day weighed down by her estrangement from her father, a situation she needed to address sooner rather than later, but her mother had advised her to wait until she could do so in person on Thursday when she went to Hampstead for his birthday. That rendered her powerless for almost a week. And today's incident at work had mushroomed from an employee sabotaging an eRock datacenter, to an attack against the local power grid that affected other businesses and potentially put the lives of hospital patients at risk, to an FBI investigation. In both situations, the personal and the professional, she had no control. Ironically, as bad as today's incident at eRock was—and the full extent of the fallout from it was yet to be seen—it had helped take Dana's mind off her father. Now she had the urge to call her mother. Her phone was blue-toothed to the car so she could talk hands-free.

"Hi, Dear," Meryl McLaughlan said, courtesy of caller ID.

"Hi Mom. How are you?"

"I'm fine. Are you OK?"

Dana was not about to unload on her mother about the situation at eRock. "Yeah, I'm fine. How's Dad?"

Meryl was pleased Dana asked. "He's fine. You know. He's strong."

"Yeah. There's one thing I'll say for absolute faith, it makes you strong."

There was a brief silence.

"Mom, I was thinking, I don't want to wait till Thursday and come to Hampstead with him still sore at me. I want to come and make up with him tomorrow. I want us to be good on Thursday. Thursday's his birthday. I don't want there to be tension."

"Hmm. I don't know."

"I've tried calling him but…he doesn't answer."

"He's hurt, Dana. I've always told you not to be so blunt."

"I know, Mom, I know. But it's like…I'm blunt with the truth."

"The truth as you see it, Dana. And anyway, if someone you care about is ugly, do you tell them they're ugly?"

"I know, Mom, I get it."

"You just have to accept him the way he is."

"I do accept him. We fight because *he* doesn't accept *me* the way *I* am. Remember when he gave me the silent treatment when he saw the Buddha statue in my living room? You were there. That was two years ago, and the two of you haven't been back to my place since."

"The silent treatment is better than saying things like you said on Sunday."

"Yeah, maybe I should try what he does, just go quiet and leave."

"Not saying hurtful things would help."

"I get hurt too, Mom. But look, I've thought about this, and if I have to choose between having a relationship with him and not expressing myself and expressing myself and not having the relationship, I choose the relationship, OK? I can't stand us not talking. I want to come up tomorrow and I'm prepared to apologize so we can put this behind us."

There was a reflective pause. "I don't know," Meryl said. "Tomorrow may be too soon."

"Too soon for what? For an apology? Tomorrow's too soon but Thursday's OK? How much sense does that make?"

"I just don't know, Dana."

"OK look. I'll do what you tell me. Why don't you talk to him, tell him we've had this conversation, tell him I feel bad and I want to come and apologize and let me know what he says. If he says no, I'll leave it alone."

"He'll be home soon. I'll talk to him."

"Call me back either way?"

"Yes."

"I love you, Mom."

"I love you too, Dana, more than you know."

"Bye, Mom."

"Dana—"

"Yes?"

"No more Cain's wife and no more Lot's daughters."

Dana suppressed a sigh. "Right."

There was a pause, and Dana could just see her mother's expression, worry and uncertainty adding to her years. "I promise, Mom."

"Bye."

Dana pressed her thumb against the roller button on the steering wheel, disconnecting the phone. She felt better now. She wanted the hurt on both sides to go away, the sooner the better, and she was of a mind to drive to Hampstead tomorrow regardless what her mother said.

The digital clock on her dashboard read 7:14 when she got back to eRock, and she noted that neither Chris Banks' BMW 5 series nor Steve Smith's Escalade were in their usual spots. Just as well, as she didn't really care to see either of them. She sent them both a brief email confirming she had reported Mike Massey to the sheriff, and telling them that it was about more than just eRock because Massey had attacked the Dominion Power overhead line.

A normal Friday evening might have involved dinner and/or a movie with friends, some wine for sure, but this was not a normal Friday. Her last conversation with Smith and Banks was still on Dana's mind, and she wanted to learn more about Mike Massey. She called the VA2 security desk and asked for the name of the associate that manned the Shipping & Receiving desk, then got his cell phone number from the employee directory on the eRock intranet. During a brief conversation he told Dana he remembered the large package that FedEx had delivered for a Richard Sloane on April 1st, because Mike Massey had alerted him of its impending arrival. Massey had explained that he was taking delivery of the package on behalf of a friend who could not be at home to receive the shipment. He also reported that he had seen Massey take the package out to his car through the delivery door at the back of the datacenter. He knew that was a violation of security policy, as employees are required to always use the front door so that their movements in and out of the datacenter are logged on the security system, but he lacked the authority to stop Massey. Dana hung up the phone with the sinking feeling that she might have missed another hole in the security policies and procedures. How had an employee arranged delivery of a shipment of personal items to the datacenter? Did the policy not specifically prohibit that? If it didn't, it should. She immediately checked and was aghast to discover that sure enough, there was nothing to say employees could not have personal items delivered to the Shipping & Receiving desk at the datacenter. Someone could have a bomb delivered by UPS and not worry about security being alerted. She thought about what Steve Smith might have to say about that, and made a snap decision. She edited the master Policies and Procedures document to close the loophole. Then she sent an email to the Shipping & Receiving team alias informing them of the policy change. Technically, changes to the P&P document had to be approved by an oversight group that she was a part of, and her unilateral action might result in her being censured. But it was a risk she was prepared to take. The alternative was allowing a serious loophole to linger and sweating about whether it being caught by the auditor Steve Smith was hiring. "Mike asshole Massey," she murmured. "What the hell are you doing to me?"

Friday night or not, it was time to learn everything she could about the bastard.

She called the Pauline Riggs, the VP of Human Resources, filled her in on what had transpired with Mike Massey, and her visit with the Loudon County sheriff. "I need to go through Massey's HR file," Dana said.

"Tonight?" Riggs asked.

"Yes. I'm at the office, and I'd like to do it now if there's a way I can access it."

"It's in a locked file cabinet behind a locked door, but security has keys to both. The guards report to you, right?"

"Yes."

"Here's what you need to tell them…"

Fifteen minutes later Dana fished Massey's file out of an HR cabinet and took it to her office. The documents in the folder were stacked in chronological order, most recent on top. She reached into her glass jar of mixed nuts, put a handful of them on the desk next to the folder, popped a few into her mouth and started from the bottom.

The earliest document in the folder was his application for employment, dated January 2013. It showed that he held a BS in Electronic and Electrical Engineering from Leeds University, UK, and an MS in Electrical Engineering from the Volgenau School of Engineering at George Mason University, just down the road, in Fairfax.

Dana leaned back in her chair. On April 8th, just two days ago, when Massey's HR representative had told her his employment was being terminated and asked her to escort him off the property the next day, she had explained that this was because his work visa was about to expire and he would no longer be legal in the country. Dana had acted on that information without asking for additional details because she hadn't needed any. On April 9th she had simply relieved him of his company laptop, his company phone, his security access badge, his company keys, and shown him out of the building and out past the perimeter security gate. Then she had ensured that the an email notification was sent to all those who needed to know so all his physical and electronic access privileges would be revoked, and they had been. Dana reflected on how she had shown him out on the morning of April 9th, but HR had informed him on the morning of April 8th that his employment at eRock would end the next day, coincident with the expiry of his work visa. And it was during the afternoon of April 8th that he disabled the generator room CCTV cameras and eliminated the time delay on the generators. He was a scheming rogue who knew exactly what he was doing. But the timing exposed another flaw in the security policy. When the company terminates a facility engineer's employment, it should happen without advance notice. Tell them, collect their stuff and show them out in one swift, seamless motion. She jotted a note on a pad on her desk and turned back to the file.

There was a U.S. Citizenship and Immigration Service I-9 employment eligibility verification document that showed he had been granted an F1 Optional Practical Training visa valid for twelve months. He had subsequently been given a 17-month extension available to foreign graduate students in STEM, science, technology, engineering or math. He had asked eRock to sponsor his application for a green card so he could stay in the country, but his request had been denied. His HR representative had handwritten a note that Massey's qualifications and experience were not unique enough or rare enough to qualify him for a green card. And when his work permit expired, eRock had to let him go. Dana also noted two performance reviews in the file, both rating Massey in the top category, *Exceeds Expectations*.

Again Dana paused. Had he harbored a grudge against eRock for not sponsoring his green card? Is that why he orchestrated the outage?

The opening strains of Weather Report's *Birdland*, her cellphone ringtone, interrupted her thoughts. She glanced at the screen and saw it was Sheriff Jason Hart.

"Hi Jason." The time they had spent together that day made for first name familiarity.

"Hey Dana. I've got an update for you. Is this a good time?"

"Sure."

"Your man is a smooth operator. We found a Richard Sloane in Reston, owner of the credit card that was used to purchase the drones. He had no idea his name and card had been used to make the purchase, which was made online, by the way. He hasn't set up any alerts with American Express to be notified when his card is used and not physically presented."

"That's credit card fraud," Dana said.

"It is. But you've got to give it to Massey. He used the identity and credit card of someone right here in Reston to preclude any red flags being raised about the billing address and delivery address being geographically far apart."

"Bad-ass."

"The FBI guys are all over it. We're gonna get this guy."

"I'm sure. Thanks for the update."

"I'll let you know when I hear more."

"I appreciate that, Jason. Later."

Her stomach rumbled, and Dana realized she hadn't had a proper meal since breakfast. She locked Massey's file in her desk, locked her office, and headed out to her car, reflecting on a bittersweet day. Bitter, thanks to Steve Smith and Chris Banks. Sweet, ironically, because Mike Massey's criminal shenanigans had produced the first meaningful work to cross her desk at eRock. It was after eight, and her mother hadn't called back. Dana imagined her parents would be having dinner, and she expected to hear from her mother within the hour. Dinner was exactly what she needed. She decided she would stop at a favored Greek diner in Herndon on her way home. They made a gyros platter with Tzatziki sauce to die for.

***

Sheriff Jason Hart was also having dinner with his wife at their home in Gainesville when he received two calls related to Mike Massey. The first one was from his deputies at Massey's apartment. Now armed with a search warrant, they had secured the cooperation of the apartment manager to gain access to Massey's unit. There was furniture, a television, a fridge with frozen pizza, milk, bottled water, eggs, some fruit, an assortment of cheeses and bread. The bed was unmade, and the closet had some clothes in it. No computer, nothing irregular. Hart ordered one of the squad cars back to the station, and instructed that two deputies remain on vigil in the other car at Massey's apartment to arrest him if he showed up. The second call informed him that the result of the background check he had ordered on Massey had just been emailed to him. In deference to hunger and his wife, he decided it could wait until after dinner. He took a swallow of beer and dug into his steak.

Thirty minutes later Hart accessed his email on the desktop computer in the den, downloaded the report and printed a hard copy. By the time he finished reading it he was glad he had already eaten dinner, because he might have otherwise lost his appetite. His brow was furrowed when he picked up the phone and called Dana. She had just devoured her meal and was getting ready to pay and head home.

"I've got some more information for you, Dana," Hart said. He didn't ask if this was a good time, because what he had just learned couldn't wait. "We've searched his apartment. There's nothing of note. He's not there, but we'll get him if he comes back to it tonight."

"I doubt he'll do that," Dana said, handing the waitress her credit card.

"You told me you fired Massey because his work visa expired, right?"

"Yes."

"I see he was on a practical training visa," Hart went on. "Something called an F1 OPT. The Citizenship and Immigration Service issues them to foreign graduate students who want to stay on after getting their degrees to get practical experience before they return home."

"Yes, I just learned the same from his HR file."

"What else did his HR file tell you?"

Dana sensed the question was leading somewhere. "What else is there?"

"Did your HR people do a background check on him?"

She hadn't seen a background check in the file. "I don't know. Unless, because he was only hired as a trainee, not a permanent employee…"

"Do you know about his name change?"

That was new, and Dana didn't know what to make of it. "What name change?" she said.

"So he comes here for grad school, spends a year at GMU, during which he petitions for a name change at a court in Fairfax, and the petition is granted."

"So Mike Massey isn't his real name?"

"Nope."

Dana knew Steve Smith would have a field day with this. No background check and an unknown name change. Surely he couldn't blame her for that too? It predated her joining eRock. "So what's his real name?" she asked.

"His real name is Mahmoud. Mahmoud Reza—let me see if I can pronounce this right—Massevadegh." He spelled it out for her.

Dana jotted the name down and stared at it. The only Mahmouds she had ever heard of were Mahmoud Abbas, President of the Palestinian Authority, who she didn't have an opinion of one way or another, and...

"You ready for the kicker, Dana?"

And Mahmoud Ahmadinejad, whom she despised. She winced and waited for Hart to tell her.

Hart cleared his throat and said: "Your bogeyman is from Iran."

Chapter Five

Amir Yazdi loved Friday afternoons. With his last class at Rice University winding down at 3 p.m., he had just enough time to make it home to his parent's house in Piney Point Village before the rush hour traffic turned Houston's West Loop into a snail-paced, road rage-infested driving purgatory. His escape during the commute was National Public Radio, for him the best source of news on America's airwaves, notably free of the sensationalist editorializing that had turned him off the likes of Fox News and CNN, where even the sunrise was presented as Breaking News. Between 3 and 4 p.m. he enjoyed catching the BBC's *Newshour*, a refreshing mix of updates on what was happening around the world. But a late departure from campus on this 10th of April meant he heard only the last twenty minutes of *Newshour*. No matter, NPR's *All Things Considered* would be next, after a minute of local news headlines.

First up was Hillary Clinton's visit to Houston to attend a fundraiser. He shook his head. Could it really be that of all the people in America, the next presidential election could come down to a Bush versus a Clinton, one a wimp the other a liar?

He had barely completed the thought when his world was rocked by the next report. Federal authorities had today raided the offices of Houston-based Mitronica for allegedly channeling microelectronics to Iran in violation of U.S. trade sanctions with the Islamic Republic. The firm's owner, Farzad Yazdi, a U.S. citizen of Iranian origin, had been arrested and was being held in custody.

The sound of the name of his father's company followed by his father's name stunned Amir. It felt like autopilot took him off the freeway at the next exit and into a restaurant parking lot. He reached into his backpack on the passenger seat next to him for his cell phone and found that he had missed six calls, all either from home or from his mother, all missed because he had left his phone on silent mode as he always did when attending lectures. He swore out loud as he called his father's cell phone. The call went straight to voicemail so he hung up and called his mother. When she answered he had never heard her sound so distraught.

"Mom, I just heard on the radio—"

"Come home, Amir. The police are here."

"Is it true? Where's Dad?"

"They took him to downtown. Come home."

"I'm on my way—I'll be there in twenty minutes."

He fought his way back onto the freeway thinking it had to be a mistake, praying it was a mistake. His father ran a clean, successful business and was a respected pillar of Houston's Iranian community. He exported electronics to the Far East and South America. He didn't need to sell to Iran! He was a tax-paying citizen, noted for his philanthropy, a lifetime member of the 100 Club, the organization that provides financial assistance to the dependents of Houston firefighters and law enforcement personnel who lose their lives in the line of duty. He was non-partisan, donating to Republicans and Democrats alike. He had even voted for Ross Perot, having worked for Electronic Data Systems in Iran in the seventies when the company was automating the Iranian social security system. He was proud of his Iranian heritage, but he wouldn't risk everything by violating the sanctions! No way! This had to be a case of government paranoia run amok.

The barrage of thoughts was incessant. Where was his father now? What were they doing to him? Who else had heard the news? Who of the family friends, his friends, his professors, his classmates? What would they all be thinking? What if it were true? How would their lives change?

It couldn't be true.

When he turned onto their street in the leafy Memorial Drive suburb it was like a scene out of a bizarre nightmare. Two Houston Police Department patrol cars, a brown ford Crown Victoria, and four media vans, one each from the local affiliates of ABC, CBS, NBC and Fox. He parked in the circular driveway and pushed through the press leeches to the policewoman standing outside the front door. With a quick glance at his driver license she confirmed his identity and home address and stepped aside.

It was a large, two-story house, typical of the neighborhood. Fine Persian carpets and ornate furnishings abound. His mother and sister were in the formal living room with two policemen and two FBI agents, the latter identified by the large yellow letters on the backs of blue shirts. Amir rushed to his mother and held her in a tight embrace. He tasted tears as he kissed her cheek. "It's going to be okay," he whispered. Then he hugged and kissed his older sister, Taraneh, who quietly assured him the same.

One of the FBI men made introductions: "Special Agent Monroe, Special Agent Simms."

Amir turned to face them. "Amir Yazdi. I'm sure this is all a mistake."

"We've spoken with your mother and your sister," Monroe said, "and we'd like to ask you a few questions. You are not under suspicion, and you can request an attorney be present."

Amir glanced at his mother, who looked devastated. She shook her head at him and wept, mascara streaking down her cheeks out of red, puffy eyes, a look of helplessness in the face of despair. He glanced at Taraneh, a model of calm and poise overlaid with concern. "I have nothing to hide," he said. "I don't need an attorney."

"Would you like to sit down?"

"I'm fine."

Special agent Monroe nodded and went on, all business. "What do you do, Amir?"

"I'm third year architecture at Rice."

"Have you ever worked at Mitronica?"

"No."

"Not even part time, like during summer vacation?"

"No. I have no interest in electronics."

"Are you aware that Mitronica has been exporting microelectronics to Iran via Venezuela?"

Again Amir glanced at his mother, who couldn't stop shaking her head. "I am not and I don't believe it." Taraneh agreed with a slight nod.

"We've been monitoring Mitronica for over a year and we believe we have evidence that proves otherwise."

Amir shrugged his shoulders adamantly. "My father has always been a good, law-abiding citizen."

"As far as you know."

There was glibness about Monroe that sickened Amir. "Everything in life is as far as we know," he said.

"Did you ever discuss with your father Iran's nuclear program?"

It was one of the most stupid questions Amir had ever been asked. Are there any Iranian-American families who *don't* discuss the mother country's nuclear program? He could think of several smart-ass retorts but he thought it unwise to antagonize Monroe.

"Amir, enough," Laleh Yazdi said, her voice cracking with emotion. She turned to Monroe. "I told you...we are not involved in the business, and our family discussions are private matters."

"Can't Amir answer for himself?"

"Yes, I can."

"Amir—" his mother interjected again.

Amir held a hand out at his mother while keeping his eyes on the FBI man. "But I won't answer any more of your questions without an attorney present," he said.

Another nod from Taraneh.

"I called Kenneth and Miles," Laleh said to Amir. "They are...both...out of the country...returning tonight."

"Then your questions will have to wait," Amir said to Monroe.

"Are you on a first name basis with your father's attorneys too?" Monroe said.

Amir squinted at the FBI man. Was that a hint of mockery he had heard in his tone? "Where's my father?" he demanded, not afraid to show he wasn't intimidated.

Taraneh replied, "They've taken him to the federal jail, downtown."

Amir kept his eyes on Monroe. "I want to see him."

The FBI man shook his head and said, "Only his attorney can visit him right now."

Amir sensed it would be futile to argue. "So that's it?" he said.

"I'm afraid so," Monroe said smugly. "We're a nation of laws."

"And we are citizens of this nation of laws," Amir said, staring Monroe down. "We wouldn't have it any other way."

"Glad to hear it." Monroe placed a business card on the coffee table. "I'm sure we'll be seeing each other again."

Long after the FBI men, the HPD officers and the media scrum had left, Amir was still cycling between joining his sister in consoling his mother, assuring her things would be alright, and cursing the Iranian regime's mullahs and their nuclear program. While Taraneh eschewed politics, Amir's mother was on his father's side of the ideological divide, and while this was no time to argue about politics, the air of family crisis led them both to vent at each other. Amir voiced his wish, repeatedly and out loud, that Iran would go back to being Iran, not a pariah state, but a respected member of the international community. His mother dissented, as she always did when the subject came up between them. Eventually they heeded Taraneh's pleas to leave the subject alone while agreeing to disagree. With his father around, Amir would have had both his parents arguing against him while his sister stayed out of it. He desperately wished it were so today.

***

The bellhop at the Dulles Airport Marriott first sensed a situation was developing when he heard two car horns doing battle with each other. He looked in the direction of the sound and realized it was two ladies vying for a parking spot. One, driving a minivan, barged her way into the spot, while the other, in a compact, reacted by leaning on her horn, eliciting a like response. When the horns fell silent vitriol was exchanged. The minivan driver got out, slammed her door, and stormed over to the hotel entrance. The bellhop judiciously got out of her way. The other lady retaliated by parking her car so that it blocked the minivan from reversing out, seemingly unconcerned that she was also blocking the cars on either side. Another door slammed, another defiant march into the hotel. The bellhop wasn't about to miss this episode of Real Soccer Moms of

Dulles, and he followed them into the lobby. The staff manning the reception desk and the patrons at the lobby bar were taken aback when the shouting started anew. The bellhop urged a colleague at the reception to call security, and then he intervened by stepping between the antagonists, whose use of the word *Bitch!* had intensified. Over the ensuing few minutes no blows were landed but tempers flailed and a variety of fingers were aimed in both directions. Things calmed down when two patrol officers from the Metropolitan Washington Airports Authority Police Department strode into the lobby. Appropriately, one was a female, and she took charge of the situation. Accusations flew as the two sides of the story were told. Agreement was clearly out of the question, and eventually it was decided to the satisfaction of all but one that since possession was nine-tenths of the law, the minivan would stay as parked and the compact would have to move. This was supervised by the police officers who thought better of handing out tickets. As the cops were leaving the scene the female officer stopped and stiffened. She took a step back and crossed over to the next row of parked cars, to the blue Toyota FJ Cruiser that had caught her eye. She stayed put while her partner went back to the hotel entrance and drove their patrol car to where she stood. The check on the onboard computer was instantaneous. The Toyota's license plate matched that of the active APB.

Backup deputies were summoned and a cordon was established around the hotel. Sheriff Hart himself arrived and took command until the FBI's Joseph Mayle joined him.

The hotel's front desk did not show that a Mike Massey had registered or held a reservation. However, a check against the name Mahmoud Massevadegh showed that someone by that name had booked a room using a Barclay's Visa credit card, had checked in to room 3017, that morning, and had not yet checked out. A search of room 3017 revealed it was vacant; the bed had not been as much as touched, let alone slept in, and the only thing out of the ordinary was a missing trashcan liner in the restroom. Surfaces were dusted for fingerprints. Undaunted, the lawmen then conducted a systematic sweep through the entire hotel, including a physical check in every room, much to the ire of sleeping guests who had to be awakened, plus all public and service spaces. When all was said and done, the only evidence that Massevadegh had been there was the testimony of the receptionist who had checked him in. She provided a positive ID when shown his photograph.

The FBI's subsequent review of passenger manifests and reservations for all airlines operating flights in and out of Dulles turned up nothing. Much to the consternation of Jason Hart and Joseph Mayle, Mahmoud Massevadegh, a.k.a. Mike Massey, had apparently disappeared without a trace.

**

It stunned Dana to learn that Mike Massey was really Mahmoud Massevadegh, citizen of Iran. The fact that she'd had no clue was mortifying. Massevadegh had hidden his true identity from everyone at eRock. Legitimate name changes happen all the time; there was, after all, a legal process in place with nominal differences from state to state, but still, this one felt like being mocked without even knowing about it. She took it as a personal affront. A mixture of outrage and revulsion welled up inside her. The deeper this Mike Massey pile of shit got, the more nauseating it smelled.

When she had escorted Massey out of VA2, it was the first time she'd spoken to him or heard him speak. Yes, he had an accent, but he looked like he could have Latino ancestry. Steve

64

Smith would go ballistic, not because Mike Massey was Iranian, but because nobody at eRock was aware of that. At least that's what it looked like to Dana. Knowing Smith, he would probably feel she should have been aware of it, even though Massey was hired before she joined eRock and she had nothing to do with the process, or a background check, or ensuring the I-9 form was filled out correctly. This was more than sickening; it was noxious. Security is all about predicting and preempting, less about reacting after the fact. Was it really easier being a Secret Service agent than director of security at a datacenter company? Or had she just lost her edge?

A chip on the shoulder was a weight, a burden, something to be discarded. Now here she was bearing one the size of an anvil. This was no longer about what Steve Smith's opinion might be, this was about her and her ego. She had actually stood within ten yards of Mahmoud Ahmadinejad once, outside the UN building in New York, and had thought he looked slimier and creepier in real life than when being interviewed by Larry King on CNN. Now here she was, being tormented by another Iranian Mahmoud. The thought was too much to bear.

She had thought she was done for the day, but there was no way she could switch off now. She had to face the music, her own music, and the chorus of self-doubt was getting louder. She had to get inside Massevadegh's head. At this point in time, there was one way she could maybe begin to do that, and there was no Gaussian genius shortcut for it.

She got in her car and headed back to eRock.

The company's employees, from CEO down, are strictly prohibited from bringing personal computers onto corporate premises, and eRock's internal IT system is geared to routinely back up every search done on corporate laptops and desktops to its private cloud. Employees know this policy; they sign off on it when they sign on. Massevadegh had worked there for twenty-seven months. He was human. He had to have done some browsing while on duty. Dana called the head of IT from her car, Friday evening be damned, and explained the situation. By the time she arrived back in Ashburn an email was waiting in her inbox with two links, one to an image of Mike Massey's hard drive, the other to his browsing history. She had barely started looking when the opening notes of *Birdland* drew her eyes to her phone. It was her mother. This was an inopportune time and she needed to keep it short.

"Hey, Mom."

"Hi, Dear."

"I'm still at the office and super busy. Did you talk to Dad?"

"Yes. You can come over tomorrow, but it'll have to be before noon because he's going to be in Baltimore all afternoon."

"Thanks, Mom. How about I call you before I leave in the morning?"

"That's fine. And Dana, it's going to be OK. His eyes lit up when I told him you wanted to apologize."

"Glad to hear it. Listen, I'm working on something pressing…let me go, and I'll call you in the morning."

Dana dropped her phone on the desk. That was one worry off her mind for the time being. She turned her attention back to the computer screen. Mike Massey—Mahmoud Massevadegh—had started off today being an unwelcome distraction; now he was a head-on menace, a challenge to her intellect and awareness because the more she discovered about him, the more her instinct told her there was to discover.

The first decision was whether to start with Massey's oldest searches and come forward in time or go the other way, starting with the most recent. With his HR file she had gone old to recent.

Now she decided to flip that approach and see what he'd been looking at of late.

Again her phone interrupted her. This time it was Sheriff Hart. She hoped he was calling to tell her they had the bastard in custody.

"Good news and bad news," Hart said. "We found his car, but there's no sign of him." He told her about the search at the Marriott and added: "He hasn't checked out of the hotel, so there are deputies stationed in the lobby in case he shows up. The FBI's checked with all airlines that operate out of IAD and he's not on any passenger list. At least not as Mike Massey or Mahmoud Massevadegh. He could be in the terminal, not yet booked on a flight. TSA has been alerted. If he tries to go through security, we got him."

Dana heart sank. "Could be that someone picked him up at the hotel," she said.

"Could be."

"There are no trains out of the airport, and he's not going anywhere on foot. He's either in one of the buildings over there...maybe he's waiting to fly out...or he's riding with someone who is either knowingly or unknowingly helping him out."

Dana thought furiously through the options. "Or he's rented a car," she said. "He knows the golfers saw his car. He could've parked it at the Marriott, taken a cab to one of the rental agencies and driven out in a rental car."

The sheriff realized that was a stone they hadn't turned over. "Yes. Yes, we'll look into that right away. Let me get on it."

After she hung up with the sheriff and turned her attention back to Massey's browsing history, Dana noticed something odd. The network access audit logs showed that some of the searches from his laptop were made under the username *mmassey*, but others were under a different username, *kturner*. She sat back in her chair and squinted at the screen. Both were consistent with the username format at eRock. She pulled up the employee directory on the company's intranet. There was one Turner, a Kevin Turner, a facilities engineer in Ashburn, so a colleague of Massey's. Why had Turner used Massey's laptop to browse the web?

She scrolled through more searches and saw it wasn't an occasional thing; the vast majority of searches were by *kturner*. She paused, thinking about what that might mean.

She reached into a drawer and took out a rubber band. With a few practiced motions she arranged her hair into a ponytail, an impulsive habit when thinking hard. It was like pulling her hair to the back of her head freed up her brain.

Why wouldn't Kevin Turner use his own laptop?

One potential answer came to mind, and the more she thought about it the likelier it seemed. If she was right, Massey was even craftier than she had thought. It wouldn't be difficult to find out. The employee directory included email addresses and cell phone numbers. She called Kevin Turner's eRock cell phone. Like a good, responsible facilities engineer, he answered.

"Kevin, it's Dana McLaughlan, director of security."

"Yes ma'am."

"Catching you at a bad time?"

"No ma'am. What can I do for you?"

"I need to ask you some questions. This is related to the power outage we had today."

"Sure."

"First understand there's nothing you need to be worried about. I'm looking at Mike Massey's web browsing history and I'm seeing some of it was done on his laptop but with your login credentials."

Turner hesitated, thought about what he'd heard and said: "I'm not sure I know what that means."

"Did you ever browse using Massey's laptop?"

No hesitation now: "No. Never."

It was as Dana had thought, had hoped. "Did you ever give him your password?"

"Give him my password? Why would I do that?"

Basic social engineering, dummy. Taking care to keep her tone more respectful than her thoughts, Dana said: "Like…did he ever come to you and say he needed your credentials to check—"

"Yes, there was one time, let's see, maybe three, four months back, we were on a shift together and he wanted to test the BMS—the building management system—to see if it would alarm if two people accessed it simultaneously from the same terminal. It's supposed to—"

"So what did you do?"

"Well, I gave him my password and he ran the test with me watching, and it alarmed."

Dana shook her head. "Kevin, Kevin. *Never* give anyone your password. Or if you do, change it."

"Yes ma'am, I changed it the next day."

"You sure about that?"

"Oh yeah."

"OK, good. Best not to give it to anyone in the first place."

"Yes ma'am."

"Thank you."

"My pleasure. You have a good night."

Dana believed Kevin Turner, and now she believed she knew what she was looking at. Again, not caring that it was Friday evening, she called the head of IT, apologized for the repeat disturbance, and told him about the conversation with Turner. Then she threw another request at him. Moments later she received another email from him, this time with a link to Kevin Turner's browsing history. She was thrilled to see it proved she was right.

Turner had been close on the three to four months, but a tad short. It had been five months back, in November 2014, when he had last changed his password. Since then, Turner had browsed using his new login password, and his activity was unremarkable. But also since then his old password was still active on searches and bookmarks. That could only mean one thing. Massey had used Turner's login credentials right after his little BMS charade was over, and, crucially, he had never logged out. So from that point in time on, despite there being a new password for Turner, the old one had also remained valid until the first time its user logged out, which the user—Mike Massey—never did. It was a simple scheme that enabled Massey to impersonate Kevin Turner while browsing at work. He was smart. He was also arrogant, because he thought no one would ever check so no one would ever find out. But Dana had checked, and she had found him out.

She jumped when her phone rang again. It was Sheriff Hart.

"You were spot on, Dana. I had deputies check with the car rental agencies. He rented one from National using his Iranian name and a British-based credit card, the same card he used at the Marriott."

Dana felt a rush of blood, a thrill that came from knowing that not only were they onto the bastard, but that it was because of her.

"We've got the details of the rental car, a silver VW Jetta, and the license plate. We've updated the APB, and extended it to all neighboring states, Maryland, West Virginia, Delaware, Kentucky, Tennessee and the Carolinas. Just in case."

"Great. I appreciate you updating me."

"I'll continue to do so. Credit where it's due, this latest discovery is because of you. I'd have you on my team any day."

Dana was giddy when she hung up the phone. This is what turned her on, solving unknowns using wits and brainpower, not worrying about access controls in a datacenter. It had been a mistake to retire from the Service. But retire she had, and there was no reversing that.

She went back to Massey's browsing trail. He had schemed to cover his tracks by using someone else's identity to browse the web. It would make sense for him to do so if he had something to hide. Dana was now manically curious to find out what that something might be.

***

The drive from Rocky Mount to Raleigh was uneventful, which is exactly how Mahmoud wanted it. His spirits had soared with the success at the ATM, and he concentrated on driving defensively and staying within the speed limit. The one distraction he allowed himself—apart from constantly re-living in his mind the incredible events of the day—was the radio, tuned to news. He half-hoped to hear about the fallout from his escapades, but the Dominion power outage was unlikely to be of interest beyond the environs of Loudon County, and the ATM caper would probably not be discovered before Saturday morning, or maybe not until Monday. Which, of course, suited him perfectly. Now was not the time, and these were not the incidents, with which to make headlines. Today's escapades were teasers. The headlines could wait for the main event. Until then, his bywords had to be *vigilance, caution.*

The only item of real interest on the radio was a shock jock talk show rant about Dzhokhar Tsarnaev's guilty verdict of two days prior. Mahmoud had mixed feelings about the Tsarnaev brothers. On the one hand, their hearts were in the right place. On the other, their bombing of the Boston Marathon had been so amateurish, they had virtually served themselves to the FBI on a platter. Besides, they were small-time players. Martyrdom was honorable, but if you're going to go out with a bang, make it a big bang.

By the time he reached the Comfort Suites at 64 and Corporation Parkway, the spot he had picked to spend the night at before he'd left his apartment in Herndon this morning, he was tired and emotionally taut. Today marked the beginning of a new phase of his life, a phase he had prepared for with intense singularity of purpose. If everything went right, if his plan succeeded, America as it was known today would cease to be. Victims of American imperialism, hubris and hypocrisy the world over would rejoice. He harbored no desire to be recognized as the hero; he would have been happy living the rest of his life as the anonymous perpetrator of the demise of the American empire, but for one development. Now that Iran and six other nations were close to concluding a deal that would defang Iran, he could singlehandedly torpedo that deal if he not only crippled America's power grid, but also let it be known that an Iranian was behind the attack. Today he had pulled off two modest successes that validated his planning and execution. His sense of optimism was based not on dreams, but the realization that he had the right tools and the wherewithal to use them. And, praise be, *Khoda* was with him.

He chose a parking spot between two other cars, killed the engine and locked the doors. He still had a long drive ahead of him over the next few days, and it was imperative to get adequate rest in order to be fully alert when behind the wheel. He had to get a good night's sleep.

The VW Jetta was cramped compared to a hotel room, but keeping his head under the parapet was paramount. Besides, he wasn't as uncomfortable as the passengers aboard Iran Air flight 655 on July 3, 1988, when an American missile blew them out of the sky. Everything was relative.

The silence was welcome, albeit deafening. Absent the numbing drone of the engine, his brain raced like it was on steroids, rewinding to the triumphs of today and sweeping forward to the master stroke yet to come, like a twister bouncing around between past destruction and future carnage. He closed his eyes and tried to no avail to block out the febrile images in his head. He thought, as he often did, about how succulent would be the taste of revenge, particularly so because he could fight fire with fire. They—America and Israel—thought they had played smart when they unleashed the Stuxnet virus against Iran's nuclear program. No need for bunker-busting bombs to be dropped from above when you can decimate a target from within. But in today's world, revenge for one act of cyber-warfare could be exacted with another. They were about to learn. Israel would be dealt with later. First, though, the enabler, the underlying evil, America. They might not be awed, but they were certainly going to be shocked.

His slid his seat as far to the rear as it would go and reclined the back all the way down. He yawned, a good sign, even though his synapses remained hyperactive. He wished he had a sleeping pill. He made a mental note to buy some over the counter when he got to Mexico.

***

It was well after midnight when Dana decided she had seen enough. The pattern that had unfolded as she'd delved deeper into

Massey's browsing history had left her spooked and galvanized in equal measure. It had been a long day, even tumultuous by the standards of what she'd come to expect at eRock, and she was tired. She wondered if she was getting carried away. She resolved to sleep on this and in the morning rethink and re-evaluate what she'd learned.

She printed out a hard copy of several of the search entries she considered most damning. She read them again and ran over some key words with a yellow highlighter. She slid the loose sheets into a manila folder and took them with her when she left the office.

She drove to her condo in Reston in a state of quasi-suspended consciousness. If the way she was connecting the dots was right, Mike Massey was planning to paralyze the country. She was willing to stick her neck out on this, and if she were crazy wrong, well, that would actually be a relief. Tomorrow she would see what Sheriff Hart and the FBI's Joseph Mayle thought, but for now, from her perspective, this affair transcended any chip on her shoulder, and it certainly transcended eRock. If she was right, this business with Mike Massey—or Mahmoud Massevadegh, or whatever name the son of a bitch wanted to use—had begun to take on the appearance of a matter of national security.

Chapter Six

Mahmoud woke up still feeling like he needed a good night's sleep. The combination of constricted space in the VW's uncomfortable front seat and overnight lows in the 40's had left him stiff, cold and bleary-eyed. It was tempting even now to get a room and a comfortable bed, but he had to keep rolling. He reached into his backpack. Seeing and feeling the wad of hundred dollar bills raised his spirits. As he surveyed the Comfort Suites parking lot, he reminded himself of the sacrifices of the martyrs. To those on a sacred mission, thoughts of comfort were an unnecessary distraction.

He didn't know much about Raleigh, and he didn't care to. It was just another American city; with few exceptions, if you've seen one you've seen them all. The coast was clear, so he got out of the car and stretched. He would have liked to go into the lobby and use the restroom, but he couldn't risk being seen. He positioned himself between the Jetta and the adjacent car, and urinated. He used some of the water he had bought at Walgreens to wash the sleep out of his eyes and brush his teeth.

He had noted that the Sunset Avenue branch of Old North Bank in Rocky Mount had lobby hours of 9 a.m. to 6 p.m. on Monday through Friday and 9 a.m. to 1 p.m. on Saturdays. So he figured he had about two hours before the earliest complaint could be made inside the lobby about the ATM being dysfunctional. It would be a little longer before any of the bank's employees discovered the ATM had been hacked. Longer still before anyone checked the CCTV footage and reported the silver VW with covered license plates to the police. It might actually not happen for days, but he had to play it safe. He called customer service at

National and reported that his car wouldn't start. The representative who fielded his call quickly established that, yes, his rental included roadside assistance, and after checking with a dispatcher, informed him his proximity to the Raleigh-Durham International Airport meant a replacement car would be delivered to the Comfort Suites at which he was located within the hour.

He checked the map of the surrounding area on his phone. There was a Burger King just down the road on the other side of 64. Following the same routine as at McDonald's in Rocky Mount the night before, he ordered in the drive-through lane and ate his breakfast in the car, before returning to the Comfort Suites parking lot. As he waited, he again studied the map. The shortest distance between two points was a straight line, and the straightest line between Raleigh and his destination for the day was 64 to Asheboro, 49 to Charlotte, then 85 through Atlanta and on to Alabama. God willing, there was no reason why he couldn't make it to the Gulf Coast before he made his next overnight stop.

America. The smartest people in the world. Albert Einstein, moonwalks, Apple. The dumbest people in the world. A democracy for sale to the highest bidder, ATMs that spew cash, and the national spine an aging, fragile power grid.

National's customer service representative was good, as she had set his expectations with a margin of safety. Fifty minutes after he hung up with her, a tow truck arrived with a replacement car. With quiet efficiency he moved his bag and backpack out of the Volkswagen and into the white Nissan Pulsar. He kept his cap and glasses on and exchanged the bare minimum of words with the tow truck driver. He was in a hurry to get on his way and he showed it. There was no reason to wait for the disabled Jetta to be towed away, so he drove off in the Pulsar and resumed his drive to the southwest. He thought about what good planning it had been to purchase the roadside assistance option from National and allowed himself a smile of self-satisfaction.

Some mechanic somewhere would eventually discover that the reason the Jetta wouldn't start was that its fuel pump relay's wiring harness had come loose, but that would take hours, maybe days. If the mechanic were a fastidious sort, he might report to his superior that this was such a rare occurrence that somebody must have intentionally separated the harness from the relay. Mahmoud's immediate goal was to ensure that by then he would also have separated himself from North Carolina.

***

Massevadegh had in fact just crossed the state border into South Carolina when the first customer of Rocky Mount's Old North Bank complained to the branch manager about the OUT OF SERVICE notice on the ATM screen on Saturday, April 11th, at 9:17 a.m. local time. Within the hour the manager had filed a report with the City of Rocky Mount Police Department that the ATM had been emptied of all its cash without any visible signs of forced entry. Review of the CCTV recordings for the previous evening showed three cars had pulled up at the ATM, the third of which immediately drove off, presumably because by then the OUT OF SERVICE message was already on display. The two cars before it were a black Chevy Tahoe, license plates legible, driver's face visible, and a silver VW Jetta, license plates and driver's face obscured. With the previous evening's APB for a silver VW Jetta still fresh in the minds of the investigating police officers, they immediately notified the FBI.

***

Dana slept sporadically, her mind agitated by the potential ramifications of what she had discovered about Mike Massey. By sunrise she was in the shower, wondering what was the earliest time that would not be too early to call Jason Hart. She decided nine would be civil enough. She dried herself while still in the shower stall, then threw on a bathrobe and wrapped her hair in a towel. She brewed a cup of mint tea and drank it while in deep contemplation on the whereabouts and intentions of Mahmoud Massevadegh. When she called Hart and told him she had some new information to share with him he told her to meet him at his office at nine-thirty. That didn't leave time for breakfast, but she didn't care. She didn't even think of makeup. She left the condo wearing faded jeans and a white V-neck sweater, her hair still damp, with not a care for her appearance.

When she arrived at the Loudon County Sheriff's Office there was a palpable ripple of excitement, like everyone was on adrenaline therapy. It was a feeling she recognized from her days in law enforcement, when the battle of wits against a live one was in full game-on mode. She discovered from one of the deputies that the buoyancy was down to the discovery of Massevadegh's Toyota. Jason Hart was in the same groove. "He's smart but we're smarter," he declared from behind his desk when Dana entered his office. "We're going to nail him."

"He's not as smart as he thinks," Dana said as she handed Hart the folder. "Or maybe his weakness is arrogance, underestimating us. I went through his web browsing history at the office last night. He's spent a lot of time researching power grid vulnerabilities and he downloaded tools that can be used to compromise the SCADA systems that control the grid. He impersonated a colleague, probably never occurred to him we would discover that."

Hart opened the folder and looked at the highlighted text on the first sheet. "Remind me what SCADA stands for."

"Supervisory control and data acquisition, an industrial automation and control system heavily deployed by the utilities. It enables them to remotely monitor and control their power systems infrastructure. But its Achilles Heel is that it's network-based, and a lot of it runs on unprotected networks that are accessible to the bad guys. Especially the older parts of the grid. The systems were never designed with protections against being connected to the Internet. And the grid itself is so interconnected, a failure in one place can very quickly domino to other areas. Remember the Northeast power failure of 2003? That started in a suburb of Cleveland and ended up affecting 50 million people in something like ten states. It even spread into Canada. It cost billions of dollars and ten people lost their lives."

Hart's expression grew sterner and he turned back to the papers in the folder. "What's Shodan?" he said. "Sounds like a James Clavell novel."

"Shodan is a search engine, like Google, only Google logs webpage contents and gives you links to the ones with content most relevant to your query. Shodan logs machines connected to the Internet. Unfortunately it's publicly available, and it pinpoints the hardware running SCADA systems which control critical infrastructure...like the power grid."

"Why the hell is it all out in the open like that?"

"The power grid's everywhere, right? Say something needs to be fixed at some substation at four a.m. The techs assigned to fix it can either get out of bed and drive—maybe for hours—to the site, or they can get on their computers and fix it remotely from where they are. Which do you think is the preferred option?"

"That doesn't explain why it's accessible to the bad guys. Why isn't it set up so that only legitimate users can log on?"

"Like I said, some of the SCADA systems are so old they weren't designed with the Internet in mind. To beef them up would require downtime. You think the citizens of Manhattan would agree to a couple of weeks without power so their grid protection features can be upgraded?"

"Whew," Hart said. "How do you know all this stuff?"

Dana smiled. "I started chasing hackers fifteen years ago. The Secret Service isn't just about protective ops. Investigating computer and telecommunications fraud is a big part of the mission."

"You think Massevadegh's planning to attack the grid?"

"If he'd only searched for Shodan, maybe not. But you can see there he also searched for—and downloaded—Energetic Bear, Havex and Metasploit."

Hart looked at her blankly.

"Metasploit is penetration testing software. It uncovers weaknesses, highlights risks. So it's basically an attack kit. Energetic Bear is an online espionage...well, I guess you'd call it an online espionage movement. Also known as Dragonfly. First appeared about four years ago when it spied on, and maybe compromised, energy systems in Europe. And Havex is what's known as a Remote Access Trojan, or RAT. It's been known to cause communications platforms to crash, which causes applications that rely on those communications to also crash. The bottom line is...the fact that he's into this stuff and downloading it strongly suggests one of two things. He's either researching ways to protect the grid from attack, or ways to attack it."

The sheriff looked like this was all starting to get over his head. "Do you think he has the skills to use these tools to attack the grid?" he said.

"I don't know," Dana replied, "but I think we have to assume he does."

"I mean, we know he used a drone, but anyone can fly a drone. This stuff here is a whole different ball game."

Hart's assistant buzzed him on the intercom and said Joe Mayle of the FBI was on the line. He took the call, and from the way he looked at Dana as he listened to Mayle, she sensed it was new information related to Massevadegh. Hart scribbled on a notepad and asked brief questions to do with the name and location of a bank. When he hung up his face was flushed with excitement.

"You're not going to believe this," Hart said. "Last night someone ripped off an ATM machine at a bank in Rocky Mount, North Carolina, just across the state line, and made off with twenty grand in cash. Nothing was broken, so it wasn't a physical attack, they're speculating it was a remote hack. We'll know for sure when they check out the machine's software to see if it's been modified, but I'll bet they're going to find it has been. The cameras at that ATM picked up a car with concealed license place and someone with a concealed face. I told you Massevadegh rented a silver VW Jetta from the airport, right?"

Dana nodded.

"The car in the video is a silver Jetta."

The only movement was blinking eyes.

"So, Sheriff," Dana said, tilting her head in a told-you-so manner. "Do we think he has the skills to attack the grid?"

Hart stood up and reached for his keys. "Joe Mayle's going to be in his office in Manassas in ten minutes. I think you should come and show him what you've found."

"You bet," Dana said.

Dana's mind was in hyper-multitask mode on the drive to Manassas. 10:00 a.m. till noon on Saturdays was a time slot she normally reserved for yoga, and ironically, while that was out of the question today, she felt she had probably never needed it more. She found the unification of mind, body and breathing imparted by yoga—together with the serenity of meditation—enhanced her physiological suppleness, heightened her awareness and sharpened her clarity of thought. Now, just coming on twenty-four hours since Mike Massey had flown a drone into an overhead power line, she felt tired, stressed and tense. It was hard to believe how what at first appeared to be a local incident involving a disgruntled ex-employee had so rapidly become a matter of grave national security implications. She expected Joseph Mayle's assessment of the threat would match hers.

The Special-Agent-in-Charge of the FBI's resident agency in Manassas was African-American and tall enough to suggest he went into law enforcement because his basketball skills were not quite good enough for the NBA. After the introductions were made, Mayle ushered them into a conference room where his laptop was already situated in front of the chair at the head of the table. Hart sat to his right. As she took her seat to Mayle's left, Dana thought the arrangement a fair reflection of the reality of the respective roles.

"Sheriff Hart tells me you spent a few years at the nation's second-best federal law enforcement agency," Mayle said with a grin.

Dana sensed that the jab was in friendly spirits and played along. "I'll take the high road," she parried, "just like I did back then."

Mayle smiled and raised his hands, as if in surrender, then he got down to business. "I understand you've got some more information you want to share with us about your man."

"Yes. Has there still been no sign of him?"

Mayle shook his head. "He's laying low. Could be holed up in a motel somewhere, waiting for the sun to go down before he gets on the road again."

Hart grunted, disappointed that it was looking increasingly unlikely he or his deputies would be involved in apprehending Massevadegh.

"I did a search of his browsing history at eRock," Dana said. "He's researched power grid vulnerabilities and downloaded tools that suggest he's planning a malicious attack against the power grid." She placed the folder on the table in front of Mayle.

Mayle opened the folder and looked at the highlighted text. His expression gave nothing away. "Do we know if he's armed?" he said.

"We don't," Hart said.

Mayle took a minute to scan through the first two pages. When he looked up at Dana his expression was one of concern. "I see what you're saying about the malware. But I don't know I can jump to the same conclusion."

"What do you mean?" Dana said.

"The attacks we see against the power grid are physical. People shooting at transformers, that kind of thing. But there has never been a successful cyber-attack against the grid. Not one."

Not the response Dana had anticipated.

"Really?" Hart said.

"Never," Mayle said. "There are probes, lots of them, all the time. It's mostly impossible to tell who's behind them, but we can be sure the Chinese and Russians are in the mix. To be honest, we probe their grids too. But the fact is, there has never been one recorded outage that resulted from a cyber-attack."

Dana had not realized that, and she couldn't refute it. It was deflating, but she wasn't ready to back off. "No terrorist had ever flown a commercial airliner into a skyscraper before nine eleven," she said pointedly. "Yet when it happened we were criticized for failing to connect the dots. All of us were criticized for failing to connect the dots."

Mayle held her gaze. "You think there are dots here we're not connecting?" he said.

"I'm saying if we connect them the threat level is way up there."

Mayle reclined in his chair and brought his hands together over his stomach. "What would you have me do?"

Dana already knew what she wanted from the FBI. "I think we should consider Massevadegh a most-wanted."

Mayle spoke respectfully, but firmly. "I can understand you feeling that was because he caused an outage at your company," he said.

"And he stole someone's identity," Dana said, "and he committed credit card fraud when he purchased the drones, and now we know he hacked an ATM—that's one we haven't seen before in this country—and we have evidence he downloaded tools used to attack the grid. This is no longer about eRock, Joe. It's much bigger than that."

Mayle frowned. "We don't know it was him at the ATM," he said. "The drone attack, granted, there's the positive ID from the golfers. Same for the purchase of the drones. But at the ATM there's only grainy CCTV footage of a silver Jetta with covered license plates and a driver with concealed features. You want it to be him, and again, I understand that. The grid malware can be downloaded by anyone; it's not illegal to have it. We don't know that he's ever used it. I really don't think we've got enough on him—yet—to elevate him to most wanted."

Sheriff Jason Hart watched the exchange with fascination but stayed out of it.

Dana was taken aback. She sighed with consternation. "I guess it's…like…how clear do you want the signs to be? What if you do nothing and it turns out you're wrong?"

"We're not doing nothing, we've got an APB out for the car we know he's driving, in Virginia and the surrounding states. If he's spotted, he'll be stopped, and he'll be arrested and he'll prosecuted for the drone attack and the identity theft. And if we can prove he was behind the ATM hack, he'll pay for that too. I really think that response is appropriate, because it's based on what we know, not what might be. What if I escalate based on a presumption and it turns out someone else hacked that ATM?"

"What if you don't and he attacks the grid?" Dana said.

Mayle shook his head and it was clear he wasn't about to change his mind. "I need more, Dana," he said. He rolled his chair back and stood up. "Let's just see what happens. He's going to show his face somewhere and we'll get him."

He didn't sound unreasonable, but Dana still disagreed with his position. "Thank you for your time," she said curtly. She perfunctorily shook Mayle's offered hand, picked up her folder and walked out of the room.

Hart could sense Dana's disappointment as they drove back to Chantilly. "For what it's worth, I'm with you on the dots," he said, "and I think it was him at the ATM."

Then why didn't you say so back there? Dana thought to herself. She didn't react.

"But you know how it is," Hart continued, "Mayle's in the lead now. We have to let the FBI do their job and wait and see what happens."

Dana was deep in thought, already preoccupied with next steps. When they got back to Hart's office, she thanked him for taking her to Manassas, told him to let her know as soon as he heard anything, and excused herself. She had already decided what she was going to do, and it was not wait and see what happens. She still had connections inside the Secret Service; it was time to leverage them.

While most people might think the Secret Service's mission is protection of key individuals, primarily the president, the truth is the agency was established in 1865 as a law enforcement force focused on investigating the counterfeiting of U.S. currency. That is to this day part of the agency's remit, but its authority has since been expanded to encompass investigation of crimes involving financial fraud, computer fraud, telecommunications fraud, false identification documents, electronic funds transfers, and, more recently, protection of the nation's infrastructure. The Mahmoud Massevadegh case involved several of those elements. There was one person at the Secret Service who she felt more comfortable reaching out to than anyone else.

Noel Markovski was someone with whom Dana went back many years. They had met on assignment with the Secret Service in Austin, Texas, where their work was key to the successful apprehension of a hacker threatening to blackmail the U.S. government. They subsequently served together on the same Protective Ops team with responsibility for the physical safety and wellbeing of foreign leaders visiting the U.S. Dana had attended Noel's wedding, and he had led her colleagues' toasts as master of ceremonies at her farewell party when she had retired from the

Service. She hadn't seen him since then, but he was still on the inside, the one person she could trust to do not only the right thing, but to also do right by her.

"Hey there, stranger!" Markovski said when he took her call. "Tell me you've cashed out and gone uptown on us lowly Secret Service folks."

"I wish," Dana said. "How the hell are you, Noel?"

"I'm just right! How are you?"

"I'm good, I'm good. Is this a good time, can you talk?"

"Linda and I were just heading out with Amy, but…what's up?"

"Please tell Linda hi for me. And how is Amy? She must be two now, yeah?"

"She turned two last month. Terrible twos is not something they trained us for, but it's a real and constant threat, you know?"

Dana laughed out loud. "I want to see you all, but 1 don't want to keep you from dinner so let me quickly tell you why I'm calling."

Markovski gestured to his wife that he had to take the call, and walked to the living room. "Shoot."

Dana kept it short. She told him about Massey, about the power line, the drone, the ID theft and credit card fraud, and told him there was more. Before Noel could think about it, Dana, in a calculated move, told him that the sheriff had enlisted the assistance of the FBI. That did the trick. The undercurrent of competitive rivalry between the two agencies was still healthy, and as Dana knew he would, Noel obliged her. They agreed to meet for lunch.

When she hung up the phone with Noel, Dana felt invigorated. There was a chance, of course, that Noel would react like Joe

Mayle had. But she had to try, because she couldn't just sit around waiting to see what happens.

She was still in the car, on her way back to Reston, when her phone rang. As soon as she saw it was her mother calling, Dana remembered she had forgotten to call her. Going to Hampstead today to make up with her father was now out of the question. She answered the phone hands-free with a sullen expression on her face. "Hi Mom, sorry I forgot to call you," she said.

"Yes, I waited for your call, then I thought maybe you were on your way up here," Meryl McLaughlan said. "I hope you're not, because your father's leaving for Baltimore in a few minutes."

"No, I'm not. I'm sorry, I should have called. It's just been one of those mornings."

"Okay, well, I just got worried, that's all."

"I'm sorry. My fault. What does tomorrow look like?"

"Let's play it by ear. You let me know."

"I will. I love you, Mom."

"I love you too."

Dana was upset with herself for neglecting to call. That was the kind of lapse that leaves people—in this case the people who meant the most to her—feeling like they were taken for granted. She had become so obsessed with Mahmoud Massevadegh that she wasn't thinking of anything, or anyone, else. Damn the son of a bitch. She just wanted him arrested, and *now!*

Chapter Seven

Noel Markovski and Dana McLaughlan were two of six Secret Service agents who attended a September 2012 briefing at the National Counterterrorism Center in McLean, Virginia, along with counterparts from the CIA, NSA and the Department of Defense. Apart from it being their first visit to the Liberty Crossing complex, which also includes the Office of the Director of National Intelligence, it was the occasion by which they discovered the Silver Diner in Tyson's Corner, just a mile away. A self-described retro diner with American comfort fare touting healthy, fresh and locally sourced organic food, Silver Diner quickly become one of Dana's favorite eateries. With Tyson's being equidistant from Reston, where Dana lived, and Arlington, where Noel's home was located, it was an easy choice for their lunch meeting on Saturday. They had agreed to meet at one, but Dana got there an hour early, still sans makeup, still in faded jeans and a sweater, still restless, and now hungry to boot.

Her meeting with Noel wasn't about lunch, it was about the contents of the folder she had brought with her, and she decided she would go ahead and eat before Noel arrived so she could talk while he ate. She hadn't had breakfast before leaving the house today so she ordered quinoa coconut pancakes. Distracted by uncertainty about how Noel might react to her threat assessment, she downed the food absentmindedly. Afterwards, as she sipped a pomegranate milkshake, she decided that—at least to begin with—she would not try to convince him, but instead let him make up his own mind. If his opinion differed from hers, then she would argue the case. It was an approach driven by her belief that she was right, and that his conclusion would mirror hers.

Bonds are forged by shared experiences, the more poignant, the tighter the bond. Bill Clinton was still serving his initial term as President in 1995 when Dana first met Noel at Austin's Robert Mueller Municipal Airport. She had already been stationed in Texas for two years when Noel arrived for his assignment at the Secret Service's field office in the Lone Star State's capital. Over the course of the next eight years they collaborated on a variety of cases involving cell-phone cloning, identity crimes, counterfeiting, computer fraud and money laundering. They were both single and third-generation of mostly European extraction, she of a strong Irish flavor, he proudly embracing the Polish national character that his parents and grandparents had preserved and handed down. While their families were both Catholic, that was where the differences between them first came to the fore. Dana was by then already beyond skeptical; Noel was a believer, but he never took offense at her positions, always invoking instead the letter and spirit of the Warsaw Confederation, which he held as the formal harbinger of legalized religious freedom in Europe, and the inspiration behind Thomas Jefferson's articulation of religious tolerance when drafting the U.S. Constitution. When Dana asked Noel how he internalized the scientifically inexplicable provenance of Cain's wife, his response was one she couldn't argue with: "The science is in my head, God is in my heart."

The first time Dana went undercover Noel gave her a miniature Lady of Czestochowa replica, telling her, "My faith will protect you." Now, as she watched him park his Volvo XC90 outside the Silver Diner, she was glad she had not only kept the Black Madonna, but had brought it with her. Maybe, if Noel was in two minds about Massevadegh, seeing the Madonna might sway him, for old times' sake. Dana watched as he ambled across the parking lot with the languid gait of a pro basketball player, which, at six feet four inches, he was tall enough to be. She wondered who was taller, Noel or Joe Mayle. It looked like Noel's blond hair had thinned, albeit without diminishing the boyish innocence of his kind, pleasant features. More than anyone else she had worked with at the Secret Service, Dana thought Noel embodied the agency's motto: *Worthy of trust and confidence.* She still found it weird to think he had a daughter. She stood as he approached the table, and they greeted each other with wide grins and a tight hug.

"I can't believe it's been six months," Noel said. "The corporate world becomes you. You look great!"

"Oh, Noel, ever the knight! You look good too! Thanks for coming out here. How's the family?"

Noel beamed. "Amy's a natural at terrible twos, and Linda's a champion terrible twos handler." He pulled a recent photograph of Amy out of his wallet and handed it to Dana.

"Oh my! What a precious little thing! Daddy's girl, I'm sure!"

"Of course! Isn't that how it's supposed to be?"

"Lucky Amy. Are you teaching her Polish?"

"You bet! I only speak to her in Polish. Linda speaks to her in English, of course, but for me, only Polish. And Amy's good! A few days ago I mistakenly said 'I love you' in English and she replied *Kohaam chye!* So she relates Polish to me, English to Linda. It's amazing! Of course, now that she's two, her favorite Polish word is *nie.* When it's me telling her something, it's *nie, nie, nie,* when it's Linda telling her, it's no, no, no!"

Dana laughed. "That is so cool! Bilingual from the get-go."

The waitress appeared tableside and offered Noel a menu.

"I've eaten," Dana told him, "so go ahead and order."

He opted for the fruit plate and a glass of fresh-squeezed orange juice.

"I've missed you," Dana said when the waitress left the table.

"I've missed you too. How are things going at eRock?"

Dana shook her head. "I'm not happy. I can't see myself staying there. But first I've got to deal with this—no, let me re-phrase that—I *want* to deal with this situation I told you about. Then we'll see."

"So, tell me more about this guy. You said he flew a drone into a power line?"

"That's the least of it, Noel."

"What do you mean?"

Dana slid the folder across the table in front of him and spoke in a low voice. "Before I tell you more, see for yourself what he's been researching and downloading and tell me what you think he's up to. I found this stuff after we talked."

Intrigued, Noel opened the folder. Dana watched him as he started reading, her eyes on his, awaiting any reaction. It didn't take long for him to glance up at her briefly before going back to the folder's contents. He lifted the top sheet of paper and read the second one, but his expression gave nothing away. He could have been sitting at the final table at the World Series of Poker. Dana was antsy but didn't show it; she forced herself to keep still, to match his stoicism.

Eventually Noel looked up again, his expression dead serious, and said, "Huh!"

Dana couldn't keep her anticipation bottled up any longer. "What do you make of that?" she said.

"Shodan and Havex? Energetic Bear, Metasploit, SCADA? Looks like this guy is very interested in grid vulnerabilities. How to find them…and…how to exploit them."

It was what Dana hoped he would say. "Thank you!" she said with relief. "And Noel, disrupting operations at eRock didn't require any of this. He did that with just a drone and changing settings on generator circuit breakers. This is...well! What's more, all his searches were done incognito. He got another engineer's login credentials and used them so if anyone checked it would look like it was the other guy."

"You found him out?"

"Yes."

Noel Nodded. "Way to go, Dana," he said softly.

"Wait...there's icing on this cake."

He looked at her quizzically.

Dana held back as the waitress delivered Noel's fruit salad and juice. When she was out of earshot again, Dana leaned toward Noel and said, "When we spoke yesterday I called him Mike Massey. That's an assumed name. A legally assumed name, but still. His real name is Mahmoud Massevadegh. This guy is from Iran. He was on an F1 OPT visa when eRock hired him after he finished a master's in electrical engineering at George Mason University."

"No shit!"

"No shit."

Noel pondered the implications, nodded slowly and said: "Have you shown this to Hart?"

"Hart and the FBI's guy in Manassas. A Joe Mayle. Do you know him?"

"No."

"He thinks they're doing enough with the APB. By the way, they found Massevadegh's car last night, at the Dulles Airport Marriott. He apparently parked it there and rented a car from National using his real name and a UK-based credit card. He's driving a silver VW Jetta, but he doesn't know we know."

Noel gulped down his juice, draining the glass in one go. He wiped his mouth with his napkin and said: "So he comes straight out of GMU to eRock on an F1 OPT, and spends two years assembling tools to attack the grid."

"Tools and, presumably, know-how."

"Wow. We've always assumed that the Chinese won't attack the grid because they're too vested in our economy, and the Russians won't because they have too much to lose. But one guy from Iran, acting alone—or maybe with support—it wouldn't be beyond that regime."

"Right. And there's more, Noel."

He raised his eyebrows at her.

"Last night someone hacked an ATM at a small bank in Rocky Mount, a town in North Carolina. Emptied the machine of about twenty thousand dollars in cash. The CCTV video shows three cars stopped at the ATM last night, one of them a silver VW Jetta with its license plates covered."

"No...*shit!*"

Dana could barely contain herself. "I'm telling you!" she gushed.

They were silent as Noel let it all sink in. "What do you think I should do?" he said.

"We don't know where he is. There's been no sign of him since the drone attack, other than at the ATM. And that's what it was, an attack, no doubt about that. I think we bring to bear all the resources we can into finding the son of a bitch before he does some real harm."

Noel handed her back the folder. "OK. I'll head down the road to Fairfax, stop by GMU, see if I can locate his adviser, see if we can learn any more about him. Maybe find out who his friends were so we can talk them, see if he ever said anything to anyone that might shed light on his motives, his plans. I know it's a Saturday, but I'll see what I can find out. Why don't you go talk to the people who worked with him at eRock and see if you can learn anything?"

"And there's something else that's bugging me," Dana said. "The golfer we talked to, one of the guys who saw him fly the drone into the power lines, he said that when they shouted out at Massevadegh, the guy just stood there, took off his shades and stared at them. He said it was almost like the guy was daring them to do something. It doesn't make sense for someone committing a crime to deliberately show his face to witnesses. You'd expect the opposite. I don't know what he's playing at."

Noel shrugged.

"Maybe it's nothing, but I don't understand it."

"You want to order anything else, or are we ready to go?" Noel said.

Dana reached into her purse and brought out the Black Madonna. "Remember this?"

Noel took one look at it and smiled. "I'm glad to see you still have that."

"I brought her in case I needed help to convince you about Massevadegh."

He tapped the folder. "This here is all the convincing I need, Dana."

"I'm glad."

Noel gestured to the waitress for the check.

"Can I get this?" Dana said.

"No way."

"Then let's split it."

"Forget it."

"Some things never change," Dana said, conceding with a chuckle. "Ever the chivalrous knight."

"Let's circle back this afternoon," Noel said after he paid. "I'll call you if I don't hear from you first."

They walked outside and hugged again before parting. Dana left him with a rueful wave as she drove off. There were times when it wasn't just the nature of investigative work that she missed about the Secret Service, it was also having the authority. This was one of those times.

Noel had read Dana's mood but decided they could talk about it later, because right now he was galvanized by what he had learned about Mahmoud Massevadegh. In 2003, the year his and Dana's assignments at the Austin field office wound down, the Secret Service was transferred from the Department of the Treasury to the Department of Homeland Security. Protection of critical U.S. infrastructure and protection of the American people from harm became part of the agency's expanded remit. In 2008, after serving five years in Protective Operations, Noel was assigned to the agency's National Threat Assessment Center, NTAC, where he remained to this day a senior analyst. So by training and experience, he was acutely aware of the risk to national security posed by the vulnerabilities of the national power grid. A long-term widespread outage would be more devastating than most Americans knew, far more than any attack the nation had ever been subjected to. It could happen due to natural causes, like a solar flare, or it could be caused by an electromagnetic pulse attack by a rogue nation like North Korea detonating a nuclear device high up in the atmosphere above the U.S. But a lone-wolf hacker armed with nothing more than a laptop and an Internet connection could also conceivably perpetrate it. Regardless, it was a nightmare scenario the country was not prepared to deal with. The lives at risk numbered in the thousands, tens of thousands, potentially hundreds of thousands. It could push America back into the mid-1900s. It was unthinkable.

He had fixated on a career in law enforcement while in his junior year at Northern Valley Regional High School in Demarest, just down the road from his parents' home in Wallington, Bergen County, New Jersey. Intense pride in his family's background, in particular Poland's centuries-long struggle for freedom, had made him intolerant of Polish jokes to the extent that he developed a reputation for using his fists if necessary to drive the point home. While a senior in high school, he wrote an op-ed published by the *Bergen Dispatch,* in which he argued that the negative portrayal of Polish people was a phenomenon started and encouraged by Hitler after the Nazi invasion of Poland, and that anyone still doing it was either unwittingly perpetuating Nazi propaganda, or knowingly engaged in racism. He felt so strongly about the subject that he chose a career in the Secret Service because he wanted to belong to an SS that was the antithesis of the Nazi Party's version, the euphemistically named *Schutzstaffel,* or 'protective squadron.' That had informed his decision to pursue a B.A. in Forensic Psychology at Notre Dame University. The more he had soaked up core courses in criminal justice, forensic law, American politics, the American legal tradition and scientific investigations, the more committed he had become to the defense of freedom and democracy, and the more certain of his career choice. He needed no external motivation to hunt down and pre-empt anyone—let alone a foreigner—suspected of planning an attack as insidiously malicious as disruption of the nation's power grid.

From the front seat of his SUV in the parking lot of the Silver Diner, Noel used his personal Wi-Fi hotspot to access the George Mason University website, and he navigated to the *Faculty & Staff* page. He accessed the *People Finder* page via a directory tab. He didn't have a name to search for, so he entered "electrical engineering" in a futile attempt to reach a departmental directory. Even if he knew Massevadegh's advisor's name, it was unlikely that the online directory would list a cell phone number; it probably listed an office phone number, which probably wouldn't be of much use on a Saturday. The next best thing would be an email address. A note told him he was out of luck there too:

To reduce spam sent to George Mason University students, faculty and staff, email addresses in People Finder will only be shown when the site is accessed through the on-campus network of George Mason University. Off-campus users must log in with their Mason Username (NetID) and Password to access the full directory. Non-affiliated off-campus users do not have access to email addresses for privacy reasons.

Noel googled 'George Mason University Electrical Engineering' and found a link that took him to the home page of the Volgenau School of Engineering's Electrical & Computer Engineering Department. From the menu on the left he tried the *PEOPLE* tab and found what he was looking for, an alphabetical listing of thirty-four faculty members that included headshots, titles, office numbers and email addresses. He scrolled down until he found a professor Brandon Mitchell, who was listed as the chairman of the ECE Department. He sent him a brief email stating his name, cell phone number, who he worked for, and why he was making contact. Then he decided to head over to Fairfax regardless, to see what he might find.

By the time he reached the GMU campus, just a ten-minute drive from Tyson's Corner, Brandon Mitchell had called him and agreed to meet him right away. He called again a few minutes later and informed Noel that he had identified Massevadegh's advisor as a professor Daniel Vergas, who was also now heading to the campus to join them.

The three men met outside the four-story glass atrium of the Long & Kimmy Nguyen Engineering Building, which conveniently faced a main entryway into campus. Noel introduced himself, flashed his badge, and told the professors about the drone attack in Loudon County. He described the evidence at eRock that pointed to Mahmoud Massevadegh.

Daniel Vergas looked genuinely shocked. "What you've described is totally out of character for the Mahmoud Massevadegh I know," he said.

"Are you aware he changed his name during his program here?" Noel said.

"Yes, of course. He wanted to live permanently in the U.S. He did it while in school so he could have his American name on his diploma."

"Were you the DSO for his OPT?" Mitchell asked Vergas.

"Yes," Vergas replied.

"What's DSO?" Noel said.

"Designated School Official," Mitchell explained. "The staff member who provides the required recommendation for a grad student's post-completion practical training – technically OPT for Optional Practical Training. It's the visa that allows foreign grad students to stay in the States and work for a set period of time."

"Did you have any contact with him after he graduated?" Noel said.

"No," Vergas said. "But he was a clean guy. Maybe there's a mistake?"

"No mistake. We have a positive ID by two men who witnessed him using the drone to trip the power line. Then he left his car at Dulles Airport and drove off in a rental, so the police are looking for a blue Toyota while he's driving a silver VW. Why would he do that if he wasn't trying to evade capture?"

Vergas frowned.

"Do you have any contact information for him?" Noel said.

"Just the gmu.edu email, but that's no longer active."

"Any idea where he might be?"

The professors shook their heads.

"One more question," Noel said to Vergas. "Did he ever express an interest in the grid?"

Vergas spread his hands out like it was a redundant question. "All of our students are interested in the grid. We're an electrical engineering department."

"Grid vulnerabilities in particular," Noel added.

"These days you can hardly talk about the grid without talking about its vulnerabilities," Vergas said.

"Did he ever show any interest in malware that can be used to find and exploit grid vulnerabilities? Havex, Dragonfly, Energetic Bear, that kind of thing?"

Vergas hesitated, as if in thought, before saying: "Nothing I would consider sinister, or even unusual, in our environment. I would make the analogy with medical students who learn about diseases. They study their causes as well as how best to go about preventing and curing them. I would argue electrical engineers must know grid vulnerabilities in order to design and build a better grid."

Noel wasn't sure he bought the analogy, but he wasn't about to argue with the professor. "Fair enough. Still, I'd like to talk to his classmates, see if any of them can shed light on what might be going on in his head. I need a list of names and whatever contact information you have on file."

Vergas turned to Mitchell. The department chairman looked uncertain. "Let me check on that and get back to you," he said.

Noel handed each of them one of his cards. "Thank you. And other than that list, if you think of anything you feel I should know, please call me immediately."

He shook hands with them and left. As he walked to his car, Noel couldn't help thinking it was insane that America opened up its institutions of higher learning to people who might do it harm with the knowledge they gain. But how do you separate the good from the bad? And how do you protect against the good turning bad?

***

Neither Kenneth Leach, nor his partner, Miles Jenkins, had answered Farzad Yazdi's phone call on Friday, because when he placed it they were both forty thousand feet above the Pacific Ocean, sequestered in adjacent flatbed seats in the Business-First cabin of a United Airlines flight from Tokyo's Narita Airport to George H.W. Bush Intercontinental Airport, Houston. Takeoff had been delayed due to bad weather in Narita, and it was after ten p.m. when they landed in Houston, somewhat tipsy. The attorneys both had U.S. Customs and Border Protection Global Entry privileges, so they breezed through immigration control, only to wait fifteen minutes at the baggage claim carousel for their suitcases. They shared an Uber Black car to their mansions off Memorial Drive in

Hunter's Creek Village, both within a mile of Yazdi's house. On the way they heard an impassioned voicemail from his wife, and they took in more details of what had happened from their assistants in voice messages and emails. Farzad Yazdi had been a client of their eponymous law firm for over a decade, and his payment history was exemplary. The business relationship had morphed into a personal one that included the wives, mainly over dinners at Houston's finest restaurants, always lubricated by fine wines from Burgundy and Bordeaux. They had debated calling Laleh Yazdi on the way home from the airport, but it was already past eleven and they decided against it. They agreed that Ken would call her in the morning after he visited Farzad at the downtown Federal Detention Center.

Leach's assistant gave him the name of one of the federal prosecutors on the case, a man he'd worked with before. There was enough mutual respect between them for Leach to call on his way to downtown on Saturday morning and find out what the charges were. On the face of it, the mountain he had to guide his client across was steep and perilous.

He walked through the front door of the Federal Detention Center at 1200 Texas Avenue, up to the single window in the lobby. He presented his driver license and his bar card to the lady behind the window, and she handed him a key to a locker in which he deposited his mobile phone. He filled out a form, including his name, the prisoner's name and the eight-digit prisoner number. He placed his briefcase and shoes on the X-ray machine belt and walked through the metal detector. He was then buzzed through a door that closed and locked behind him, leaving him in a mantrap. Once through a second door, he signed in on a visitor logbook and had his hand stamped with invisible ink. He put on his shoes, gathered his briefcase and was escorted by a guard through another mantrap into the visiting area, access to which came after a black light illuminated the invisible ink on his hand. It was a large room designed for visits by prisoners' family members. Leach found his way to the far end and waited in one of the five smaller rooms dedicated to private visits between prisoners and their attorneys. Moments later, Farzad Yazdi was shown in dressed in brown overalls and looking predictably disheveled, emotionally as well as physically.

"Ken, this is not acceptable," Yazdi started as soon as he was alone with his lawyer.

"My apologies, Farzad. Miles and I were both in Taipei and Tokyo. We got back late last night. This all took us by surprise."

"It took you by surprise? What am I to say?" There was an air of desperation about him. "Get me out of here."

"We're going to get you out, but, uh, I've made some calls... there are pretty serious charges leveled against you and—"

"Lies! All lies! You know what this is? I'll tell you what's going on. There are powerful people in America who want the nuclear talks with Iran to fail so Iran's facilities can be attacked and destroyed. So they orchestrate the arrest of an Iranian-American under fabricated charges, all lies, because if they convict me of going around the sanctions and selling to Iran, that means Iran is not to be trusted, and maybe the talks break down. It is so clear. You see it, don't you?"

Leach had expected this. The Middle Eastern appetite for conspiracy theories was legendary, and it wasn't limited to the Arab Middle East. "We're set to appear before a federal magistrate on Monday, when the indictment will be unsealed," he said. "We'll know more then—"

"You know I have health issues, Ken," Yazdi protested animatedly. "I can't stand to be in this jail for another day. I—"

"There's nothing I can do today, Farzad. Nothing we can do before the hearing on Monday. Then we'll request bail and get you out."

"This is unbelievable! There's no proof! What happened to innocent until proven guilty?"

"That still holds, but there's a process we can't circumvent."

Yazdi despaired. "Fuck this country."

"Now come on, Farzad—"

"No! Fuck this country! All these years I've been a good citizen, paid my taxes, played by the rules, and they just come and put me in handcuffs in front of my staff and stick me in a prison with a tiny cell with another prisoner. Where are my rights? Look at what they force me to wear. It is the color of shit. Like I'm a prisoner in Guantanamo. Where is justice? Where is respect for dignity? This kind of thing happens in the third world, it's not supposed to happen in America!"

Ken Leach had represented Farzad Yazdi long enough to know he was a feisty, combative, unyielding sort, so none of this surprised him. "Calm down, Farzad," he said. "There will be due process. I'm with you every step of the way. But we will have to wait until the hearing on Monday before we can decide how we're going to deal with this."

Yazdi ran a hand through his gray hair, pushing it back from his brow. In an anguished voice he said, "How are Laleh and Taraneh and Amir? These fuckers won't even let me call my wife and children!"

The attorney thought his client looked like he had aged ten years in the last two weeks. Instead of his usual Mr. Universe straight-back posture, he was now looked fatigued, his shoulders hunched. "I know," Leach said. "I'm not even allowed to bring my phone into the building. Just... rules and regulations we have to live with. I'm going to swing by your house as soon as we're done here. I wanted to see you first."

Yazdi's desperation was clear in his eyes, like those of a cornered prey unsure which way to lash out. "We have to fight this, Ken," he protested, smacking the top of one of his hands into the palm of the other. "It's all lies."

"Oh, we'll fight it, Farzad," Leach said, unable to sound as reassuring as his client wanted him to be. "Just stay calm, trust me...and let me call the shots."

With that Ken Leach gave Yazdi a firm handshake and a sturdy smack on the shoulder. "Keep your chin up, Buddy. We'll get you out of here."

"You get me out of here," Yazdi replied miserably, "so I can keep my chin up."

***

There were several cars parked outside the eRock administration building when Dana pulled up, which was not unusual for a Saturday afternoon at a 24x7 datacenter campus. Apart from the facilities engineers and security guards—whose cars were parked in front of the specific datacenters they were assigned to—there were operations personnel who work in shifts around the clock out of cubicles in the ground floor of the administration building, ready to respond to a variety of paid 'remote hands' requests from customers, such as change-out of a hard drive or a server reboot. Dana noticed that Chris Banks' black BMW 535i was also there, also not surprising given yesterday's outage. He was probably still dealing with the aftermath, maybe finalizing the customer-facing incident report. Dana took a moment in her car to ponder whether to stop by his office and update him. She decided against it. He had openly sided with Steve Smith yesterday when the CEO had all but scapegoated her. Her update could wait until he asked for one. Besides, she had two important matters she urgently wanted to attend to.

She left her car at the administration building and walked to VA2. She asked at the security desk who was on shift from the facilities engineering team and was surprised when told it was Susan Morton, whom she hadn't met before. The surprise was that it was a female, and Dana realized it was the second stereotyping gaffe she had committed that day. The first was in Manassas, when she had subliminally assumed Joe Mayle was white, and now again when she learned of a female facilities engineer. Dana knew that of all people, it was inexcusable for her to err like that. She couldn't count the number of times people had looked bemused—some of them bewildered—to learn the woman they had just met was a secret service agent. Old habits might die hard, but old preconceptions were best quashed.

She found Susan Morton in the facilities engineering office adjacent to VA2's central plant, studying building management system status parameters on three large wall-mounted screens. She introduced herself and asked if she could have a minute of Susan's time.

"Sure," Susan said. "Here, or—"

"Yes, right here's fine," Dana said. "I just want to ask you a few questions related to yesterday's outage."

Susan had been on duty during the incident, and Chris Banks had already debriefed her.

"Nothing related to the technical aspects of the outage," Dana clarified.

"Okay…"

"I want to ask you about Mike Massey."

Susan flinched. She hadn't expected that. "What about him?"

"How well did you know him?"

Susan was clearly surprised by the question. "I didn't know him outside of work, if that's what you mean," she said.

"Did you ever do any shifts together?"

"Yeah, when we were scheduled together."

"Did the two of you ever talk?"

"Well…yeah, of course. Just…work stuff, you know."

"Did he ever talk about anything else, other than work? Hobbies, likes and dislikes, that kind of thing."

"No," Susan said without hesitation. "He was…probably the most introverted one of the engineers I work with.

"What do you know about him, other than that he's an engineer at eRock?"

"I know he's originally from Iran," Susan said matter-of-factly.

Now Dana was startled. "How do you know that?"

"I heard him speak a foreign language on the phone once, and I asked him what it was. He told me it was Farsi. So I asked him if he was Iranian—his English did have an accent—and he said yes. Why?"

Dana suddenly realized that because she hadn't known that Massey was Iranian before Sheriff Hart told her, she had assumed nobody else at eRock knew. "Did the other engineers on the team know Massey was from Iran?" she said.

"I believe so. Why?"

"What else do you know about him?"

"I know he got a master's at GMU. And I believe he said he got his bachelor's in England somewhere."

"Did he ever talk about the power grid, about the grid's vulnerabilities?"

"Not to me."

107

"What about hacking? Did he ever talk about hacking, cyber-tools, malware, that kind of thing?"

"Not to me."

"Are you sure?"

"Yes. I would remember that. No one here has mentioned hackers and malware to me. Why these questions?"

"Never mind," Dana said. "Thank you. I'll let you get back to work now."

"Sure."

"Well…one more question. Did you ever hear any of the other engineers say anything about Mike Massey?"

Susan thought for a second and said: "Just that he is a loner. I guess he didn't open up much in a personal way to anyone on the team."

"Thank you."

Dana walked back to the administration building thinking about what Susan had said. When she got to her office she used her desktop computer to access the eRock intranet employee directory, and looked up the cellphone number of Kevin Turner, the facilities engineer she had spoken with yesterday, the one whose login credentials Massey had performed so much of his web browsing with. Turner was just as forthcoming with answers to Dana's questions as he'd been the first time they spoke, and he pretty much seconded what Susan Morton had said. He too knew Massey was from Iran, he also thought Massey to be somewhat of a loner, a guy who mostly kept to himself, and they had never had any conversations about grid vulnerabilities or malware related thereto.

Dana had three more telephone conversations about Mike Massey, two with other engineers on the team Massey had belonged to, the last with the engineer who managed the team.

Every answer she was given confirmed what Susan Morton and Kevin Turner had reported, and Dana was left satisfied there was nothing more she could learn about Mahmoud Massevadegh from anyone at eRock.

It all gave Dana cause to stop and rethink her conclusions about Massevadegh. She had been stunned when Hart told her the guy was from Iran, but now that was obviously not something Massevadegh had tried to hide. But because of the way she had learned about it, she had presumed—evidently wrongly—that he had kept it a secret. What other wrong presumptions was she acting under? She grimaced, upset at herself. Maybe Joe Mayle was right. Maybe her connecting of the dots was rash. What if it was in fact not Massevadegh who had committed the ATM hack?

She thought of something she had learned in a course on probability theory at the University of Maryland. The professor had started the first class with an open discussion of probability, and the words people commonly used to describe how probable they thought things were. He'd driven home the notion that being 'certain' about something means you assign a probability of 100% to it happening or being true. And he posited that a simple benchmark to check how 'certain' any of his students were about anything was to consider if they would bet their life on it. For example, he had said, are you certain there will be a tomorrow? There was a unanimous show of hands for yes. Would you bet your life on it? Again, everyone said yes. Which made sense, because if there turned out to be no tomorrow, you won't worry about losing your life.

Dana asked herself if she was willing to bet her life that Massevadegh had hacked the ATM. The answer was no.

Dana asked herself what probability she would assign to Massevadegh having hacked the ATM. She started off above 90%, but the more she thought about it the lower it dropped. After a few minutes she settled on 65%. With dismay, she accepted that maybe Joe Mayle had a valid point. Maybe for now the APB was enough.

She called Noel, who answered on the second ring.

"Hey, Dana, I was about to call you. Anything new?"

"I've spoken with the people he worked with," she said with a sigh. "There's nothing new, other than they all know he Iranian. I don't know why I assumed he was hiding that…the name change, maybe…but he wasn't hiding it."

"Okay."

"What about you? Anything at GMU?"

"I met with his advisor and the department chairman. They both seemed surprised to learn about the drone attack. There was nothing about his time at GMU that raised any eyebrows. I'm waiting for them to send me a list of name and numbers of his classmates."

"Noel, I've been thinking. Maybe Joe Mayle is right. Maybe the APB is good enough right now. Truth be told, we don't know for sure it was him who hacked the ATM last night."

"It would be a pretty big coincidence if it wasn't him," Noel said. "And if I remember right, you don't believe in coincidences."

"Yeah, yeah, I know. But I think we should wait before we do anything else. Let's see if he gets picked up today, tonight. Let's circle back tomorrow."

"Okay. There wasn't anything I was going to do before talking to his peers at GMU anyway. Let's talk tomorrow."

"Thanks, Noel."

Dana hung up with mixed emotions. She felt out of sorts and in need of a reboot. She looked up at *Ananda* and thought she was overdue some. She popped a few roasted chickpeas in her mouth, grabbed her purse and left the office. As she drove away she noticed that Chris Banks' car was no longer in the parking lot. She wondered if he'd seen her car when he left. If he had, it would have made sense for him to come to her office and see if there was anything new on Massey.

Back at home she changed into running gear, leggings with mesh sides, sports bra, tank top, Adidas Supernova glide shoes, and a LifeProof case on her iPhone. She drank a large cup of water and walked across the surface parking lot from her condo to the Washington and Old dominion Trail. She ran west, past the Reston Town Center, too preoccupied to decide how long of a run it would be so she could pace herself. After half a mile she realized she had started too fast and she slowed down. Her breathing rhythm was steady, her pace comfortable, but there was too much mental churn for her to achieve a zone, that state of consciousness runners reach where mind and body are one. At three miles from her starting point she turned and headed for home.

After a quick shower Dana made herself a smoothie. As she consumed it in silence she decided that what she needed most of all was a session of *zazen*, Zen Buddhism's meditative discipline that, when performed correctly, purges the mind of all thoughts, ideas, judgments and images, achieving the closest state possible of conscious mental nothingness.

She kept her *zafu* cushion atop a *zabuton* mat in the corner of her living room, next to the balcony. She sat and folded her legs in full-lotus style. With a settled spine holding her back erect, she folded her hands together into a simple *mudra* over her belly, her fingers gently nestled against each other under her thumbs, the tips of which came together. She focused only on breathing from her *hara*, the center of gravity in her belly. She relaxed her eyelids so her eyes were half-closed. This was a meditative form she was practiced at, and her mind slowly slipped into oblivion.

***

On North Carolina's 78,000 miles of roadways, the primary mission of the State Highway Patrol is safety. Divided into eight troops that cover the state, the patrol is headquartered in Raleigh, and it was there that the FBI's notification about a silver VW Jetta driven by a wanted fugitive was received. By the time it was disseminated to the Highway Patrol's 1,600 troopers, a force second in size only to that in Texas, the specific car they were to keep an eye out for was nowhere to be seen. The word coming back to the FBI Resident Agency in Manassas from the field office in Charlotte throughout the day was constant: Of all the silver Jettas spotted on North Carolina's roads, none bore the license plate number of the wanted one.

***

When Dana first scrutinized Massevadegh's browsing history, she had started with an open mind, and then gradually focused on anything to do with power grid vulnerability. When her mind snapped into the present after forty minutes of meditation, one of the first thoughts that came to her was that she needed to revisit the browsing history, review it again, this time focusing on different keywords. The indecision that had had engulfed her that afternoon now dissipated, and she headed back to eRock with fresh vigor and a renewed sense of purpose.

Dana toiled late into the night, a relentless application of grit, driven by her nagging discomfort with the way things stood. The incentive was primarily an aching for a truth her every fiber demanded she find. As the hours passed, she resisted the tendency to quit. A glass of wine beckoned, a bottle promised the reprieve of induced oblivion. Temporary reprieve, she knew, unless she could wake up to the gratification of a triumph of her will and intellect over those of her tormentors, including Mahmoud Massevadegh, Joseph Mayle, Steve Smith and Chris Banks.

She scrolled through Massevadegh's search history line by excruciating line. She revisited the entries she had earlier highlighted, all to do with the grid, it's vulnerabilities, and how to exploit them. She found new entries that interested her, and she printed screenshots and highlighted them for further investigation at a later time, after she had exhausted her search for the new words she was now fixated on. Drowsiness set in before midnight, intermittent nodding off shortly thereafter. It was just after 2 A.M. when she was jolted back to full alertness by one Mahmoud Massevadegh search entry that was exactly what she had hoped to find: *ATM Jackpotting.*

Chapter Eight

Mahmoud's phone alarm woke him from a deep sleep on Sunday morning in Mobile, Alabama, the surroundings unfamiliar but safe. It had not been difficult to fall asleep in the car; the fitful sleep on Friday night and the twelve-hour drive on Saturday had taken their toll. Yesterday had gone according to plan; he had drawn a straight line on the map between Raleigh and Mobile and driven the closest possible route to that line, pausing only for gas and drive-thru food and answering nature's calls during the stops. Mobile was the chosen destination because it put him on I-10, setting him up nicely for what should be no longer than an eight-hour drive on Sunday, maybe even less, traffic permitting. An Internet search for a good spot to spend the night had coughed up the *I-10 Kampground* in Theodore, on Mobile's western outskirts, and it had turned out to be not just good, but ideal. A call ahead from one of his 'burned' phones—prepaid in cash and dispensable, so not traceable—secured him a tent spot to park in. Best of all, the campground's office closed at 6 P.M., and the manager agreed to leave him a brochure at the office door with his reserved spot marked on the map. All he had to do was leave $18 in cash in an envelope and slide it through the mail slot on Sunday, which he did on arrival. There was even a bathroom with a private shower, and he set his alarm for 6 a.m. so he could be in and out before any of the other patrons stirred.

The shower was refreshing, but he kept it brief, all business, just long enough to shampoo his hair and soap and rinse his body down. When he resumed his drive westbound on I-10 the sky behind him was ablaze in shades of orange and red. The distance he had put between himself and Virginia—and Rocky Mount—gave him comfort. Today the open road was therapeutic, conducive to quiet reflection. As he crossed the state line into Mississippi, he assessed his situation.

These were seminal days. It was mind-bending to think of the cataclysmic change at hand, in his hands. Outside of a small familial circle in Tehran, the world didn't know who Hamid and Fariba Massevadegh were. No one knew or cared that on March 4, 1987, the couple's second son, Mahmoud, was born, six years and seven months junior to their first, Bahram. Thirteen months later, in April 1988, Hamid was with the Iranian 84th infantry division which fell victim to the deadliest chemical weapons attack of the Iran-Iraq war, when Saddam Hussein's Republican Guard and other Iraqi artillery divisions launched over 1,000 chemical shells while America nodded in approval and Saudi Arabia and its Sunni Gulf sycophants applauded. Outside of Iran, historians didn't care to acknowledge that extensive exposure to—and inhalation of—sulfur mustard gas, had left Hamid Massevadegh permanently blind and stricken for the rest of his days by chronic respiratory disease and incessant infections.

There was indeed an axis of evil in the world.

There was also poetic justice. Mahmoud was now twenty-eight, the age his father was when he was gassed.

There was also serendipity. The birthday of Lionel Messi, one of Mahmoud Massevadegh's heroes, and arguably the greatest soccer player of his generation, was also March 4th. Mahmoud had Messi in mind when he changed his name to an American-sounding Massey, especially as it was a derivative of the original. It all loosely tied together to the first time he had come to think of the USA in the context of a rivalry. He was eleven years old at the time, and Iran was in the same group as the USA in the France 98 FIFA World Cup. An Iranian victory would mean the USA would be eliminated from the competition. Excitement in Tehran had built to fever pitch as kickoff approached, and went stratospheric when the match ended Iran 2 – USA 1. Delirium reigned in the streets of Tehran; people danced and drank, women ditched their headscarves, and even the Revolutionary Guards, deployed to maintain law and order, joined in the revelry, because they were football fanatics first, Revolutionary Guards second, and on the receiving end of the spanking was none other than *Amreeka*.

The gleeful mayhem was an awakening for the young Mahmoud. In the days and months that followed he learned from his father that America, the country that claimed the mantle of Champion of Democracy, had in 1953, in collusion with the British, overthrown the democratically-elected prime minister of Iran, and replaced him with the Shah. The CIA had then helped to establish and train the new regime's secret police, the SAVAK, which became an institution loathed and feared for its brutality, its use of torture, its assassination of regime opponents. He learned that the Iraqi chemical weapons that had killed or injured over 100,000 Iranians—and left his father wheelchair-bound and breathing from an oxygen tank—had been developed under American aegis. He learned that in 1988, the year after he was born, the American Navy shot an Iran Air civilian airliner out of the sky above the Persian Gulf, killing 290 innocent civilians, sixty-six of them children.

Evil indeed.

As the boy became a man he saw for himself the Americans making a mockery of their claims of championing democracy by supporting the Sunni ruling family of Bahrain in discriminating against the overwhelming majority of the country's citizens who were Shia. He saw America turn a blind eye to nuclear weapons proliferation in India, Pakistan and Israel, non-signatories of the

Non-Proliferation Treaty, while applying sanctions against NPT-member Iran, and never once acknowledging America's failure to live up to its own commitments under the NPT.

Now the world was about to change. Things were about to come full circle. An Iranian cockerel was coming home to roost.

Mahmoud's thought train persisted through Mississippi into Louisiana, and he arrived at the same conclusion he had drawn many years ago, a conviction that only hardened with time. There are two camps of people in the world: The Fuck Me flock that always bends over for America, and the Fuck You front that steadfastly refuses ever to do so. He was proud to belong to the one with head—not ass—held high.

***

The white Nissan Pulsar was still approaching the eastern fringes of Louisiana's Lake Pontchartrain when Dana and Noel met for the second day in a row at the Silver Diner in Tyson's Corner. This time Dana had brought her laptop with her because what she wanted to share with Noel had to be seen to be believed. She waited until they had ordered breakfast before summoning YouTube.

"When I saw he'd searched for ATM Jackpotting, I did the same, and the first link was this," she said, swiveling the laptop around on the table so the screen faced Noel. What followed was a ten-minute presentation by a man named Barnaby Jack, a video titled *Jackpotting Automatic Teller Machines*. She had watched it the night before at her office at eRock in silence, in turn shocked and dismayed that information like this was out there in the public domain. Noel was engrossed. He reacted by shaking his head and muttering "unbelievable" over and again. "I'd read about Barnaby

Jack," he said at the end, "but I had no idea this video was out there."

"I know," Dana said. "Distressing, huh? So, when I saw it last night, and I saw that Massevadegh had researched the topic, that eliminated any thoughts that it was anyone else but him at that ATM in Rocky Mount."

"Agreed."

"So then I did some research of my own, just to get my head around what we're looking at if he goes after the grid." Dana pulled up a Word document she had created by copying and pasting text from different sites on the web. "Read these bullet points," she said, and walked away to get a coffee refill.

Noel took it in.

- The US power grid serves more than 300 million people and comprises more than 200,000 miles of transmission lines. Private companies and other non-federal institutions own the vast majority of grid assets.
- Grid operations and control systems are increasingly automated, incorporate two-way communications, and are connected to the Internet or other computer networks. While these improvements have allowed for critical modernization of the grid, this increased interconnectivity has made the grid more vulnerable to remote cyber-attacks.
- Secretary of Defense Leon Panetta identified a "cyber-attack perpetrated by nation states or extremist groups" as capable of being "as destructive as the terrorist attacks on 9/11."
- The National Academy of Sciences found that physical damage to large transformers could disrupt power for months to large regions of the country.

- The Department of Homeland Security reported that in 2012 it processed 68% more cyber-incidents involving federal agencies, critical infrastructure, and other select industrial entities, than in 2011.
- More than one public power utility reported being under a "constant state of attack from malware and entities seeking to gain access to internal systems."
- In May of 2013 the Department of Homeland Security warned industry of a heightened risk of cyber-attack, and reportedly noted increased cyber-activity that seemed to be based in the Middle East, including Iran.

When Dana came back to the table, Noel was statuesque, lost in thought. "See that last one?" she said.

He nodded gravely.

Dana slid into her chair. "What do you think?"

Noel leaned back with a sigh. "I think the question is, what can he do and when can he do it?"

"Thank you."

They stared solemnly at each other until Dana asked: "What do you think we should do?"

"Well, I don't think we should sit back and wait for a cop somewhere to spot the Jetta and pull it over."

"Amen," Dana said. "What can he do and when can he do it? We have to assume, based on what he's been up to on the web, that he knows how to use the tools he's downloaded."

"Agreed."

"As to when, we can't guess, so we must assume it's imminent." She took a sip of her coffee. "Clear and present danger, I think."

Noel looked at her and nodded.

"So," she said. "Next steps?"

Noel reached into his backpack and pulled out his own laptop, an IBM ThinkPad. "First, you're going to help me write a one-page summary of what we know and what we think. Then I'm going to put it in front of the right set of eyes and recommend it be included in tomorrow's Presidential Briefing."

Dana could have screamed with relief. "Fuck the FBI," she said, relishing her choice of vernacular. "I knew I could trust you to do the right thing."

They composed the brief together, outlining what they knew, first the drone attack against the Dominion Power overhead line and the related fraudulent purchase of the drones, then the hack and heist of the Old North Bank ATM, followed by Massevadegh's browser history, his downloading of tools used to scan the Internet for power grid vulnerabilities and malware designed to penetrate and compromise the grid. They added background information on Massevadegh, his entry into the U.S., his graduate studies at George Mason, and his successful name change petition. They stressed that Massevadegh was at large, location and destination unknown, and ended the brief with a professional assessment that the fugitive posed an imminent threat of disruption of unquantifiable scope to the national power grid. After Dana read through it one last time, she handed Noel back his laptop and they gave the document a joint final blessing. With a few clicks on the ThinkPad's keyboard, the brief was on its way, in encrypted form, fast-tracking all the way up to the top of the Secret Service hierarchy.

Dana said: "I'd love to be in the room when Joe Mayle learns this has reached the President."

"Let's hope it reaches him first thing in the morning," Noel replied. "We've done our part, but we still need help getting it there."

Dana was sure it was now just a matter of time. "I can't see it not happening," she said. "What do we do now?"

"I guess…now we wait."

Waiting was too passive, and Dana too restive. "It occurs to me…we know Massevadegh rented the car at Dulles, I wonder where the rental contract says he's going to return it."

Markovski shrugged. "Could be anywhere. But I don't know that I'd put too much stock in what the contract says."

"It wouldn't hurt to find out, maybe get an edge on the FBI boys."

Noel knew what Dana was up to. First, she was antsy. He knew her well enough, she wasn't the type to sit back and let a situation like this play out. She had to be doing something, anything that might push the investigation forward, no matter how minutely. Second, she was playing on the traditional rivalry between the FBI and the Secret Service, something she knew he was likely to respond to. Third, although she left it unsaid, she was asking him to find out what the rental contract said because he had the authority that she had forfeited when she retired from the Service. He didn't have any pressing plans for the day, and this wouldn't take long as Dulles was a fifteen-minute drive away. "Do you want to take two cars or one?" he said.

Dana beamed. "If you're coming back this way, I'll ride with you and get my car when we're done."

Traffic on the 267 Dulles Access Road was light, so getting to the airport was a breeze. As soon as Noel presented his credentials the National location manager became a model of cooperation. He pulled Mahmoud Massevadegh's contract up on his screen and told his visitors it said the car would be returned to Dulles. Noel handed him one of his cards and asked to be notified when the car was returned, regardless of location.

"I'll bet you this is the last place he intends to return the car," Dana said as they walked away. "He's not going to tell us where we can sit and wait for him."

"I think you're right."

Noel's phone rang on the drive back to Tyson's Corner. The caller ID showed a 703 area code, so local, but not a name from his contacts list and not a number he recognized. He answered anyway. "Markovski."

"Mr. Markovski, this is Daniel Vergas."

The name wasn't new, but he couldn't place it. The phone was bluetoothed to the car, so Dana could hear both sides of the conversation.

"Daniel Vergas, from GMU, George Mason Uni—"

"Yes, Professor Vergas, what's up?" Noel whispered to Dana: "Massevadegh's advisor."

"I have that list of his classmates that you asked for, and also another document you might be interested in seeing."

"Great! What's the other document?"

"I was looking through his files and found a paper he wrote about grid vulnerabilities for one of his classes. I'm sure you will find it interesting. I have a copy for you...if we can meet somewhere."

Noel glanced at Dana, who gave him an emphatic thumbs-up. "I'm not far from campus," he said. "I can be there in ten or fifteen minutes, if that's good for you?"

"Yes. Let's meet at the same place as yesterday, in front of the engineering building. You remember how to get to it?"

"Of course. Heading there now."

123

With the light traffic they were there in twelve minutes, and Vergas was waiting. Dana thought you could tell he was a professor from a mile away. Jeans, sneakers and jaded corduroy jacket with elbow patches. He wore horn-rimmed glasses, had a thick, graying goatee and unruly black hair. Noel made names-only introductions without elaborating on who Dana was or why she was there. Vergas handed Noel a folded printout. "That's the list of Massevadegh's classmates names…and the contact information we have on file for them," he said.

Noel glanced at the list. "And you said there was a paper he wrote?"

Vergas reached into an inner jacket pocket. "Here it is. You'll see it is about grid vulnerabilities and how to protect against them."

Noel leafed through the pages. "Anything in here that stands out to you?"

"Standard stuff, you know? But yesterday you mentioned malware. Havex, Dragonfly. You're going to see he mentions them in the paper."

"In what context?"

"Just in the paragraph where he identifies some of the tools used to probe and compromise grid infrastructure. I think this paper explains his interest in them."

"Can you email me a copy?"

Vergas turned apologetic and dropped his voice to a whisper. "I can't. I shouldn't even be giving you a hard copy, but I trust you will be discreet with it."

Noel's phone rang and he stepped away to answer it.

"How long did you know Massevadegh?" Dana asked Vergas.

"I was his advisor during his stay at GMU, so it was…a little over a year."

"Did you stay in touch after he graduated?"

124

"No. I knew he was working on a practical training visa, but no more contact, no."

Noel rejoined them, and Dana could tell he had news.

"That was the National manager we just talked to in Dulles," he said. "He called to let me know that Massevadegh switched cars yesterday."

"Switched cars?"

"Yesterday morning, in Raleigh."

"How come?"

"He reported a problem with the Jetta."

It was like a kick to the gut for Dana. So for the past twenty-four hours the cops had been looking for the wrong car! "I'll bet he did," she muttered.

"Professor Vergas, thank you," Noel said. "We don't want to keep you any longer on a Sunday."

"No, my pleasure to help in any way!" Vergas replied. He handed both of them cards. "Anything I can do to help, I'm here, just call me."

They walked back to Noel's car. "Raleigh, huh?" Dana said as they drove away.

"The guy's covering his bases," Noel replied. "Surely he would have known the Jetta was caught on video at the ATM."

"Has National notified Hart?"

"I don't know. He didn't say."

"We need Hart and Mayle to know. I don't want to tell them because they'll want to know how I know, and I haven't told them about you."

"Well maybe you should. Maybe it would be a good thing to light a fire under Mayle's ass."

Dana's mind was going through the gears. "Yeah. I'd love to keep him in the dark about you, but we've got to do whatever is most conducive to finding the bastard before he does some real damage."

"Mayle's going to find out tomorrow anyway if my report gets to the President."

"You think it's going to?"

"I hope so. We'll know tomorrow."

"Okay, I'll call Hart and he can tell Mayle. I don't have to agree with the guy, but we need his resources."

"And this list of names from GMU...how about we split it down the middle, you call half and I'll call half."

Dana knew that probably killed her plans to drive to Hampstead and talk to her father that afternoon, but there was no way she could ask Noel to handle it on his own. Of the two pressing issues she needed to resolve, only one could wait. "Deal," she said.

By the time Noel dropped Dana off in Tyson's Corner, she had reached Hart and filled him in, first on Massevadegh switching cars, then on Noel and the Secret Service being on the case. There was a hint of annoyance in Hart's voice, uncharacteristic of him when he was speaking with her, and she couldn't tell if it was because she had found out about the car switch before he had, or because she had pulled in the Secret Service without first coordinating with him and the FBI. As she drove away from the Silver Diner back towards Reston, Dana decided she didn't give a damn who might be upset or why. The only thing she cared about was nailing Mahmoud Reza Massevadegh.

***

A short time after he finished his Sunday brunch with his wife and two children at the Four Seasons Hotel in Georgetown, the director of the Secret Service checked his inbox and read an email with an attachment that made him stiffen. Alarmed by its implications, he cursed the proliferation and diversity of the threats to U.S. national security emanating from the Middle East. He thought about the memorandum he had just read for all of two minutes, before he endorsed it and forwarded it to the Director of National Intelligence, the man responsible for presenting it to the President.

***

Mahmoud had just crossed over the Mississippi River at Baton Rouge when one of his phones rang. He was startled because it was the first time that had happened since Virginia. He could tell from the ringtone that it was not his main phone, the iPhone 6 he had purchased upon its release last September, but one of the two disposable pre-paid 'burner' phones, the one that was switched on. Only one person had that number. He didn't know if Louisiana had a hands-free law, but he answered and brought the phone to his ear. He listened for fifteen seconds and said, "Understood." Then he hung up. The next exit was a minute down the freeway. He took it, turned right off the feeder onto the first cross street, and pulled into a Chevron station. He used his iPhone to check what stores were in the vicinity and found two that suited his needs. He would have to backtrack, but only for a couple of miles.

He got back on I-10, now eastbound, and took the last exit before the Mississippi River, Alexander St. A block north of the freeway he found the AutoZone store at the corner with Oaks Avenue, right where the map showed it to be. He was in and out in no time, his purchase a set of wrenches that included both metric and standard sizes. The second store was one he needed not for a purchase, but for its large parking lot that would contain a large number of vehicles. It was a Walmart Supercenter on the other side of the freeway, and again, it was exactly where the map said it would be. He drove around until he found a parking spot between a car on one side, and a truck on the other. He waited a few minutes until he was sure there was no one around, and then he went about his business. It took less than two minutes to find the right-sized wrench and remove the front and rear license plates from the truck to his left. On the way to the Walmart he had passed the Port Allen Magnussen Hotel, and now he went back there and pulled into the hotel's parking lot. No one came after him. He removed the Nissan's North Carolina plates, replaced them with the Louisiana plates he had just lifted off the truck, then walked over to a trash dumpster and tossed the North Carolina plates.

It was still mid-morning, and he was itching to get back on the Freeway, to resume his push to the west, but prudence dictated he wait until dark. He climbed back into the Nissan, fleetingly wondering why, if *Khoda* was on his side, shit happens. He comforted himself with the usual answer: Because God tests your faith, your belief, your patience and your endurance. All of those qualities together give you the mental strength to overcome all obstacles. If everything were easy, faith might easily be eroded. He believed that one of the building blocks of mental strength was to identify those things he had no control over and set them aside, not fret over them. The situation at hand was a case in point. He knew the bastards would be after him sooner or later, but it still felt discomfiting to know they had mobilized. He just had to stay calm, not panic, bide his time, and complete the next leg of his fateful journey under cover of darkness. The minutes were going to feel like hours, but he had to stay disciplined and minimize his exposure to the highway patrol. He would stay right where he was, try to get some more sleep, stay rested, and hit the road after sundown.

Besides, the fact he had just been warned confirmed God was with him.

While Mahmoud patiently waited out daylight behind the Magnussen Hotel, out of sight of cars on the road, a widening perimeter of law enforcement vehicles of various insignia received an update to an All-Points-Bulletin describing a combination of make, model, year, color and license plate number that could no longer be found on any road in America.

Chapter Nine

The brief that Special Agent Noel Markovski composed in his car in Tyson's Corner under the watchful eyes of Dana McLaughlan remained virtually unchanged when the Director of National Intelligence included it in the President's Daily Brief of Monday, April 13th. Named the President's Intelligence Check List during its first iteration in 1961, the PDB is arguably the most highly sensitized classified document in the U.S. government, so much so that former CIA Director George Tenet once warned the National Archives and Records Administration that none of the daily editions could ever be released for publication, no matter their age or historical significance. On rare occasions the PDB has been "For the President's Eyes Only", but it is more often briefed to other high officials, most notably the Secretary of State, the Secretary of Defense and the National Security Advisor. All four men read the April 13th edition. The group discussion was followed by a private one between the two of them whose political legacies would be most impacted by the success or failure of the negotiations with Iran over its nuclear program. The President initiated it, and he spoke first.

"One of the most important things I take away is there's nothing so far to indicate that this Massevadegh guy has the support of the government of Iran. We don't know that he's not working alone. Which isn't to say that he isn't."

"There's too much at stake for them," the Secretary of State opined. "I wouldn't think anyone from Rouhani's government is involved, but it wouldn't surprise me if some of the Basij or Revolutionary Guard hard-liners in Tehran are in on it."

Barack Obama nodded. "So here are the possibilities," he said. "A. He's working alone and he succeeds in sabotaging the grid before the June 30 deadline. If it becomes public knowledge that an Iranian did it, the Republicans will be up in arms. Hell, the country will be up in arms. Forget a comprehensive agreement. Depending on the scope and scale of the damage, we might even find ourselves at war with Iran.

"B. The hard-liners in Tehran are behind him and he succeeds. Our response would have to be one that ensures no one else— country or individual—will ever contemplate doing that to us again. So if he succeeds, whether he's working alone or with people behind him, at a bare minimum the nuclear agreement is shot.

"C. He's thwarted, nothing happens, the negotiations continue on course and hopefully we reach an agreement."

When it was clear the President was finished, his Secretary of State added a fourth possibility. "D," John Kerry said. "The Mossad is behind this. I wouldn't put it past Netanyahu. He's staked his political future on the failure of the negotiations."

The President rolled his eyes. "Let's not go there. Even if it were true, we'd never be able to prove it."

"Yeah, I know. Bottom line is…this guy's got to be stopped."

"Agreed. But until we know exactly what we're dealing with, and what the threat level is, we need to keep this quiet. Any mention of this in the press will send the Republicans ballistic and blow the prospects of a deal out of the water." The President leaned forward and placed his elbows on his desk. "Here's what I want you to do…"

***

Even before last Friday's outage and its aftermath at eRock, Dana's Monday morning drives from Reston to Ashburn had already become increasingly depressing because of her growing distaste for life in the corporate world. Today the feeling was more pronounced than ever. She wanted to be fully engaged in the battle of wits with Massevadegh. She had three weeks of vacation time accrued and was tempted to use it. Compared to the open-ended unpredictability of law-enforcement, eRock was not only boring, it was stiflingly so.

The first order of business was to update Steve Smith and Chris Banks on the developments since their last conversation on Friday. They convened in Smith's office, and Dana gave them the blow-by-blow. Massey's name change, the drone, the credit card fraud to buy drones, the car rental at Dulles, the ATM hack, the car change, the browsing history, the malware, and the FBI. She left out only the Secret Service.

In the days that followed that meeting, upon further reflection, she should have predicted Steve Smith's reaction.

"Let me get this straight," he began when she was done briefing them. First off, this guy's real name is Mahmoud Massedaveh—"

"Massevadegh," Dana corrected.

"Whatever. And to us he's always been Mike Massey? How could we be so in the dark about something like that?"

"I checked his HR file," Dana said assertively. She had come into the meeting with the mindset that she had nothing to be defensive about. She was not going to accept an iota of blame for any of this. "They did all the required background checks, but there's nothing there to indicate they knew about the name change. Even if there was, it's legal."

"It should've raised a red flag, goddammit!"

Dana thought he had a point, but she didn't respond.

"And all of his browsing, on our computers, using our network..."

Dana nodded.

Steve Smith glared at her. "And you just go and report that to the fucking FBI without checking with me first?"

Dana flinched. "Steve, you told me you wanted to prosecute. You told me to contact the police. Once it was clear what we were dealing with, the sheriff pulled in the FBI."

"You should have stopped him right then and there and contacted me. Bad decision, Dana! Bad decision!"

"Wait a second," Dana retorted. "It so happens that I too deemed it information material to the investigation of a potential threat to national security, and I wouldn't withhold it from any branch of law enforcement."

Steve Smith's face was flushed with anger. "That's right, *you* deemed it. But it's information that is the property of this company, and it should not have been shared with anyone without my approval. At the very least, I would have wanted to seek legal counsel before releasing it. There's no telling what liabilities we might face now. That was a rash decision, and you should've known better."

Chris Banks was a silent spectator. Dana stood her ground. "There's a guy out there who could be plotting a cyber-attack against the national grid with potentially disastrous ramifications not just for this company, but for our country." she said. "You should be worried about your liabilities if that happens and it becomes known that you withheld information that might have led to him being preempted."

"Oh, that's great! Now you're giving me legal advice?"

Dana had had enough. Self-control was becoming near impossible. "I'm not giving you advice. Your world is eRock. Mine extends way beyond that, it always will, and that's something I'm proud of." As she stood up she removed the lanyard that held her eRock ID and access badge from around her neck and threw it on Smith's desk. "The only thing I'm giving you is my resignation, effective immediately, because I can't stand to be in the same room as you for another minute!"

"You're fucking fired, Dana!"

"Too fucking late, asshole!"

"Oh, that's really impressive!" Smith shouted after her as she stormed out of his office.

Chris Banks ran after her. "Dana!"

"Stuff it, Chris. You guys make me sick!"

"No need to be so crude," he said, sounding half-apologetic. "I'm just going to show you out. You know you can't just walk through the doors without setting off alarms. You got stuff you need to get from your office?"

"Maybe I'll send the FBI to pick it up."

She held back her tears until she was alone in her car. The release was overwhelming, a mixture of pent-up frustration with the tech world's alpha-male chauvinistic egotism, anger at her weakness—she should not have allowed herself to snap—and relief that she was never coming back to a job she was never cut out for in the first place. As she drove back to Reston the frustration dissipated and the anger subsided. Snapping at Smith had felt good. The asshole had it coming. The more she thought back on it, the better she felt.

**

Amir Yazdi could not bring himself to get out of his car. His Monday morning commute to the campus of Rice University had been hell, and not because of the traffic. It was bad enough having to spend the weekend knowing his father was in jail. Bad enough being unable to do or say anything to ease his mother's angst. But the press! Oh, the heartless, ruthless press, uncaring of what detritus people's lives might be reduced to by a story based on allegations as yet unproven. Saturday's Houston Chronicle had put a brief account of the arrest of his father on page 2. But the Sunday edition smacked it up to front-page-center status. He was enrolled at Rice University, whose students are bound by the strict Honor Code, enforced by a student-run Honor Council, and Sunday's paper had dragged his family name through a mire of allegations so toxic they were virtually a life sentence in and of themselves. He might as well walk around campus bare-chested with Iran Nuclear Bomb Enabler tattooed across his forehead. Maybe his headshot was on the front page of today's Rice Thresher, a suitable public lynching for the student from the nefarious family that sends microelectronic nuclear bomb components to the Death-to-America choir.

He feared the worst was yet to come. He knew his father, knew where his sympathies lay, and would not bet half a rotten penny that he would be found innocent. The arguments they'd had at the dinner table stretched back years, since high school, when Amir had started expressing his disdain for the mullahs and his wish that Iran would reform and rejoin the family of nations. He never could reconcile his father's ramblings about dignity with the reality of Iran's international isolation. And he had been horrified by his father's applause whenever Mahmoud Ahmadinejad had opened his mouth on television.

136

Mohammad Javad Zarif, now there was a man Amir could identify with, cultured, highly educated, well spoken, affable, the best Iranian politician of his generation. And his father called Zarif a white-haired poodle. The only real problem with Zarif was he was on the wrong side! He reported to the mullahs.

He dreaded the day when his father would be found guilty. If he felt hollowed out today by mere allegations, how would he find the will to breathe when they became indictments? What future was there for the family in America?

He started his car and drove away from campus, destination unknown. There was no way he could face going to class and wondering what people were thinking when they looked at him or looked away.

Thank you, Dad, for all your lectures about dignity. Because of you, if I stay in this, the country of my birth, I will have to change my name. Not because of my dignity, but because of my shame.

***

The announcement that was made on April 2nd in Lausanne, Switzerland by the foreign ministers of the United States, Russia, China, The United Kingdom, France, Germany, Iran and the European Union, was one of the most anticipated international diplomacy milestones of recent memory. They had reached consensus on the framework for a comprehensive agreement on the Iranian nuclear program, thus significantly boosting the prospects of a negotiated resolution to the toxic program, as opposed to the military one Israel and Saudi Arabia clamored for. The joint statement addressed four key areas, enrichment, reprocessing, monitoring and sanctions, in outline form, and set June 30th as a self-imposed deadline for hashing out final details. As soon as the announcement was made, the degree of difficulty of the process to date and going forward was made crystal clear when the United States and Iran issued separate fact sheets that displayed contradictory narratives of the agreement. But they also confirmed what observers already knew, that the United States was leading the negotiation with Iran on behalf of the five permanent members of the United Nations Security Council plus Germany and the European Union. Less appreciated by the general public was a truth acknowledged by all of the diplomats involved in the negotiations: they would never have progressed so far without the mutual respect underlying the relationship between the American Secretary of State, John Kerry, and his Iranian interlocutor, Mohammad Javad Zarif Khonsari, a relationship described by aides in the know as friendly, but not friends. This was a result of random twists of fate that were seen as either serendipitous or unfortunate, depending on which side of the negotiate-with-Iran vs. bomb-Iran debate one was on.

Zarif, as western media refer to Iran's Minister of Foreign Affairs, had spent more than half his adult life living in the U.S. After an early education at Tehran's Alavi School, a private religious institution, he had attended, at age 17, Drew College, a private college-preparatory high school in San Francisco. He had gone on to attend San Francisco State University, Columbia University and the University of Denver, earning multiple degrees in International Relations. His two children, a girl and a boy, were both born in the U.S. He had served for five years as Iran's ambassador to the United Nations. Prior to that he had been credited with having played an invaluable role in securing the release of Western prisoners held in Lebanon.

Kerry, on the other hand, has an American-Iranian son-in-law who has family still living in Iran. In 2011, while Chairman of the

Senate Foreign Relations Committee, Kerry led an overture to Iran by flying to the Arabian Peninsula and meeting with Sultan Qaboos of Oman, who facilitated the establishment of a secret channel of diplomatic dialogue between America and Iran.

At the 2013 United Nations General Assembly, Kerry and Zarif met formally for the first time in a small room off the main chamber of the Security Council. By the time they parted company some twenty minutes later, they had exchanged email addresses and phone numbers. As the negotiations between them over Iran's nuclear program got under way, the two men quickly developed a shared intuitive sentiment: the result of the negotiations would either be win-win or lose-lose, and their political legacies would be thus embellished or tainted. As would the legacies of the two presidents they reported to. As a result, since that initial meeting in New York, the two diplomats had spent more time one-on-one with each other than with any other foreign minister. And it soon became evident that there was one more shared reality that fostered empathy with each other's position, hardline opposition at home. For Kerry, it was the republican-controlled U.S. Congress that openly aligned itself with the 'Bomb Iran' policy of Israeli Prime Minister Benjamin Netanyahu, rejecting any deal that would leave Iran as a threshold nuclear state. Zarif's detractors had raised their voices with undisguised vitriol in January, after photographs were published of him strolling with Kerry along the banks of the Rhone in Geneva. The commander of Iran's paramilitary *Basij* force considered the episode an ill-conceived dalliance with the "enemy of humanity," a mistake he called "unforgivable." All of which informed John Kerry's decision as he pondered the marching orders his boss had given him at the Oval Office on the morning of Monday, April 13th.

The need for a face-to-face meeting with Zarif was urgent and immediate. Thanks to Edward Snowden, an email exchange or a telephone conversation would be too risky. It had to be in-person, and it had to be secret. No press, no cameras, only the bare minimum of aides from both sides to establish and maintain a secure perimeter. He was thinking Europe, because that would be halfway, a diplomatic no-brainer. Geneva, or Lausanne maybe, but maybe too obvious because of how often they had been used. The next round of negotiations was going to be held in Vienna, at the Palais Coburg Hotel. There was a park just one block away…

***

Dana was still smarting when she got back to her condo in Reston, but it was less because of what had happened than how. That she was no longer at eRock was actually a relief, but she wished she had not snapped at Steve Smith, even though he deserved it. She wished she had handled that situation with more professionalism and less raw emotion. But what was done was done, and now she wanted to stop thinking about it and refocus her energy. She owed her mother a call to explain why she hadn't called or driven up to Hampstead on Sunday, but that could wait. Turning to what couldn't wait, she called Noel.

"Hey, Dana," he said when he picked up, "your timing is perfect! I just heard the memo was in the President's Daily Brief this morning. The word is we're authorized to make stopping Massevadegh a top priority, but we're to keep the effort under the radar. No press."

"That's great!" Dana gushed. "Can I take it Joe Mayle is going to hear that word?"

"Yes, and he won't know you had anything to do with it."

Dana couldn't suppress her smile. "Fantastic."

"Did you have any luck with your half of the names on the GMU list yesterday?"

"Zero. You?"

"Same. That's a blind alley."

"There's something I need you to do."

"What?"

"We need a warrant to secure Massey's laptop at eRock, and his browsing history. That's crucial evidence if and when we get to prosecuting him."

"Yeah, you're right. I'll make that happen today."

"Oh, and Noel, you should know, I'm no longer at eRock."

Noel was blindsided. "No longer there as in—"

"As in I quit this morning."

"Whoa!"

"I met with the CEO, told him about the developments since Friday, he got overly aggressive about how this might embarrass the company, how I was out of line getting the FBI involved—I didn't even tell him about you being involved, I imagine he might have a heart attack if he finds out about the President's Brief—anyway, I lost it and snapped and told him where to put it."

"Wow!" Noel said. "So what now?"

"Now we need to get Massey's laptop."

Noel thought for a moment, then said, "Do you want me to make sure the CEO knows it's happening?"

It was Dana's turn to think, and she pondered with relish the prospect of how a warrant to seize an eRock laptop and the records of an ex-employee's browsing history would sit with Steve Smith. "Yes," she said, enjoying the thought that Smith was going to go through the roof. "The more visible you can make it to him…well…on second thoughts, I need to keep my feelings toward

Steve Smith out of this. This is not about him. It's about Massevadegh. You know what? Just do what you need to do."

"What are you going to do?"

"I'll figure something out."

"About work, I mean."

"I know. I'm all right…for a while. I'm going to help you get Massevadegh, and I've got a few personal…wrinkles…I need to straighten out, then I'll find something. But don't worry about me, let's focus on Massevadegh. Can you send me a copy of the paper his advisor sent you yesterday? I want to read it."

"Sure, I'll scan it and send it over. And I'll work on that warrant and get someone over to eRock today. I'll let you know when it happens."

"Great. Later."

"Later."

***

City of Baton Rouge police officer Joe Calvin did a double take at the truck that passed him westbound on I-10 at and shook his head. A native Louisianan, he had grown up and gone to school around these parts, and in his seven years with the force he had witnessed so much stupidity that he often wondered what people were ingesting. He switched on the lightbar mounted on the roof of his cruiser and accelerated. The truck pulled into the right hand shoulder and stopped, Calvin just a few yards behind it. With his lights still flashing to ensure he was visible to passing motorists, Calvin got out of his car and walked up alongside the truck as the driver's window came down.

"What seems to be the problem, officer?" The voice was wary, the face callow. Late teens, Calvin thought.

142

He walked on, took a quick glance at the front of the truck and came back to the driver, once again shaking his head. "Where are your license plates, son?"

"What do you mean?"

"I mean you're driving without plates."

"No way! Can I get out and see?"

"C'mon."

The kid got out of the truck and saw for himself what Calvin was talking about. "I swear, officer, they were on there yesterday. I wash my truck every weekend, and yesterday I wiped down the plates myself when I dried it. That's the truth, I swear to you!"

"So where'd they go?"

"I got no idea!"

Calvin nodded wearily like he'd heard it all before. "Gonna have to give you a ticket and you can explain yourself to the judge."

"May be someone's pulling a prank here, but I'm telling you the plates were on there yesterday."

"I heard you, son. Let's see your license and insurance."

"For the record, I want to report that my plates have been stolen."

"You can do that when we're done here. Go down to the station and report what you want."

Half an hour later a puzzled and frustrated nineteen-year-old high school senior presented himself at the Baton Rouge Police Department at 9000 Airline Highway and did precisely that.

***

Amir Yazdi needed to be alone and to clear his head and he knew of one way to do both. He drove back to his parent's home in Piney

Point Village, changed into his biking gear, and set off on his $3,500 ten-speed road bike. He cut a westerly route along Memorial Drive then Boheme Drive for a mile until he reached the Sam Houston Tollway, the starting point of the Buffalo Bayou Bike Trail. It was in fact a running, hiking and biking trail that wound along the banks of Buffalo Bayou for five miles to the George Bush Park at Highway 6, and from there another ten miles to Fry Road for a round trip total of thirty miles that normally took him under two hours. The ride was a Sunday morning staple with a group of a dozen or so Iranian-American friends, but he had missed it yesterday, grounded by the Houston Chronicle spread about his father's arrest. Now it was the perfect getaway; with his bike helmet and his Adidas Evil Eye half rim pro sunglasses, he was virtually incognito and free to pedal away his anger. He just wished he could expunge his cares with his sweat.

The only uncomfortable part of the ride was the start and end at the tollway, where some genius had located a malodorous wastewater treatment plant. Amir held his breath for as long as he could while he rode past it. After that it was clear, few people on foot and even fewer bikers. He rode fast and thought hard. His mother was hopeful that Kenneth Leach would be able to get the charges against his father thrown out, but he had spoken to Leach after the attorney had visited his father on Saturday, and the prospects were not good. The fact that Leach had kept the conversation focused on securing his father's release—a temporary one—on bail or bond, meant he didn't want to dwell on what they were looking at in the long-term. As Amir dealt with his resentment, he came to the realization that realistically, his father probably was guilty, at least of conspiring to violate the sanctions against Iran. That he could be locked up for years was unthinkable, but Amir knew he had to start planning for the eventuality. He also knew he didn't know where to start. He could probably count on his father's friends for advice, although who knows, maybe now they'd be reluctant to be seen by the authorities as close to the Yazdis. He didn't know the state of the family finances. He assumed they were good but how good? Rice was being paid for out of pocket, as had been all the private school tuition for him and Taraneh, which wasn't cheap. They all drove expensive cars, all paid for, as far as he knew. He didn't even know if they had a mortgage on the house or if they held clear title. They could sell the property if need be and move into a smaller place. The legal bills were sure to be hefty. Would Mitronica have to be shut down? What would happen to things like health insurance if that happened?

He felt no pain on the bike. The exercise was good, but it was also numbing. Questions begat questions to which he had no answers.

When he got back to the house he put his bike in the garage and checked his phone. There were several missed calls from his mother. He hadn't heard the phone ring for a simple reason. He always put his phone in a shockproof case when he rode the bike. It fit so tight that when he put it on the case pushed the button on the side of his iPhone to silent mode, and today he had been so preoccupied he had forgotten to reset it back to ring mode. There was also a text message from his mother, asking him when he was going to be home and telling him not to be late as there was a surprise waiting for him at the house.

Had his father been released? He pulled his helmet and gloves off and kicked off his biking shoes. A connecting door from the garage led into a utility room, and a corridor led to the kitchen. He walked through another door into the den where CNN was on the TV and his mother was sitting with a man he didn't immediately recognize. The man saw him, stood up, and stepped towards him with outstretched arms, saying: "Finally! Here is my dear cousin, Amir!"

The voice clinched it, and yes, it was a surprise. "Oh my God!" Amir said. "Mahmoud!"

They embraced, right hands clasped together, left arms locked in a hug as they kissed with brio on alternating cheeks.

Chapter Ten

While Dana's outburst at eRock had initially felt bittersweet, the passage of a few hours erased the bitterness, and by early afternoon on Monday she felt good about herself. She felt she would do it all again, maybe slightly differently, without the profanity, perhaps, but she was not going to harbor regrets. She had a year's salary worth of savings in the bank, so money was not an immediate problem. She now also knew that the corporate world was not for her. She had connections, and when this Massevadegh affair was over, she would find a position that enabled her to practice her passion for investigative work, a private eye-type setup, or a small security firm. Maybe even start a cyber-security consultancy, for that was a field in which women were vastly under-represented. Whatever it was going to be, it would not entail working for men who felt they could intimidate her or push her around. She would never again compromise on that particular aspect of her life and work.

It crossed her mind to drive up to Hampstead and visit with her parents. Today's separation from eRock was a milestone, a good time to turn the page and start anew. But there was pressing work to do. She was impatient for Noel to email her the scanned copy of the paper Daniel Vergas had given him. Anything written by Massevadegh was of interest if it offered the slightest possibility of peeling back a layer of skin and revealing something new about his psyche. She decided Hampstead could wait till tomorrow.

Her newfound sense of freedom felt refreshing. She uncorked a chilled bottle of her favorite sauvignon blanc and poured herself a glass. On her only trip to Napa Valley she had toured the estate and taken to its wines. The fact that the winery's CEO was a woman may have had something to do with that. The wines were lovely, and at under $15 a bottle, a terrific value. She had just started to swirl the glass when her phone vibrated, indicating a new arrival to her email inbox. It was from Noel. She sent the attachment to her wireless printer and watched with anticipation as the machine performed its magic. She collected the seven fresh pages from the output tray, slid into one of the two high chairs at the kitchen counter, and started to read.

Scholarly Paper Seminar Series
October 23, 2012

Grading the Grid

Presented by   : Michael Massey
Advisor   : Professor Daniel Vergas
Attending Faculty : Professor Keith Braithwaite

I. Abstract

The National Academy of Engineering (NAE) rated the electric power grid as the top engineering achievement of the twentieth century. How does it rate today?

II. Grid Overview

From its humble beginnings on September 4th 1882, when Thomas Edison inaugurated the Pearl Street Power Plant in Manhattan as the nation's first electric utility, the United States electric power grid is today the largest single capital-intensive infrastructure in the country, comprising a national network of over 9,000 electric generating units, 4,491 nodes and 6,594 edges, with over 200,000 miles of high-voltage (230KV or greater) transmission lines, enough to wrap around the earth's equator eight times. While vastly integrated, the national grid is divided into three separate systems: The Eastern Interconnection (which serves approximately 70% of the U.S. population and electrical load), the Western Interconnection (virtually defined by an extension of the north-south line separating Montana and North Dakota), and the Lone Star Grid of Texas. The division is designed to limit a disruption in any one region from cascading into a nationwide outage.

III. Grid Importance

All other national infrastructures rely on electricity and are therefore dependent on the electric grid to produce, transmit and distribute the power that is their lifeblood. Electricity enables—and the lack of it disables—the nation's water infrastructure, food infrastructure, comfort infrastructure (heating and cooling), emergency services, transportation infrastructure (including fuel and natural gas delivery), healthcare, telecommunications, financial services (including banking and money access) and city, county, state and federal government services, in other words the very fabric of life as Americans know it. The longer and more widespread an outage, the greater will be the degree of societal paralysis, with production of goods and services—the U.S. economy itself—coming to a standstill. The Northeast Blackout of 2003 varied in duration between seven hours in some areas to two days in others, and it contributed to ten deaths. A prolonged grid outage, one lasting a month or more, will result in much higher fatalities, depending on geographic scope and time of year. The U.S. electric grid is the combination circulatory and central nervous system that sustains the heartbeat of American life.

IV. Grid Vulnerabilities

The traditional design and evolution of the electric grid—centralized, vast, complex and interconnected—combined with the reality that so many of its critical components have aged beyond their design lifetimes, render the grid vulnerable to a variety of threats, both natural (storms) and man-made (physical and/or cyberattacks). Two key grid components are particularly vulnerable, extra-high voltage (EHV) transformers and electronic control systems.

- EHV Transformers. While they only account for at most 3% of the transformers in U.S. substations, up to 70% of the grid's capacity is routed through them. Those rated above 345KV are of special concern due to their large size (comparable to the size of the average new single-family dwelling), their weight (400 – 500 tons) and their high cooling oil content (30,000 gallons). There are approximately 2,000 in service. Most are unique, of custom design and specifications to suit specific applications, with long lead times for labor-intensive manufacture (the copper windings around the core must be wound by hand) and delivery of replacement units, 12 to 24 months being typical as limited U.S. production capacity means some units must be imported from overseas. Due to the size and cost of EHV transformers (up to $8 million), utilities do not typically maintain a sufficient inventory of spares to enable rapid replacement of disabled units. Physical security at the typical EHV transformer installation is largely inadequate. Simultaneous attacks causing disruption of multiple units could result in an extended outage over a large geographic area with potentially catastrophic impact.

- Electronic control systems. The digital revolution has spawned a transformation in the way grid elements are monitored and controlled, from original electro-mechanical means to any combination of modern electronic systems, including Supervisory Control and Data Acquisition (SCADA), Digital Control Systems (DCS), Industrial Control Systems (ICS) and Programmable Logic Controls (PLC). These computer-based systems offer radical improvements in grid monitoring and control, but when connected to the Internet with poor security measures (ID & Password), as many are, they entail elevated cyber-security risks. These systems provide would-be saboteurs with access points to control electric grid infrastructure. Examples of readily available tools used to identify and penetrate targets are Shodan (filtered search engine for any type of device connected to the Internet, e.g. SCADA ports), ERIPP (Every Routable IP Project, a comprehensive searchable database), Google Dorks (advanced Google search operators), THC-Hydra (Siemens PLC password-cracker), and HAVEX (remote access Trojan malware targeting ICS).

V. Remediation and Safeguarding the Grid
- Utilities should regularly use the tools mentioned above (and others like them) to discover what devices and/or information on their networks are visible/accessible on the Internet.
- Utilities should either block scans and searches known to come from aforementioned tools, or simply remove their devices from the Internet. The tradeoff is between convenience (connected devices) and security.

151

- In the long term, transitioning from the traditional centralized power generation model to a distributed generation model would significantly reduce the threat of widespread outages.

VI. Regulatory Environment

- The U.S. Electric Power Reliability Act of 1967 stimulated the creation of an industry-based electric reliability body and led to the establishment in 1968 of the National Electricity Reliability Council (NERC). In 1981 the name changed to North American Electric Reliability Council in recognition of Canada's role.
- In 1987, the National Security Council and the Department of Energy directed NERC to safeguard against disruption of the electric power supply by terrorism or acts of sabotage. NERC developed policies and criteria but lacked the authority to enforce compliance with them.
- In 2000, the US government designated NERC as its primary liaison for critical infrastructure protection policies.
- In 2004, the final report on the 2003 Northeast Blackout included as its top recommendation the need to make reliability standards mandatory and enforceable by the U.S. government.
- The Energy Policy Act of 2005 mandated the creation of a self-regulatory North American electric reliability organization with oversight of the USA portion by the Federal Energy Regulatory Commission, or FERC.
- In 2006, FERC officially designated NERC as the United States' electric reliability organization. In 2007, NERC's name changed to North American Electric Reliability Corporation, with a membership base representing a cross-

152

section of industry players. NERC essentially became an industry-funded non-profit corporation that writes industry standards. As the federal agency having jurisdiction over the power grid, FERC approves or disapproves NERC's standards. NERC was also assigned responsibility for enforcement of its standards. The industry was thus writing its own regulations and expected to self-enforce them, at a minimum a classic conflict of interest, and potentially a recipe for disaster.

- In 2010, NERC successfully fought against legislation known as the Grid Reliability and Infrastructure Defense (GRID) Act that would have eliminated the industry's self-regulation. The bill passed the House of Representative by unanimous vote but the measures to protect the power grid were stripped out of it in the Senate.

- Statutory authority to address risks, including cyber-security risks, to the electric power grid can only be vested by an act of Congress. To date, Congress has failed to act.

VII. Notable Quotes

"Critical missions are almost entirely dependent on the national transmission grid. In most cases, neither the grid nor on-base backup power provides sufficient reliability to ensure continuity of critical national priority functions and oversight of strategic missions in the face of a long-term (several months) outage."
-- Defense Science Board's Task Force on Department of Defense Energy Strategy, 2008

"Down the road, the cyber-threat, which cuts across all programs, will be the number one threat to the country."

-- FBI Director Robert Mueller in testimony before Senate Select Committee on Intelligence, July 2012

"The United States faces the possibility of a cyber-Pearl Harbor. An aggressor nation or extremist group could use cyber tools to shut down large portions of the power grid across large parts of the country."
-- Secretary of Defense Leon E. Panetta, October 10, 2012

VIII. Summary
Digitization of the electric grid has improved its efficiency, flexibility, resilience and reliability, at the cost of increasing its vulnerability to external threats. A prolonged (several months) outage of the national grid due to natural (geomagnetic storm) or man-made (cyber-attack or electromagnetic pulse weapon) causes represents a nightmare scenario for the United States.

IX. Conclusion
The top engineering achievement of the twentieth century has become the top national security liability of the twenty-first century.

Dana realigned the pages by standing them on edge and tapping them against the kitchen counter before setting them down. She realized she hadn't touched her glass of wine, reached over and picked it up. The motions of swirling, sniffing and sipping were instinctive and did not distract from her single-minded focus on what she had just read.

First off, the quality of the writing had surprised her, but maybe it shouldn't have. The guy had an undergraduate degree from a British university, so of course he was fluent in English. But there was pithiness to the paper, an economy of words that she found impressive. The section on the regulatory environment was a bore, except for the fact it highlighted the bizarre reality that the electric power industry writes its own rules and has oversight over its members' implementation of them. Unbelievable! The bottom line was there could be no doubts about the level of the threat posed by a cyber-attack against the power grid, especially a successful one that caused a widespread outage of significant duration. Leon Panetta's comparison with Pearl Harbor was too conservative. Terrible loss of life and limb, to be sure, but the immediate physical impact of Pearl Harbor had been limited to the naval facility in Oahu. A successful grid attack had the potential to be far more debilitating in scope and scale.

She sipped on the wine and wondered if there was a warning system in place, one whereby the nation's utilities could be told an attack was imminent and could take precautions to minimize its impact. Could they even do that? Maybe operators could be put on high alert and override automated controls to preclude the cascading effect that had been so instrumental in the 2003 Northeast outage? Maybe that would at least help to localize an outage? There were more questions than answers.

She refilled her glass, re-corked the bottle and placed it in the refrigerator. She took another sip of the wine and her spine tingled with the onset of its high. Today's separation from eRock was absolutely a time to turn over a new leaf, and she found herself buzzing on another level, a very personal one. There might never be a more appropriate time to cross a line she had toyed with for way too long. Wine glass in hand, she went back to the computer desk that held the printer, slid open its one drawer, and took out a business card. She took another sip. With a salacious smile, she reached for the phone.

***

The spread on the dining table reflected the common provenance of the diners: *Gheimeh Bademjan,* a tomato-based split-pea stew with chunks of beef and eggplant; *Ghormeh Sabzi,* a vegetable stew; charbroiled ground beef and chicken *Koubidehs* served kabob-style with grilled tomatoes over a bed of crust-charred Basmati rice. Sides included bilberries sautéed with onions and saffron, and fresh yoghurt peppered with cucumbers and dill.

Laleh glanced at her watch and said: "Taraneh will be here any minute now. Would you like to start or shall we wait for her?"

Amir didn't hesitate. "I'm hungry," he said. "She won't mind if we start. I say let's eat."

"I don't mind waiting," Mahmoud countered.

It was instantly settled when the lights of a car reflected through the window onto the dining room wall. "She's here," Laleh said.

Moments later Taraneh entered the room from the kitchen. She was on the petite side, with flowing black hair parted on one side framing a classy visage that boasted endearing features. She wore navy blue three quarter leggings and a sports bra, yet she looked so fresh she could be mistaken for being on her way to a gym as opposed to having just left one. Her tiny waist imparted an hourglass shape that oozed sex appeal. Exuding confidence, she was possessed of beauty, grace and elegance that took Mahmoud's breath away. Her eyes were locked on his as she approached him with a warm smile warm, her mien welcoming. "Oh my God!" she said as they embraced. Mahmoud suppressed a gasp at the electrifying sensation of her breasts rubbing up against his chest. After the customary exchange of innocent kisses on cheeks, Taraneh stepped back and looked him up and down her hands still

156

on his shoulders. "How many years has it been?" she said, all playful pussycat.

Mahmoud was not prepared for how disarmingly alluring she was. "The last time I saw you I was ten and you were, what? Six or seven?" he said. "Amir was three or four. It was in 1997."

"I was too young to remember," Taraneh said with a quick squeeze of his shoulders before she let go.

"Of course!" Mahmoud said, the words streaming out. "You all came to Tehran. I remember because it was the time when Iran beat Australia to qualify for the ninety-eight World Cup in France."

"What a memory!" Taraneh said.

"You look wonderful," Mahmoud said. Then he remembered that Laleh and Amir were there too. "All of you," he added, "just wonderful."

"Are you going to change into something more—" Amir started.

Taraneh responded firmly: "I'm fine."

Mahmoud sensed Amir's displeasure, and he understood it. Taraneh's workout outfit left little to the imagination.

"Suit yourself," Amir said. As his mother broke a loaf of *Barbari-nan* flatbread, he uncorked a bottle of cabernet sauvignon.

"That's a western vice I have not succumbed to," Mahmoud said, consciously turning his attention away from Taraneh.

"Nothing western about it," Amir retorted. "Viniculture history extends back to Neolithic times and the origins of the vine reach geographically back into central Asia. Are you having any, Mom?"

Laleh let him pour her a glass and didn't let on that she had already drank several shots of vodka that afternoon. She started filling Mahmoud's plate before Amir's and her own. Amir poured two more glasses of wine, one for his sister and one for himself.

"Are you sure you won't have any wine?" Taraneh said to Mahmoud.

Can anything, *anyone,* be more seductive? Mahmoud thought to himself. If it were just the two of us, I might just damn well do anything you want me to! "No, thank you," he replied. Then he changed the subject from the wine before succumbing to the temptation. "So, the bail hearing is set for Wednesday?"

"Yes," Amir said.

"Have you been to see him?"

"He doesn't want us to see him in the jail uniform," Laleh said. "Your uncle is a very proud man. And a stubborn man."

"Proud and patriotic," Mahmoud said. "I've always loved him and looked up to him for that. My mother, God bless her soul, always said she could not have had a finer brother. She always said that whenever his name came up. Has the attorney said anything about how he expects the bail hearing to go?"

Laleh sighed dejectedly. "He says we're in for a fight. So many government agencies are lined up against Farzad. Plus there is a bad political atmosphere now, with the sanctions and the nuclear talks, he fears this might be a complicated situation, not so easy. But he assures me Farzad will get out. I can only hope."

"Well, I'm going to remain optimistic," Mahmoud said. "With your permission I will stay in Houston until he comes out, hopefully on Wednesday, so I can see him before I leave. I want to tell him personally how proud I am of him."

"Where are you going?" Taraneh said. She was sitting across the table from Mahmoud, and it took all his discipline not to drop his eyes to her chest when he looked at her.

Before Mahmoud could respond, Amir, who had been noticeably quiet while the discussion centered on his father, suddenly chipped in. "For what?"

Momentarily flustered, Mahmoud said, "Excuse me?"

"Why are you so proud of him?"

Mahmoud said: "For having the courage of his convictions. For defying the sanctions. If that is even true."

"And if it gets him locked away for twenty years, will you still be proud?" Amir said, a cold edge to his voice.

Mahmoud quipped: "Even more so."

Amir shook his head.

Mahmoud realized he had to be careful. Uncle Farzad had funded his education, the school in Switzerland, university in England, and then GMU. Mahmoud was sure that Laleh knew that, but he didn't know if Amir and Taraneh had ever been told. He proceeded courteously. "Amir," he said, "You should respect our history, the sacrifices, the blood of our martyrs, the centrality of our collective experience to our identity. I'm sorry to see you have been so Americanized."

"I was born and raised in Houston, Mahmoud. This is my country. I am not Americanized, I am American."

"Iran is—"

"Iran is the country my parents left when it fell into the hands of repressive and backward-thinking mullahs. Here, we have freedom of thought, freedom of religion, or of non-religion."

"Do we have to talk politics?" Taraneh said.

"Besides," Amir went on, "over a year ago you sent me an email saying you planned to get a green card and stay in America. What happened to that plan?"

"That didn't work out. The company I was working for declined to sponsor my application. When the time came for them to sign my petition they said they couldn't represent to the government that I wouldn't be displacing an American citizen in the workforce because my qualifications and expertise are not

159

unique enough. And it was late in the game, too late for a plan B. They screwed me."

"So what are your plans now?" Taraneh asked.

"I'm going to Mexico for a few days, then Venezuela, then back to Tehran."

"What's in Mexico and Venezuela?" Amir said.

Mahmoud paused for a moment before saying, "Just visiting friends. People I met at GMU."

"Of course you are most welcome to stay with us as long as you like," Laleh said as she refilled her wine glass. "We have a self-contained guest apartment above the garage, bedroom, living room, restroom and kitchenette. God willing your uncle will be released on Wednesday and he will be delighted to see you. It will be a nice surprise for him to find you here."

"God willing," Mahmoud said.

Amir rolled his eyes as he swallowed a mouthful of food. "Was it God's will that he was arrested in the first place?"

"Tsk!" Taraneh glared at her brother and shook her head.

"Stop it, Amir!" his mother said. "You know I don't like to hear you talk like that."

"You should just hear yourselves talking sometimes," Amir argued. "Good things happen, praise God; bad things happen, help us God. If you're going to praise him for the good, why not blame him for the bad?"

"Oh please," Taraneh said. "Can't we just enjoy dinner with Mahmoud without arguing?"

"Is that what they told you at that Baptist school you attended?" Mahmoud said, emboldened by Taraneh's words.

Amir said: "It's what I taught myself when I decided to think for myself instead of blindly believing in folklore. My beliefs are based on my experiences, not some arbitrary set of rules that make no sense in today's world."

"So, based on your experiences," Mahmoud persisted, "does Iran not have the right, under the non-proliferation treaty, to develop a nuclear energy infrastructure? Or is that a rule that doesn't make sense to you?"

"Energy, yes. Weapons, no."

"Are you not aware that all the American intelligence agencies have said Iran has not made moves to develop nuclear weapons? Even the Mossad says that."

Taraneh had paused eating and was now following the discussion with heightened interest.

"So why does Iran build secret facilities?" Amir said.

Mahmoud said: "Because there are countries that would like to bomb Iran back into the middle ages, to keep it from progressing, leave it impotent in the face of American and Israeli hegemony in the Middle East."

"Progress does not necessarily mean nuclear programs."

"I agree. Let everybody dismantle nuclear programs and I will say Iran must also do so. But don't tell me we don't have the right to develop the technologies other countries have had for years. And not just technologies, Iran has the right to develop nuclear weapons. Why should Israel, India, Pakistan, America, and so on, why should they have the right but we don't? Sunnis, Catholics, Protestants, Jews, Hindus, Sikhs, all have nuclear weapons. Shias don't have the right to the same deterrence? That's bullshit." Mahmoud turned to Laleh and Taraneh and added, "I apologize for my language."

Taraneh smiled at him. Laleh raised her glass like she was toasting him. "You echo your uncle's sentiments." She brought her glass to her lips and drained it.

"And look where that's got him," Amir said.

Later, after the leftovers had been stored in the refrigerator and the dishwasher had started running through its cycles, after Laleh and Taraneh had retired for the evening, Amir and Mahmoud stayed at it in the family room, their conversation typical of cousins who had not seen each other since their pre-teen years. They hit on a wide range of subjects, soccer, music, women, ambitions, architecture and engineering, all of which they predominantly saw eye to eye on. But the conversation inevitably wound back to identity, politics and U.S. foreign policy, and common ground dissipated. As Mahmoud's watched his cousin uncork another bottle, his disdain for Amir got the better of him. "You know," he said, "it really boils down to this: The world is divided into two camps. One camp bends over in accordance with America's whims. I call it the Fuck Me camp. The other stands proud and refuses to march to the beat of the American drum. I call it the Fuck You camp."

Amir chuckled, as if amused by the absurdity of what he was hearing.

Mahmoud went on: "So, Amir, which camp are you in?"

Amir rose from the couch, turned off the muted television and dropped the remote on the coffee table. He swirled his glass and downed another swallow of wine. He grabbed the bottle and walked off with a scathing, "Fuck you, Mahmoud."

***

The Westin Washington Dulles Airport hotel in Herndon was five miles farther from Dana's condominium than the Westin in Reston Heights, but its room rates were lower, so Dana favored Dulles. It was early evening when she arrived, and she was pleased to see there were two vacant stools next to each other at the lobby bar, either of which would give her a good view of anyone approaching the bar from the lobby. She sat on one and put her purse on the other. Her hair was in a chignon and she wore a black cardigan, as had been agreed. She was the only patron with that particular combination of visual cues. She ordered a glass of sauvignon blanc and instinctively stole a deep breath to settle her nerves. An airline crew arrived in the lobby, several guests came and went, and two men nursing beers at the end of the bar let their eyes dwell on her for long enough to register interest. Dana ordered water, no ice, in a wine glass, and positioned it in front of the stool holding her purse. The beer drinkers stayed put. Moments later Dana watched as a tall, curvy blonde materialized from the direction of the elevator leading to the self-parking garage. She headed for the bar, took one look at Dana and didn't look at anyone else as she approached with a confident smile. "Dana?" she said.

Dana reciprocated in kind and picked up her purse, vacating the stool. "Brandi?"

"May I?"

"Please."

Hopes were rekindled at the beer end of the bar.

Brandi took the stool. "I hope I didn't keep you waiting?"

"No," Dana replied.

"Good."

There was an awkward silence. Dana looked Brandi over while trying not to make it obvious. Aware of that, Brandi looked the other way. A bartender brought a drinks menu.

"Are we having a drink?" Brandi asked.

"Sure." Dana said. "You into that?"

"Whatever you like."

"I just thought we would chat for a while."

"That's cool." She turned to the bartender. "Do you have any pinot gris?"

"We have two, a Julien Meyer from Alsace, France, and Seven Hills from Oregon. And we have two pinot grigios, Yellow Tail from Australia and Bella Costa from Italy."

"A glass of Seven Hills, please."

As the bartender turned his back on them Dana resorted to small talk. "What's the difference between pinot gris and pinot grigio?"

"As far as I know they're the same grape. I think gris is the French name, grigio is Italian."

The bartender confirmed this when he brought Brandi her glass. Dana eyed a corner table that offered more privacy than the bar and suggested they move. After settling into their chairs they raised their glasses and, at Dana's behest, toasted the unpredictable nature of life. Brandi used that to segue into the evening's business. "Amelia told me this is your first time."

Dana was relieved the subject had been so directly broached. "Yes. So...this is a personal test for me. It's rare that I'm attracted to a man. It's not necessarily that I'm often attracted to other women, but there is a void. A sexual void. Companionship, too. I've struggled with it and...it's taken me a while to decide to try...you know?"

Brandi patted the top of Dana's hand. "I do. I went through a journey of self-discovery myself. It was filled with uncertainty at first, but that soon went away and it ultimately became liberating."

"I'm..." Dana hesitated. "I'm unsure about where I stand."

"And I'm here to help you find out. We'll do what you want, whatever you're comfortable with."

"I think it's more a question of seeing if I can overcome discomfort. You know?"

"Yes. That's a good way of putting it. I will tell you, you have to be relaxed. Do you get high?"

Dana shook her head.

"It would help you relax."

"It's not for me. Not now, anyway. I'm out on enough of a limb. Besides…" she raised her glass, "I've had a few glasses of wine. If I ever try getting high it'll be when I'm completely sober."

"That's smart. You're a beautiful and smart woman. I hope you find yourself as attracted to me as I am to you."

Dana couldn't decide if Brandi was sincere or just a good professional.

"I'm not just saying that, Dana. You must know that about yourself, right?"

Dana nodded. Amelia, the agency's owner, had told Dana to always remember she had as much control as she wanted during the time with her escort, including the freedom to end the encounter at any time with no explanation. Unlike a date that had the potential to develop into a relationship, this was an exploratory experience with no strings attached. The hourly rate had been agreed, her credit card details had been filed and approved, the total sum charged would be based on the time she spent with Brandi, and that was entirely up to her, the sole caveat being a one hour minimum. She looked at Brandi and decided that she liked what she saw. She felt a tingle of excitement. "I'm ready to go upstairs," she whispered.

Again Brandi touched Dana's hand. "Me too."

The two men at the bar watched the ladies leave, fantasized, and ordered another round.

***

165

Late on Monday night Mahmoud lay awake in bed with his laptop and took stock of where things stood. It was good to be in Houston, off the streets and in the relative shelter of his uncle's house. The guest apartment above the three-car garage was very comfortable, maybe even larger than his apartment in Herndon. The past few days were a blur. His departure from Virginia had gone mostly as planned. He had expected eRock to discover the zero time delay on the breakers, and link him to the outage, but not quite that fast. Still, he had made them pay for refusing to sign his resident alien petition, and for the humiliating way that Dana bitch had escorted him out of the building in front of his colleagues like he was a common criminal. But he had been taken aback by the speed with which the cops had discovered he'd rented from National, and that he had switched cars in Raleigh. They had found his Toyota at the Marriott quicker than he thought they would. In hindsight, he should have hid it better. But as far as he could tell from the Internet, they hadn't put his name out in the public domain and there was no indication they knew where he was or where he was going. Searches for his name—both Mike Massey and Mahmoud Massevadegh—on CNN.com and FoxNews.com rendered nothing. So for now he was sure he was safe and still on track.

He had planned to stop in Houston for just one night, long enough to visit with his uncle, to warn him to get himself and his family out of the country, and get a good night's sleep before the final leg of his drive to the border. But that was before today's unexpected, shocking news. If the charges against his uncle were true—and he had to think breaking the sanctions would not be out of character for Farzad Yazdi—then they would lock him up for years, decades maybe, and he might never see him again. So he had to await the outcome of the bail hearing on Wednesday, hope that bail is on the cards, see his uncle for what may well be the last time, then split to Mexico. If bail were denied, Mexico would still be there, and if he decided there was time then he had the wherewithal for a little retribution.

A plan had begun to crystallize in his head before dinner, just moments after Laleh had told him his uncle had been arrested. He had thought he might recruit Amir to help, but that was obviously not on, and he didn't need him anyway. The guy was a hopeless case, politically naïve and more interested in wine than dignity. No big deal. He would lay the groundwork tomorrow, and ping and probe and build a target library from the sanctuary of this very room in this very house, with no one the wiser for it. Once in Mexico, he would be one strong Internet connection away from unleashing the havoc America deserved. There were unknowns, like how bad things would be, depending on the scale and success of the attack. The 2013 attack on the Metcalf Substation in San Jose had failed to bring Silicon Valley's power grid down because it targeted only one substation, and the utility had worked around it. Besides, it was a physical attack, inherently limited in scale. But he had read one assessment that if the top nine substations in the U.S. were to be disabled simultaneously, the majority of Americans would lose their electricity. If it lasted for a few months…

His world had changed in September 2010, during his final year at Leeds University, when he heard a BBC News report about the Stuxnet virus attack against Iran's nuclear facilities. The next day the British papers quoted the director of information technology at Iran's Ministry of Industry and Mines as saying that an electronic war had been launched against Iran. His life suddenly had meaning. It was a war he welcomed. In less than a year he would earn his bachelor's degree in electronic and electrical engineering, a great platform, but only a starting point. On a whim he decided he would go to America for graduate school, with a dual mission. While pursuing a master's degree at an American university, he would learn everything there was to know about the U.S. national power grid. And his extracurricular activities would focus on acquiring the hacking skills to paralyze that grid. Now he was ready, willing and able.

There was sublime beauty in the fact that America had destroyed Iranian centrifuges by deploying malware, and here he was on the verge of deploying malware that would cripple America. And the sweetest irony was that the Internet is what made it possible. The Internet, the data network first conceptualized in 1962 by the head of the computer research program at DARPA, the Defense Advanced Research Projects Agency. An agency of the U.S. Department of Defense, DARPA's mission is to create breakthrough technologies for use by the military to safeguard national security.

Revenge was all the motivation he needed. Revenge for all the past wounds, the past suffering, past humiliations. But then something else kicked his ambitions into overdrive. He had long fervently believed that Iran's security could never be guaranteed unless it developed nuclear weapons. He had never believed the Iranian government's assurances to the rest of the world that its nuclear program was only for peaceful purposes. That was just a cover story, necessary to buy time for progress. But now Iran was about to sign on to a deal that would restrict its program, deprive it of most of its enriched uranium, and seriously curb its ability to develop a nuclear deterrence capability. On April 2nd, less than two weeks ago, Iran and its interlocutors announced that they had reached consensus on a framework for what they were calling the Joint Comprehensive Plan of Action. No details, other than the widespread understanding that the deal would neuter Iran's nuclear program. Iran was going to do a deal with the devil, one that would keep it vulnerable to attack by its enemies. A deal that would block Iran's path to acquiring the only deterrence that counts in today's world. They hadn't learned from the war with Iraq, and their inability to defend themselves against weapons of mass destruction. And they hadn't learned that America, home of the CIA, could never be trusted. The timing oozed divine intervention. He had already acquired the know-how to avenge the Stuxnet attack, and it had become just a question of when. After April 2nd, the simple answer was: before the nuclear deal was signed. He alone was positioned to sabotage it, because if it became known that an Iranian had attacked the U.S. power grid, the negotiations would end. And if he had doubted for one fleeting second that he was the key player in a divine plan, the doubt was laid to rest when eRock fired him. There could have been no clearer signal from the heavens.

The serendipity of it all gave Mahmoud goosebumps.

It was intoxicating to think of the consequences, for America, and potentially for the rest of the world from an America gone berserk. He had to stay resolute, stay composed and banish fear. He found himself thinking of the consequences for Taraneh. Would she suffer? And why was it that of all of his uncle's family, it was the thought of making Taraneh suffer that concerned him the most?

He put Taraneh out of his mind and googled his uncle's name. He found details of the arrest on the Houston Chronicle website. An even more detailed account on the FBI's website, which made the situation look ominous for Farzad Yazdi. The array of government agencies and officials lined up against him was disheartening: Assistant Attorney General for National Security, U.S. Attorney from the Southern District of Texas, Assistant Director of the FBI's Counterintelligence Division, Special Agent from the FBI's Houston field Office, Under Secretary from the

U.S. Department of Commerce, Special Agent in Charge from the Department of Commerce's Office of Export Enforcement, and Special Agent in Charge of the Houston office of the Internal Revenue Service.

Mahmoud's mind flashed images of Iranian heroes courageously defending the homeland, inhaling Saddam Hussein's mustard gas—sanctioned, if not delivered by, the United States—on their march of martyrs to the heavens.

Everything was relative.

He set aside his laptop. It was time to get some sleep so he could be clear-headed and recharged for what he had to do tomorrow. He laid flat in bed and arranged the pillows under his head. The past two nights he had fallen asleep with images of transmission lines and transformers and generators swirling in his head. Now when he closed his eyes the dark abstracts of his mind were filled only with visions of Taraneh.

***

Vienna's Stadtpark dates back to 1862, making it the city's oldest public park. Its 28 acres are dissected by the River Wien and dotted with monuments to famous Viennese composers, artists and writers, one of which, the Johan Strauss monument, is a gilded bronze statue framed by a marble relief. Unveiled in 1921, it quickly became one of the best-known monuments in Austria. At 3:45 a.m. on April 14th the air around it was still and the grounds vacant when four men approached it on foot from the north, south, east and west. They took their time, walking softly, standing still, their trained eyes peering through the darkness, their ears straining to pick up the slightest sound. In choreographed movements they crossed each other's paths with only a slight nod to indicate to any observer that there was mutual recognition. But no one else was there, and once they had established that they whispered it into microphones hidden under shirtsleeves. Moments later two other men, each watched and closely tailed by more aides, entered the park, one after emerging from the Intercontinental Vienna and crossing Johanesgasse to the south, the other from the Palais Coburg and Wiehburggasse to the west. Their builds could not have been more different, one tall and lanky, with a shock of silver hair, the other short, stout and balding. As they approached the monument the moon appeared from behind a cloud, as if the heavens were blessing the assembly.

"Javad," the tall one said, extending his right hand.

"Hello, John," came the reply as they shook hands.

"Thank you for coming at such short notice. Sorry about the time. I wanted to preclude a repeat of the January media circus."

"Understood and agreed."

Around them in every direction, aides maintained their vigil.

"Besides," Kerry said, "this really can't wait." He touched the screen of a mobile phone, illuminating it, and handed it to Zarif, who adjusted his glasses and began to read. The Iranian scrolled through the document and didn't look up until he reached the end.

"Do you know anything about that?" Kerry asked.

"No."

"I didn't think you would. This just came to light within the last 24 hours."

Zarif handed the phone back to Kerry. "So this fellow…"

"He's disappeared."

The shadow of a grimace flickered on Zarif's face.

"If he were to mount a successful attack on the grid, everything we have achieved so far will unravel. The Republicans will have a field day. Schadenfreude gone wild."

Zarif nodded. He didn't have to vocalize his thought that many in Tehran would react in like fashion.

"The President and I need your help," Kerry said. "For everyone's sake."

Zarif looked up at the moon before turning back to Kerry. "What can I do?"

"We need to know if this guy is acting alone, or if anyone in Tehran is behind him. People who oppose a deal. And any information that might help us locate him…before he does anything."

Zarif smiled. "That's all?"

"We're in this together, Javad."

It was true, and both of them knew it. They were going to succeed together or they were going to fail together.

"I'll see what I can do. What else can you tell me about him?"

Kerry reached into his pocket and handed Zarif a sheet of paper folded twice. "Everything we have is here. His full name, taken from the admission documents at George Mason University and his visa application. The university in England, the name of the high school he attended in Switzerland. We don't know what's true and what's invented, but it's everything we have."

Zarif used the flashlight on his smartphone and glanced through the information. He turned the light off, re-folded the paper and slipped it into the inner breast pocket of his coat. "Strange irony, no?" he said to Kerry. "The greatest military power the world has ever seen has this huge vulnerability that is threatened by one man armed with a laptop computer."

Kerry couldn't tell whether there was any joy behind Zarif's words, but the mere possibility irked him. "I won't read too much into that statement," he said sternly. "That vulnerability is common to all countries that have a national power grid, which means all countries." After a brief silence during which the two men held each other's gaze, Kerry added a final riposte: "Including Iran."

Zarif's stoic expression gave way to a wry smile. "I will see you back in this beautiful city in a few weeks," he said.

"That won't happen if we don't stop your compatriot first. I need to hear back from you very soon."

Zarif nodded and said: "Take care, John."

"You too, Javad."

As they parted, both men looked forward to the day they could add the words "my friend" to their conversations. While they both felt they were close, they knew it could all still unravel, so they weren't there yet.

Chapter Eleven

Mahmoud slept at the margins of consciousness. When he opened his eyes shortly after 5 a.m., he reran hellacious notions that had flitted through his mind and realized he had been dreaming. It was a relief to know he had actually slept for a few hours. He remembered Taraneh and thought to himself that there was magic in the world.

He got out of bed, booted his MacBook Pro and pulled up a map of Houston. There was a Starbucks less than a mile away, just on the other side of Memorial High School. Of course there was. In America there was a Starbucks less than a mile away from anywhere, which was a godsend because regardless what you thought about the coffee, they all had good WiFi.

He ran through in his mind what he was going to do. In the most basic sense a cyber-attack is like a conventional attack in that a list of targets is drawn up, the tools of the attack are determined, then the attack is executed. A common element between the two is the need for stealth, to avoid detection before—and if possible even during and after—carrying out the attack. Stealth came first, and that was what he would set up today. Which is where Starbucks came in.

He was still in his room when he heard the rumbled exhaust note of Amir's BMW M3 come to life, then fade away as his cousin drove off, destination presumably Rice University. Amir was a disappointment, but that was neither here nor there. His politics stank. He couldn't grasp that once Iran joined the nuclear club, no other country would ever again dare attack it. The Americans knew that, of course, which was why they were so intent on negotiating a deal that would preclude Iran building nukes. It was invigorating to think that he could sabotage the deal so Iran would build the bombs. It was his destiny. *Khoda* was with him.

He found Laleh in the kitchen, drinking coffee and looking at the newspaper though bleary eyes. She looked rough, like she hadn't slept well. His uncle's situation was clearly taking its toll. A middle-aged, overweight, Hispanic-looking housekeeper was emptying the dishwasher. He guessed Laleh had already scoured the paper to see if there was anything new related to her husband's arrest. "Good morning, Laleh-jun" he said.

"Good morning," Laleh replied, instinctively adjusting her hair. "How did you sleep?"

"Well, thank you. Anything new?" He gestured at the Chronicle.

She looked at him with tired eyes and shook her head. She noticed he had his backpack. "Mahmoud, this is Leticia, she's always here during the day, except on Sundays."

"Hi Leticia,"

"Hola Senor."

"Would you like some coffee?" Laleh asked.

"No thank you, I'm not much of a coffee drinker. Are Amir and Taraneh still here?" He knew very well that Amir had already left, but he hoped Taraneh was still home.

"No, they've both gone, Amir to university, Taraneh to work. Some juice?"

Mahmoud concealed his disappointment. "No thanks," he said. "Taraneh works in public relations, right?"

"Yes. How about breakfast?"

"Thank you, I'll get some later. I'm going to the Galleria, I have a little shopping to do."

"It opens at ten."

"I know. I thought I'd drive around and see some of Houston first. Memorial Park, maybe downtown."

"If you take Memorial Avenue that will bring you to the park first, and then all the way straight into downtown."

"Yes, I've looked at the map. It's easy. When do Amir and Taraneh get home today?"

"Not before six. Will you be coming home for lunch?"

"I'll probably just grab something in the Galleria."

She took a key out of a drawer and handed it to him. "Leticia is here till five, but here's a house key, just in case. The alarm code is 21323. You can remember it by thinking BMW. B is the second letter of the alphabet, M the thirteenth and W the twenty-third."

"That's clever."

"It was your uncle's idea. He drives a 750. For as long as I've known him he's liked BMW."

"Do you drive one too?"

Laleh shook her head. "Range Rover. I like being high up in something sturdy. Houston's roads are not the best."

"Nice."

"You have my number. Call me if you need anything."

"I will. See you later."

"Mahmoud, watch how you drive around here. The village police are overly strict about speed limits, a complete stop at stop signs, that kind of thing."

"That's good to know. Thanks. I'll be extra careful."

As he walked out of the house Mahmoud thought his uncle had done well in choosing his wife. Laleh was a fine lady, head and heart in the right place, and it was no surprise that she appeared to be showing the strain of her husband's arrest. He knew she was of like mind as her husband when it came to Iran, its rights and its rightful place in the world. Amir was maybe not so much an anomaly as he was a product of the environment in which he was born, the schools he had attended, the friends he had made and the influences to which he had succumbed. Taraneh…well she was the epitome of an angelic presence on earth.

Laleh's warning about the village police was spot on. Mahmoud saw two police SUVs in the few minutes it took him to drive to the shopping center at I-10 and Echo Lane. One was by the side of the road, the officer writing a ticket for an infraction, probably speeding in the 30-mph zone; the other one was cruising with intent. Mahmoud was ever aware that his Louisiana plates stood out, so he drove by the letter and spirit of the law. He coasted down Echo Lane, past the high school, and pulled into the Hedwig Village Shopping Center. The Starbucks was right there, where the map had shown it to be, the corner spot of the one-story building fronting the road, the same kind of prime location Starbucks' scouts always held out for. Mahmoud drove slowly around the parking lot. The property came right up against the I-10 feeder to the north, Echo Lane to the east, Memorial High School across Gaylord Drive to the south, and Mustang Lane to the west. That figured because several signs announced Memorial High School to be home of the Mustangs. The anchor tenant was a Kroger grocery store, adjacent to a Walgreens, a triple-A office, a Mattress Firm, a dance studio and a tortilla restaurant. A typical urban shopping center in America. The spaces in the parking lot were mostly vacant, but that was down to the time of day; he imagined it would fill up as the neighborhood ladies completed their morning exercise routines and stopped to pick up groceries on their way home. The high school parking lot was full, as he had expected, with a predictably healthy percentage of Ford Mustangs.

The Starbucks was in the same building as Kroger and Walgreens, which was good, because it meant the rooftop air-conditioning units would probably be spread out, leaving ample roof space for landing the drone, a fact Google Earth's satellite view would confirm later that afternoon. He turned his attention to finding a good spot from which to launch the drone. Ideally it would be away from the street, hidden from the view of passing cars, yet still with line of sight to Starbucks. The shopping center parking lot was not good, as he could see there was a security guard patrolling it on a bicycle, although he probably wouldn't be there in the middle of the night, but that was a chance best not taken. The Gaylord side to the south was exposed to the high school parking lot, which could also be expected to have a security patrol, or at least CCTV cameras. Mustang Lane lacked the line of sight connection, so he drove back to Echo Lane and parked directly in front of Starbucks. There were two low-rise office buildings across the street, separated by a driveway virtually in line with Starbucks. There were plenty of trees, which was good and bad. Good because they provided cover; he could stand behind a tree trunk to hide from passing cars, bad because the overhead branches and trees could make for a tricky launch. He backed out of the parking lot onto the street, made a U-turn and turned right into the driveway separating the office buildings. At the far end he found surface parking for twelve cars, no trees. It was perfect. He could park there, launch the drone straight up, high enough to mute the sound of its rotors. He could walk back along the driveway to Echo Lane, fly the drone over across the street and quickly land it on the roof above Starbucks. The whole process would take two or three minutes, maybe less. The only risk was someone might see the LED lights on the bottom of the drone's shell. They were the means of maintaining visual contact with the drone during night flights, so that was a risk he had to take. All in all, it was good enough. It should be fine if he timed it for somewhere between midnight and 5 a.m. Closer to midnight might be less suspicious than just before the crack of dawn if a police car happened to drive past.

Satisfied that he would not find a better location, Mahmoud pulled back onto Echo Lane and headed for his second stop of the morning, the Radio Shack at 14356 Memorial Drive, five miles due west. He followed the directions on the map, took the I-10 freeway and was at the store in less than fifteen minutes. He spent no more than a few minutes inside, paid for his purchase in cash, and walked out with a 100-pack of plastic zip ties, a Raspberry Pi 2 Model B and a Netgear USB card that collectively set him back less than $100, tax included.

A British-made credit card-sized computer, the Raspberry Pi was originally conceived in 2006 by a group of computer scientists at the University of Cambridge, in response to the declining number and expertise of students applying for undergraduate computer science programs in Britain. The team behind its design wanted to rekindle hobbyist programming in kids and figured a capable, low-cost computer was the way to do so. By 2011 the Raspberry Pi was in mass production, and over two million units were sold during its first two years on the market. It can be connected to a standard computer monitor, keyboard and mouse, and can be used for routine computing activities like web browsing, spreadsheets, word processing and high-definition video gaming. The Model B has four integral USB Ethernet adapters, enabling networking and WiFi connectivity, a feature crucial for Mahmoud's needs, as he would plug the WiFi card into one of those USB ports. His final shopping stop was at an AT&T store, where for under $10 he picked up a 4G modem card that would plug into another of the Raspberry's USB ports.

He drove back to the house, now in possession of the components he needed to cover his tracks, to establish the stealth screen that would make him, if not invisible, anonymous online. Leticia was alone in the kitchen.

"Senora?" he said.

"No esta, Senor," Leticia replied with a shake of her head.

Perfect. That meant he basically had the house to himself. He went back out to the car and fetched the drone. He closeted himself in the bedroom and went to work.

He interconnected the Raspberry Pi with the Wifi card and the 4G modem and fastened them securely to the underside of the drone using four of the zip ties. Next he wired the Raspberry's power supply to the drone's battery. On full charge the battery would run the Raspberry for well over a week. Had he needed more he would have added a little solar panel to the rig, but a week was plenty for his needs. He took the drone with its new payload down to the car and drove back to the Starbucks. Time to test the combo and verify the parts were talking to each other to create a working whole. This he verified from inside his car while parked right up next to the coffee shop. Now all that remained was to drop the drone onto the shopping center roof above Starbucks, which he planned to do after midnight. From his location in the car he used Google Earth to zoom in to the satellite view of the corner of the building where Starbucks was. Just as he had hoped, there was ample clear rooftop space at the very corner, where he could land the drone without worrying about any air-conditioning units or piping being in the way.

Back at the house he took the added precautionary step of removing the drone's battery and plugging it into the wall charger to ensure it was at 100% at the time of launch.

He left the guest apartment and went to the main house. Leticia was going about her daily chores, dusting, cleaning and doing the laundry. Other than acknowledging him with a respectful smile, she kept to herself. Yesterday he had only seen the entry foyer, the living room, family room and kitchen. Now, with time to kill, he wanted to see more of the house. Mansion, actually. Off the entry foyer was a room that was clearly his uncle's study. Wood paneling all around, wall-to-wall bookcases, parquet floor adorned with an exquisite Persian carpet, substantial antique desk, everything telling of a man of worldly reach and refined taste, a man Mahmoud loved, was proud of, was indebted to, and wished he knew better. He was drawn to the picture frames on the bookshelves, family photographs spanning his uncle's life, his childhood in Iran, his wedding, his life in the U.S., and of Taraneh and Amir, from newborns to toddlers to teens to high school graduates, and, in Taraneh's case, university graduate. One photograph in particular tugged at Mahmoud's heart. It was of his mother and his uncle with their parents, Mahmoud's grandparents. He picked it up and stared at it. His mother must have been seventeen or eighteen, Uncle Farzad maybe fourteen. And now he was in an American prison.

Bastards.

He came upon another photo that had an even more mesmerizing impact. He was in it, ten years old, along with his parents, his uncle and his brother, Bahram, who would have been seventeen at the time. Bahram was standing behind his father, who was in his wheelchair, the oxygen mask removed from his face for the photograph, smiling bravely as if life were good. There were a few other relatives in the frame, and Mahmoud remembered the occasion, an impromptu celebration at his parents' home in Tehran, in 1997. His uncle had been visiting from the States, and the photograph was taken the day Iran beat Australia to qualify for the 1998 World Cup in France. Those had been heady times in Iran, which made for some serious bonding between uncle and nephew. His father had died the following year, just before the World Cup. This must have been one of the last photographs of him. Mahmoud made a mental note to ask his uncle if he could scan these precious photos so he could have high quality digital copies.

He instinctively returned to two of the photographs of Taraneh, the university graduation and a more recent portrait photo. He took close-up shots of both with his iPhone camera. His heart beat faster; he was aware that he was doing something he shouldn't be doing and didn't want anyone to know about. What the hell was that about? It was one thing to be attracted to her, another to be sneaking around taking pics of photos of her. What would his uncle say if he knew? He felt mildly ashamed of himself and stepped back, telling himself he should delete them, but stopping short of doing so.

There was a see-through humidor that Mahmoud opened. Of course the cigars were all Cuban, what else did he expect? Maybe if his uncle came home tomorrow they would light up in celebration of freedom and reunion.

He sat at the desk, where his uncle would sit. The view of the garden and pool was uplifting. It was a great place, a position of comfort, of means, befitting a man of his uncle's stature. He noticed what looked like a pool house, a stand-alone structure with an attached summer kitchen separated from the main house by an open area containing a generator. He stared at the open space and wondered if it was accessible by car from the street. It seemed like it would be, because it was just behind the garage. If so, it would be a good place to park the Nissan, as that would hide it from the street. He made a mental note to check later. Then he thought maybe not. Amir, and maybe also Laleh, would likely wonder why he was going to the trouble of parking the car there. Besides, the cops didn't know where he was; no point hiding something no one is looking for.

He turned his attention back to the desk. There was a slim center drawer and a stack of three drawers to the left with two deeper ones to the right. He slid open the center drawer. Normal desk accessories, stapler, letter opener, paper clips, pencils and the like. The drawers on the right, the deeper ones, contained hanging file folders. When he opened the top drawer on the left, Mahmoud's pulse raced again. He instinctively looked around as if fearing someone might be watching. The drawer contained a gun. Mahmoud reached into the drawer and picked it up. He had never before held a gun, or any kind of firearm. Cradling this one now gave him a bizarre thrill, part power, part security, a sense of having a first line of defense. He realized that he cared less about defending himself than defending his mission. The mission was paramount. So much so that he was prepared to give his life, or take someone else's, if that was the price of success.

The engraving on the stainless steel barrel told him it was a Smith & Wesson SW1911. It was a beauty, matte silver finish with a wooden grip panel. Mahmoud thought about what he would be doing after midnight, how he might have to defend himself against a nosy, or maybe even drunk, passerby. He made a snap decision. His uncle certainly didn't need the gun tonight. He stood up and slipped the gun under his jeans at the small of his back where his un-tucked shirt covered it. He slid the drawer shut. His heart was pounding as he headed back to the guest apartment. When he reached it he closed the door behind him and locked it, his emotions conflicted about his behavior. The photos of Taraneh and the gun…he didn't know which of the two misdeeds he felt guilty about more.

***

Dana awoke on Tuesday with a sense that the night before had been one of the seminal moments of her life. Her time with Brandi had been a revelation of pent up sexuality previously untapped, four hours of gentle interplay that would be impossible with a man. She hadn't climaxed; that was an experience yet to be had, but she had enjoyed touching—and being touched by—another person like never before. Brandi had been soft, encouraging, understanding, frictionless in her approach and attitude. She had urged Dana to relax more, not physically, but mentally. She had sensed that Dana was preoccupied by something—work, a relationship—something that prevented her from achieving the relaxed mental state that would be necessary, albeit maybe insufficient, to reach orgasm.

Dana hadn't been able to relax, and hadn't explained why. Brandi's instinct and insight were impressive, but then she was a pro. That was an experience to be repeated, and hopefully built upon, when the time was right. And the time would not be right before Mahmoud Massevadegh was behind bars. Part of Dana's preoccupation was the niggling question in her head about whether she had done, whether she was doing, everything she could to further the cause of stopping Massevadegh. The answer now was there were two things that might help and certainly wouldn't hurt. She was on the phone with Noel before taking her first sip of coffee. "I've been thinking," she said.

"Uh oh," Noel replied in jest.

"We know he headed southwest, but we don't know how far he's gone or where he is. The guy's been in the country for three and a half years. We know of one personal cell phone he's used during that time. Let's get the NSA's call log for his number, see if there's anyone he's called that lives in a state southwest or west of us, someone he might be going to see or he might have contacted more recently, someone who might know where he is, where he's headed."

"The NSA's not renowned for sharing information, as you know."

"I know. They'll share if Obama orders it."

"Yeah, they will. It's worth a try."

"One other thing. Maybe we should put the word out to Infragard. You still a member?"

"Of course."

"Me too, although I haven't been to any meetings or kept up with the emails and postings. But it's a national network. We should make them aware of this."

"Agreed. You want to do that or do you want me to?"

"It would be more credible coming from you. I'm an ex."

"I'll do it."

"Thanks, Noel. Let me know if you hear anything."

"Stay tuned."

"Bye."

Infragard was a no-brainer. A partnership between the FBI and the private sector, the organization provided a forum for information and intelligence sharing between law enforcement, the corporate world, academic institutions, and other interested parties, all with one common goal: the prevention of hostile acts against the United States. It delineated sixteen critical infrastructures at risk: chemical, commercial, communications, critical manufacturing, defense industry, dams, emergency services, energy, financial services, food and agriculture, government facilities, healthcare and public health, information technology, nuclear (reactors, materials and waste), transportation, and water/wastewater systems. Seventy percent of the nation's Fortune 500 companies had representatives in Infragard, which has over eighty chapters spread out across the nation. Chapters held regular local meetings to keep members abreast of threats in their area. All members are bound by a seven-point code of ethics: to promote the protection of critical US infrastructure, to cooperate in the interchange of knowledge for mutual protection, to support the education of members and the general public and not engage in illegal activities, to serve in the interests of Infragard and the general public, to maintain confidentiality when instructed to do so, to abide by the organization's bylaws at the local and national level, and to protect and respect the privacy, civil rights and property (physical and intellectual) of others. With someone like Massevadegh on the loose harboring potentially nefarious motives regarding critical infrastructure, there was no better organization than Infragard to raise both awareness of the threat and vigilance for telltale signs of activity potentially related to that threat. Getting the word out via Infragard was absolutely the right thing to do, and it was gratifying for Dana to have suggested it herself. She didn't know then that it would have happened anyway. It was now twenty-four hours since the President had issued his directive, and it was being acted on. Word had been disseminated from FBI headquarters to all of the agency's fifty-six field offices of a heightened threat of a lone wolf cyber-attack against the power grid. The instructions were for a below-the-radar full court press, yet no indication of the identity of the attacker was provided. But one special agent in charge of a field office, Joseph Mayle in Manassas, was privately willing to bet he knew who it was. He cringed when he thought about his disagreement on Saturday with Dana McLaughlan, and he feared for his job, let alone promotion prospects, should anyone other than McLaughlan and Sheriff Hart become aware of it.

***

Taraneh was tantalizingly distracted at work, and she couldn't fight it. She could not remember any other occasion when she had been so viscerally attracted to a man as to her cousin Mahmoud yesterday. She realized now how little she knew about him and how much she wanted to know. At dinner he had said he would stay at least till tomorrow so he could see her father—hopefully her father would be released tomorrow. But if Mahmoud was no longer tied to a job in America and was going to Mexico, Venezuela and then Iran, surely he was in no rush? Maybe he could stay a few more days, a week—or more—and they could get to know each other better? She blushed when it occurred to her that if they got to know each other better, maybe he would stay longer.

The thought put a wistful smile on her face. More thoughts flooded her mind, and they tingled her spine.

***

Mahmoud spent a couple of the afternoon hours on the web, on sites like smith-wesson.com, gunbroker.com, gunsandammo.com. He watched a few reviews and instructional videos on YouTube, from which he learned everything he needed to know about his uncle's gun, and more. He learned the .45 1911 model was considered by many gun aficionados to be the greatest handgun of all time, and that it had been around for over a century.

"Masterpiece" and "classic" were accolades in review articles, and although he was not into guns, Mahmoud did agree that it looked and felt top of the line. But that was not why he was looking. Functionality – how to use it – is what he was interested in, and to that end he learned how to remove and reinsert the eight-round magazine and verify that the gun was loaded.

Anticipating that Leticia would include the guest apartment in her housekeeping chores, he took the drone and the gun and stored them in the car. He had told Laleh that he was going to the Galleria mall, and now he thought he'd better do that, as she might ask if he did, and it would give him a broad-stroke way to account for his time. Once again he used the Apple map on his phone, and again it was unerring. He bought a t-shirt from J. Crew and ate a late lunch in the food court by the ice skating rink. Then he passed time overlooking the rink from the third level coffee shop, of course, a Starbucks, while looking at the photographs of Taraneh on his phone. It was crazy. What would Uncle Farzad think? He had to get her out of his mind. But there was no way he was going to delete the photos.

He noted that this was not a location that would lend itself to what he had planned for later that night, because there was no roof, per se. Instead there was a huge skylight surrounded by a walking/jogging track. Besides, the Echo Lane Starbucks was much closer to the house.

The day's second rush hour was in full swing by the time he headed back, and even though he avoided the freeways, it still took over an hour to get to the Memorial Villages area. He could tell from the Range Rover and M3 in the open garage that both Laleh and Amir were at home. His uncle's 7 series BMW was the only other car there, so it looked like Taraneh wasn't home yet. Mahmoud noted that the space he had seen behind the garage was indeed accessible, making it perfect for hiding the Nissan, but he decided to take his chances and park on the street. No need to raise Amir's eyebrows.

He first stopped in the guest apartment to drop off the t-shirt and found Leticia making his bed. He put the t-shirt in a drawer, crumpled the J. Crew bag and placed it in the Radio Shack bag he had earlier put the Raspberry carton and AT&T SIM card wrapping in.

"Basura, senor?" Leticia said.

"Trash."

"Si."

He found Laleh and Amir in the Kitchen. "Am I interrupting anything?"

"No," Laleh said. "We were talking about dinner options."

"I'll probably just have a salad. I had a late lunch." He turned to Amir. "How was school?"

Still smarting, Amir felt like starting this conversation with his cousin the way he had ended the prior one last night, but he held back. "Routine."

"Well I had a quiet day at the Galleria. Nice mall."

"We can order Italian or Mexican," Laleh said. "Indian is another option. There's a place nearby that makes excellent curries. Your uncle thinks it's as good as the curries he eats in Dubai."

"Please, you decide and I'll have a little of whatever it is."

"Let's order Italian," Amir said. "Hopefully dad will be here tomorrow and we'll celebrate with Tikka Masala."

Leticia walked in carrying a basket filled with the tools of the housekeeping trade and the Radio Shack bag, which she proceeded to deposit in a larger black plastic trash bag.

"You were at the Galleria?" Amir said, looking puzzled.

"Yes," Mahmoud said. "Why?"

"Radio Shack?"

Mahmoud shrugged and nodded. "Yes."

Amir straightened his posture. "The Radio Shack in the Galleria closed a year ago." His tone and look were accusatory. Even Laleh noticed.

Mahmoud stared back at his cousin, his mind in overdrive. "So?" he said at length.

"So how were you at Radio Shack in the Galleria?"

"Amir," Laleh started.

His eyes still on Mahmoud, Amir put the palm of his hand up to his mother in a gesture that told her not to interfere. The vibe in the kitchen suddenly went from strained courteous to venomous.

"What is this, Amir?" Mahmoud asked. "Interrogation, inquisition, what?"

"Just answer the question."

Laleh wanted to stop Amir, but she also wanted to hear Mahmoud's explanation.

Neither man flinched.

"You asked me if I went to the Galleria, I said yes. You asked me if I went to Radio Shack, I said yes. You didn't ask me if I went to the Radio Shack *in* the Galleria." Mahmoud was of a mind to add "Asshole," and he would have had Laleh not been there.

Amir was cornered. "Why do I feel you're hiding something?"

"Because you either have a regrettably suspicious nature, which will weigh you down in life, or you're venting your frustration and anger over your father's circumstance in my direction. Either way, I don't appreciate it." Mahmoud started for the door.

"Mahmoud, wait!" Laleh said.

"Please, Laleh-jun," he said. "I told you I'm not hungry. Have dinner without me. I will move to a hotel to diffuse this…this bad atmosphere."

"You will do no such thing! I will not forgive you if you do that, and neither will your uncle! If you move out I will take it as an insult to me personally!"

"Laleh-jun–"

"No! I won't have this in my house! Amir, you apologize now!"

"I have nothing to apologize for," Amir said. He stormed out of the kitchen toward the family room.

"Mahmoud, I apologize for him. I think you're right about the stress we are all under because of Farzad's situation. Please don't take it personally."

"I understand. And I will respect your wishes. But please, I will stay in the apartment while Amir is home so we don't have any more confrontations."

Laleh watched him go. Then went after her son. He was in the family room, simmering in front of the television. "What has gotten into you?" she said, raising her voice.

"You don't have to shout."

She took the remote control from Amir and switched the TV off. "Mahmoud is right. Ever since your father's arrest you have been on edge, unbearable. But you don't have to take it out on him!"

"I've been on edge? What about you? You think I don't know how much vodka you're drinking?"

"Stop! This isn't about me. I want you to be nice to Mahmoud!"

"I don't like him, okay? I don't like his politics. He thinks the sun shines out of the mullahs' assess. I don't like his worldview.

192

He romanticizes martyrdom, I think it's obscene. He divides the world into two camps, in his words, the anti-America camp, which he calls the fuck you camp, which he champions, and the pro-America camp, which he calls the fuck me camp, which is people of my mindset. So I don't like him. In fact, I hate him. He gets under my skin, and after he gets the fuck out of our house I don't want to ever see him again!"

Amir strode back to the kitchen and Laleh followed. "Where are you going?" she said.

"I'm curious." The large black trash bag was still on the floor where Leticia had left it. Amir retrieved the Radio Shack bag and emptied its contents on the floor. There was a J. Crew bag with an invoice inside it for a t-shirt bought at the Galleria, and packaging for something called a Raspberry Pi and an AT&T card with invoices showing they were purchased from stores on Memorial Drive.

"Satisfied?" Laleh asked.

Amir bundled everything back into the black trash bag and stood up, hands on waist, shaking his head.

"So he was telling the truth," Laleh said. "And it's so ironic how you're acting with your cousin like the government is with your father. Guilty until proven innocent."

Amir said: "I'm out of here."

"Where are you going?"

"Anywhere. I just can't stand to be under the same roof as him." He was sullen-faced as he grabbed his keys off the rack on the wall of the kitchen. His mother watched him go. She heard the door to the garage slam and decided against following him out there and making things worse. She herself was highly stressed and needed to relax. She went to her bedroom, shut the door behind her and locked it. In the bathroom she swallowed a pill and washed it down with a shot of vodka. She grimaced at herself in the mirror. Then she brushed her teeth. She lay on the bed and felt the calming fog begin to descend on her.

***

In the guest apartment Mahmoud heard the growl of Amir's car and looked out of the window at the street below in time to see the red BMW accelerate away. Fuck him, he thought. I won't let that asshole disrupt what I have to do. *Nothing* is going to get in my way. He put Amir out of his mind and went about ensuring he had everything ready for tonight.

The drone was the 3D Robotics Solo model, advertised by 3DR as a smart drone for good reason. It was offered either with a camera-stabilization gimbal designed specifically for GoPro cameras at $1,400, or without the gimbal for $1,000. Mahmoud had purchased his sans gimbal, as videography was of no interest to him, and without the gimbal he had more room to attach payload like the 4G radio he'd built with the Raspberry Pi, the WI-FI card and the 4G modem. Battery flight time was 25 minutes, ample for his needs. He ran over every component one last time:

- Charged batteries, both drone and controller. Check.
- Visual inspection to ensure no loose components after assembling the 4G radio. Check.
- Undamaged propellers. Check.

The remaining items on the list were location-specific and so had to wait until he was at the launch site. He was satisfied that he was ready. All he had to do was wait until after midnight, then execute. It was a few minutes before seven, so he had five hours to kill. He turned on the TV and sat down to see what CNN had to say. It can't have been anything interesting because he soon succumbed to sleepiness and dozed off.

He was woken by knocks on the door. He glanced at his watch and saw he had slept for thirty minutes or so. But it had been a deep sleep, a good power nap. He thought back to the confrontation earlier with Amir and hoped his cousin hadn't come back for more. He warily opened the door. His pulse surged when he saw Taraneh.

"What are you up to?" she said.

Mahmoud's relief was plastered on his face. "Nothing!" he said.

"It looks like Mom has retired early, Amir's not here and Leticia's gone. I'm going to order pizza, I wondered if you want some."

Her words were sweet music. "Yes!" Mahmoud said. "Of course! Thank you!"

"Great! How do you like it?"

"However you eat yours is fine with me."

"I have margarita with sautéed spinach."

"That sounds awesome."

"Cool. I'll order it and go pick it up. I'll be back in twenty minutes."

He couldn't bear to see her go. "Do you mind if I come with you?" he said.

"You sure?"

To the ends of the earth, Baby, he thought. "Let me just freshen up and I'll meet you downstairs."

"Great!"

He watched as she turned and walked away with a sensuous slink. He wondered if she always walked like that. Of course she does, he told himself. You're flattering yourself if you imagine that's for you.

She insisted on driving her Mercedes SLK. In such close proximity to her in the confined space of the two-seater convertible, Mahmoud was in heaven. When he insisted on paying for the pizza she rested her hand on his forearm as she thanked him. On the drive back home he silently obsessed about the length of time she had maintained the physical contact—surely longer than she had to—and whether she had done so deliberately. He told himself he was a fool for dreaming that might be so.

They ate at the breakfast table in the nook in the kitchen, and he realized he had never felt as weak as he did around Taraneh. She had him under a spell, and he relished every minute of being with her. When they were done eating he helped her rinse their plates in the kitchen sink and stack them in the dishwasher. The magnetism between them was palpable, and Mahmoud felt near powerless to stop where it was going. He reminded himself of his uncle, languishing in the federal jail in downtown, and what *he* would think of this dalliance between his nephew and his daughter. That was the only way Mahmoud could restrain himself, and it worked only until Taraneh put her lips on his and gently caressed his tongue with hers and his elation transcended his judgment. The bliss was punctured by his nemesis and the sound of Amir's M3 pulling into the garage. Taraneh pulled away. She whispered: "Until tomorrow."

***

An unbelievable calm engulfed Mahmoud as he sat alone in the apartment above the garage. His life had new meaning, one he wanted to embrace forever. But the peace was juxtaposed with a new conflict, the poignancy of which tortured his soul.

What would have happened had Amir not come back home? How could he have let his feelings for Taraneh get so out of hand, so out of control? How could he have betrayed his uncle so?

In a way, he was lucky that Amir had come home because the innocence that had been squandered was measured. It could all have been so much worse. He took solace from the fact that the betrayal was not whole.

He told himself he was also lucky that he had so much important work yet to do tonight. He forced himself to come to his senses. He needed all his wits about him.

It was past midnight when he left the house through the side door at the garage and walked to where he had parked on the street. It was a still night, clear sky, good flying conditions. The drive to Echo Lane was uneventful and he saw only three other cars on the road. When he pulled into the driveway opposite Starbucks he realized he didn't have to go to the end of it, there was a perfectly clear launch spot with no overhang of tree limbs right there at the first set of six parking spots. He could launch the drone, fly it across the street and land it on the Starbucks roof without physically moving from his spot. He parked the car and turned off the lights. All was quiet. He removed the gun from where he'd placed it in the glove compartment and slipped it under his belt. He got out and readied the drone.

This was a short-distance, short-duration flight, but he wanted to get it right the first time, so he pulled out his phone, pulled up the Notes checklist and went through the remainder of the precautionary steps. He made sure the self-locking propellers were correctly attached and spinning smoothly. Again he ran his fingers along them one by one until he was satisfied none had been chipped or damaged en route from the house. He bent the two controller antennas down and away from the controller, then out 20 degrees, the position that would best leave them perpendicular to the drone in flight. He glanced up and down Echo Lane and at the shopping center parking lot across the street. Headlights approached from his right, from the freeway. He picked up the drone and stepped back a few yards. The headlights passed. He walked back to the launch spot, set the drone down on the concrete driveway and switched on both drone and controller. The LED lights of the drone came on, but it was still silent. Within a minute he saw the signal that told him the drone had locked onto GPS satellites in the sky above, which meant it was ready for launch. He turned on the motors and the propellers started spinning, emitting a low buzz. It was now an attention-getter, so he had to move fast. He launched it straight upwards to a height of about 200 feet. That would easily clear the overhead power lines that ran along the street. At that height the sound of the motors was lower, but the LEDs were still lit. On first glimpse an observer at street level might do a double take and think it a UFO. He put it on a horizontal path for fifteen seconds, until he estimated it was now above the Starbucks. Then he initiated the descent, correcting as it came down, correcting again when it was ten feet above the top of the building. Satisfied that it was as well positioned as could be from his vantage point, he bit the bullet and landed it on the roof what looked like six feet from the edge. He killed the power and the sound of the motors died. He held his breath. All was quiet. He got back in the car and put the front windows down. Still silence. He started the car and pulled out of the parking space onto Echo Lane, southbound, in the direction of his uncle's house.

That could not have gone smoother, he thought to himself as he started breathing easy again. He took the gun out from under his belt and placed it back in the glove compartment. Starbucks' WiFi routers stayed on around the clock. With the first step of his plan—

securing online anonymity—now complete, he couldn't wait to get back to the safety of his lair above the garage and get rolling with step two. Taraneh was in every breath he took, tugging at his heart and his mind, but he still had to maintain his focus.

Chapter Twelve

During his first university lecture on network fundamentals, Mahmoud learned important basics about the Internet. Digital information is transported from one device, like a computer or printer, to another, in packets that take different routes to get from source to destination, where they are reassembled as a whole entity. It is analogous to mailing a six-page letter in six different envelopes each containing one page and bearing the same address, with the postman combining them into one upon delivery. And just like each mailing address in the world is unique, each device connected to the Internet in a way that allows it to send and receive information also has a unique address. The system for communicating over the Internet is called Internet Protocol, or IP. The unique address assigned to an Internet device is called an IP address, in its most common variant a collection of four numbers separated by dots. An IP address can either be static, which is rare because that requires a user to self-configure it by editing his or her computer's network settings, or dynamic, vastly more common and assigned by a service running on the Internet in a manner that makes it transparent to users.

The Internet continues to increase in size because the number of devices connected to it keeps increasing. And the devices are no longer just computers and printers. To enable people to remotely control things like garage doors, thermostats, ovens and the like, each such device needs a unique IP address. At the start of 2015, the number of devices was roughly four billion and counting. That posed a problem. The most common IP addresses are on an original standard called Version 4, or IPv4, inherently limited to 4.3 billion addresses. A newer standard was developed, version 6, or IPv6, and it blew away that limit.

During a subsequent lecture, Mahmoud learned about port scanning. Just like airports and seaports are places where the two-way flow of people and goods takes place, a port on a computer is a physical element where information flows in and out of the device. Port scanning is a process by which a computer's ports are systematically scanned to identify what are in effect open doors to the machine. Port scanning can be legitimate, as when used for network management tasks, or malicious, a means by which an unauthorized individual seeks to gain access to a computer or other networked device. It would have been prohibitively difficult for Mahmoud, sequestered in the guest apartment of the Yazdi residence in Houston, to scan the ports of every device connected to the Internet using only a laptop to find his targets. But he didn't need to do that, because someone else, someone with greater expertise and far more computing power than a mere laptop, had already mapped out the Internet—for fun—and published the results.

In 2012 a cyber-security researcher decided to do something that had never been done before: perform a comprehensive IPv4 census. In his own words:

"I did not want to ask myself for the rest of my life how much fun it could have been or if the infrastructure I imagined in my head would have worked as expected. I saw the chance to really work on an Internet scale, command hundred thousands of devices with a click of my mouse, port scan and map the whole Internet in a way nobody had done before, basically have fun with

computers and the Internet in a way very few people ever will."

Named Carna, after the Roman goddess for the protection of inner organs and health, the project's goal was, in layman's terms, to develop a globe-spanning phonebook of IPv4 addresses that identified what kind of device each address was associated with, and its physical location. But there was more to it than that. The researcher wanted to expose the Internet devices that were either unsecured or easily penetrated, akin to putting an asterisk next the phone numbers or addresses of homes to indicate that the doors were either never locked, or could be opened using one of a set of four keys available at the corner convenience store. One argument says that's an invitation for unauthorized access, or at least an enabler. The flip side says it's a rude wake-up call for the owners to secure the premises.

It took the researcher, who worked solo, half a year to develop a strategy to accomplish his goal and set up the infrastructure to ping all the IP addresses—the equivalent of knocking on all of the world's doors. There was no magic involved, only an ingenious strategy. He wrote simple software that tried to access Internet devices using a few known default credentials, a username like ADMIN, and passwords like ROOT or PASSWORD. Default credentials are those that device manufacturers load before shipping equipment to customers. The expectation is that customers will change them to customized versions so malicious access attempts can be resisted and repelled. In many cases that happens, and the devices are considered protected. But far too often the default credentials remain in place, or devices are connected with no credentials whatsoever, making malicious access to them a laughably simple matter. When an unprotected device was identified, its IP address was logged to an online database, and the same software was loaded on it so it became a launch pad for additional port scans. It was like a pyramid scheme, only sustainable. The software never interfered with the normal operation of any device it was loaded on, the total number of which eventually reached 420,000. But the software did include a readable file containing a short explanation of the project and an email address for feedback from anyone who noticed the activity. And the activity most certainly was noticed. The government of China's Computer Emergency Response Team asked the U.S. authorities to intervene and stop the ongoing "hacking". Remarkably, the data produced by the exercise remains freely available online today on the Internet-Wide Scan Data Repository, a public archive hosted by the University of Michigan.

When all was said and done, the data showed an alarming number of unprotected devices spread out across the globe as far as the Internet reached. It also showed that at the time, there were 1.3 billion used IP addresses and an additional 2.3 billion that did not appear to be in use. Most ominously, the data revealed that, again in the researcher's own words:

"While everybody is talking about high class exploits and cyberwar, four simple stupid default passwords can give you access to hundreds of thousands of consumer as well as tens of thousands of industrial devices all over the world."

In the pre-dawn hours of Wednesday, April 15th, as he sat hunched over his laptop in his uncle's house in an upscale suburb of Houston, Mahmoud was not interested in the tens of thousands of industrial devices all over the world. His focus was on identifying subsets that narrowed things down geographically (The U.S., Texas, Houston) and functionally (devices used to control the power grid, or systems that could impact the power grid). And he used a top penetration testing software suite, Metasploit, to cull that information from the vast database that Carna had produced, and to sort it along meaningful parameters in the new proprietary database that would become his target library. Those parameters included whether or not a device was still active and unprotected, what type of system it was part of and what known vulnerabilities it had. All information he would then use to select which systems to attack, and how, in order to achieve maximum impact.

The 4G bridge he had established on the roof above Starbucks gave him complete anonymity. His laptop connected to the Internet through the Yazdi's home WiFi. From the Internet he was connected to the 4G radio on the drone via AT&T's cell towers serving the area, and the 4G radio connected him back to the Internet through the Starbucks' WiFi. All of his digital footprints on the web would lead back to Starbucks. Anyone noticing his port scanning would see Starbucks as the source. Mahmoud had scripted his port scanning and information gathering processes to run on autopilot, so he wouldn't have to stay glued to the laptop, and he had programmed his system to alert him via text message if any errors occurred.

At 4:17 a.m., with a few keystrokes, he initiated the process.

***

Dana was two miles into her Wednesday morning jog when she stopped to take Noel's call. The news was frustrating. Just as he had feared, the National Security Agency wasn't cooperating. It was going to take intervention by the President to get them to release Mahmoud Massevadegh's personal cell phone records to the Secret Service. The President could not be disturbed for a couple of hours, so the word had come back to Noel that it would be mid-afternoon before he could expect to receive the requested records. Dana nodded and sighed. It was a dismal state of affairs.

The events of 9/11 resulted in a massive budget increase for the NSA, which enabled it to swell its ranks with thousands of new recruits, making it easily the largest single U.S. intelligence agency. New operations centers cropped up in Utah, Texas and Colorado, Georgia and Hawaii, and even the already massive listening post in England was expanded. But a concomitant rise in the levels of compartmentalization and bureaucracy at the agency brought an erosion of efficiency. Other agencies, most notably the FBI, didn't know whether lack of ability or muted desire was behind the NSA's failure to share information, and they didn't care. The bottom line was the NSA hogged intelligence other agencies—and by extension, national security—might benefit from.

Dana hung up the phone and resumed her jog. The thought was never far from her mind that while she was enjoying her newfound freedom from eRock, an alternate means of income had to be found. That was tempered by the persistent resolve to only assess her options for the future as soon as there was closure in the hunt for Mahmoud Massevadegh.

After the run she showered, had a quick breakfast, then headed to the National Rifle Association Headquarters shooting range in

Fairfax, just a ten-minute drive away. She was a regular at the facility, knew all the range officers, and was rightly regarded by them as a top-level expert. They all respected her not only for her marksmanship, but also for whence her expertise. She owned a SIG Sauer P229, the same handgun that is standard issue for Secret Service agents. The only gripe she had ever had with it was that even though it was manufactured in the U.S., it was designed and made by a foreign company, Schweizerische Industrie-Gesellschaft, or in English, Swiss Industrial Company. But she couldn't fault any of the U.S. or foreign law enforcement agencies that relied on SIG SAUER firearms, for she agreed they were the best. She spent an hour at the range and shot through two 50-round boxes of bullets. It was a stress-purging activity, like running, but a different kind of detachment from the outside world, one she looked forward to and enjoyed for both the sense of enablement it gave her and the sense of achievement when she nailed the middle of the target time after time. Once, when a group of men at the firing range noticed her performance in the lane and commended her on her marksmanship, she wondered if her mastery of firearms might have something to do with her history of shallow and failed relationships. But after thinking about it, she had let that notion go. There were too many women who knew how to handle guns— some of them range officers—who were happily married.

On the way back home she stopped at Panera Bread and ordered a Greek salad and fruit for lunch. As she scanned the seating area she made momentary eye contact with a woman sitting alone with a laptop open on the table in front of her. A brunette that looked in her late twenties, there was something about her that Dana found interesting, a combination of looks and aura. Dana hesitated, and then picked a table close and with line of sight. While waiting for her food, Dana glanced over at her several times.

The brunette noticed and looked at Dana again, this time as if trying to decide if this was someone she knew. She gave Dana a fleeting smile and turned back to her laptop. Dana's pulse quickened and she thought about asking the lady if she could join her. Maybe after she picked up her tray of food at the service counter? That bought her a little more time. The buzzer vibrated and its red LED lights blinked. Dana stepped to the counter, took her tray and grabbed utensils and napkins. Looking up, she saw that a man had joined the brunette, who had now closed her laptop and was putting it away. Dana meandered over to a table in another section of the restaurant feeling mild shock at what had gone through her mind, and relief that she hadn't set herself up for rejection. The serenity she'd felt at the firing range was gone. Back on familiar emotional turf, she wondered how long it would be before there was any information she could work with to push forward the stalled search for Mahmoud Massevadegh.

***

It was just before 4 p.m. on Wednesday when Kenneth Leach rang the doorbell at the Yazdi's house. All afternoon he had dreaded having to tell Laleh the bad news, but it had to be done, and in person, not on the phone, so here he was, telling himself to stop grimacing and put as positive a spin on it as he could. Leticia opened the door, recognized him, and didn't conceal her relief at seeing him.

"Is Mrs. Yazdi home?" Leach said.

"Si, Senor," she replied, pulling the door back to let him in.

"Leticia…Who is it?" came Laleh's voice from the family room.

"It's me, Laleh," Leach said as he stepped in. "Ken."

"Ken! Dear Ken….did you bring Farzad?" Her speech was slurred and dripping with cynicism.

Leticia showed Leach into the family room, and it was not a pretty sight. The normally coiffed and elegant Laleh Yazdi was in sweats and trainers, hair unkempt, eyes bloodshot, breath reeking of vodka. She coddled a glass of the transparent liquid on her lap and didn't get up to greet Leach. She probably can't, he thought. Leticia retreated to the kitchen.

"Isn't it too early for that, Laleh?" Leach said softly.

She gave him a disparaging grin. "Why?"

"You need to stay strong."

"Strong? St…For what? To fight…for justice? I leave that for you."

He sat down on the sofa across from her. "Come on, Laleh. This is far from over. Yes, we're going to fight, and we need you to fight with us."

She raised her glass. "I fight," she said, and took a sip.

"Please, not like that."

"You come to tell me my hujband… must stay in… jail." Her look might have been piercing had her eyes not been half-closed.

"It's my job to get him out. I—"

"Then get him out!" She stood up slowly and unsurely and he thought she might fall over. He rose and came to help her but she pushed him away. "Don't come to tell me…why you…fail." She started towards the master bedroom, unsteady on her feet. "Just…get out and…get him out." She laughed as if tickled by her wordplay.

Leach watched her wobble away and realized he was fighting a losing battle here. There was no positive spin, no sugar-coating the reality. He was a lawyer, not a psychiatrist. He'd tried, and it was actually a relief that the visit had been cut so short. He hadn't had to try to explain the inexplicable nuances of Innocent Until Proven Guilty.

He found Leticia in the kitchen.

"*Hay...otra...*vodka?" he asked in a low voice.

The maid sighed worriedly. *"Si, Senor. En su cuarto."*

Leach frowned.

"Y medicinas, Senor." Leticia whispered.

"Que medicinas?"

"No se."

"Yeah, that's all we need," he muttered. He thought of one thing he could do to make himself feel better about leaving. Amir had called earlier in the afternoon to check on the outcome of the bail hearing. Now Leach scrolled through the recent calls on his phone, found the one he thought was Amir's and touched it. When Amir answered Leach recognized the voice and knew he had got it right.

"Amir, Ken Leach."

"Hi Ken. Tell me the judge reversed himself."

"I wish. We'll keep working to get him to do that. Listen, I'm at your house, just visited with your mom. Wanted to touch base with you and tell you I'm worried about her."

"So am I."

"She's been drinking." He heard Amir sigh. "She was barely coherent, and it's...like, four in the afternoon. How long has this been going on?"

"She hasn't been starting this early. I called her after I talked to you earlier and told her about the bail hearing. She started crying and hung up on me. I called back and she didn't answer. She's been stressed and depressed ever since the arrest, but I guess today was more than she can handle."

"Do you know of any medication she's taking?"

Amir hesitated. "I know she's taking something for her anxiety, Valium...or something like that."

"Well, as prescribed by a doctor that's alright. We don't want her popping it excessively, and we sure don't want her mixing it with vodka."

"I'll talk to her when I get home."

"Alright. I won't mention this to your dad, he's got enough to deal with."

"Thanks, Ken."

"We'll talk soon."

"Bye."

***

Mahmoud had heard Leach arrive because the lawyer drove a convertible Aston Martin DB9 with exhaust sounds that could be described by many adjectives, discreet not being one of them. He had watched from the window above the garage as the well-dressed man walked from the curb to the front door. Mahmoud figured the man might be his uncle's lawyer. He wanted to know what had happened at the bail hearing, but he stayed put; it was best not to show his face to anyone who hadn't already seen it. When he heard the exhaust rumble again he watched as the Aston Martin pulled away, made a U-turn and disappeared back down the street. Amir and Taraneh hadn't come home yet. The fact that his uncle had yet to show up bode ill. Had the bastards denied bail? He left his computer doing its thing and headed to the house. He found Leticia was cleaning up in the family room. "Senora Laleh?" he asked.

"En su cuarto." Leticia replied, pointing.

Mahmoud left her and went to the master bedroom. The door was shut. He knocked. After a while he knocked again. There was no response, not a sound from inside the room. He couldn't try the door to see if would open, that was a line not to be crossed. Maybe Laleh was in the bathroom, or maybe she just didn't want to be disturbed.

He returned to the guest apartment. He guessed the bastards had denied bail. Would they have done so if his uncle were not of Iranian extraction?

He would make the bastards pay.

***

The call from Noel came just before six in the evening and none too soon for Dana. She had run errands after lunch, grocery shopping, laundry, and odd jobs around the house to keep from opening a bottle of wine while she waited for something to happen.

"Are you close to your computer?" he asked.

"Yes."

"I'm sending you two emails now. The first has a link to a secure file containing Massey's call log. The second has the password."

"Have you looked at it?"

"No. I just received it. I'm working on something else right now. I figured you could run through it."

"Hell yeah!"

"Let me know if you have any trouble opening it."

Dana was at her computer within seconds of hanging up. A few moments after she accessed her inbox, Noel's emails showed up. She opened the second one first and highlighted then copied the password. She opened the first one, clicked on the link and pasted the password into the window that appeared. She considered printing the call log but decided to have a quick look through it first. It was in chronological order, most recent first. As she scrolled through the list she immediately saw that most calls were to local Virginia area codes 571 and 703, plus a spattering of others she recognized as being local, most obviously Washington, D.C.'s 202. She saw a couple of calls to a 510 number, which she quickly discovered was Berkeley, California. That brought to mind the drones he'd purchased from 3D Robotics, which was headquartered in Berkeley. She kept going, reinvigorated by being back in the thrill of the hunt.

***

When he heard the knocking on the door of the guest apartment Mahmoud looked up from the screen of his laptop and with raised eyebrows. It can't be Taraneh, because he had positioned himself next to the window overlooking the street so he could see her car when she pulled up at the house, and that hadn't happened. It wasn't Amir because his car didn't need to be seen, it could be heard, and he wasn't yet home either. It had to be either Laleh or Leticia. There was another knock, and now, *"Senor?"* He set the laptop aside and opened the door.

Leticia held out a sleek curvilinear cordless telephone handsets from the home phone system and said, "Senora Taraneh."

"Taraneh?"

"Hi Mahmoud."

"It's magic to hear your voice. Where are you?"

"I'm leaving work now. I want you to meet me somewhere."

Yes. Clever lady. It would be good not to have to worry about Amir and Laleh being around. "Of course. Where?"

"The address is 2006 Peden Street." She spelled it out. "Write it down and map it. It's about a twenty-minute drive from the house. Call me when you get to the parking lot." She gave him her cellphone number.

"Shall I leave now?"

"Yes."

"Did you hear that they denied Uncle Farzad's bail?"

"Yes, Amir told me."

"Bastards."

"If mom sees you as you're leaving—"

"I'm going to run an errand."

"I'll be waiting."

Mahmoud moved the laptop to the desk and made sure the power cord was attached. He changed his shirt and brushed his teeth. He skipped down the stairs and placed the handset in the base on the kitchen counter. "Senora Laleh?" he asked Leticia.

"In her room," came the reply.

Probably in the pits of depression and despair, Mahmoud thought. The news of her husband was harsh. He would make them pay. But that could wait. For now, he was giddy with the thought of what the next few hours might have in store for him.

He left the house quietly and followed the iPhone map directions with mounting anticipation. He told himself he had to be responsible and stay in control of the situation with Taraneh. It threatened to become a major distraction, a complication that could skew his attention away from the mission at hand. He had to stay focused on the big picture and see what happens with Taraneh later.

Easier said than done. The way he felt since yesterday, Taraneh *had become* the big picture. Girlfriends had come and gone in Switzerland, England and, to a lesser extent, Virginia. But they were ephemeral, fleeting affairs, more for carnal gratification than anything else, mostly forgettable. He had never before known the omnipotent intensity of feelings like he had for Taraneh. It had

214

happened so fast, so unexpectedly. The simple reality of the effect she had on him was that where she would lead, he was bound to follow.

She had been spot on with her twenty-minutes estimate. He pulled into the parking lot off a street that looked like it was a high-end shopping district. There was nothing he could identify as number 2006, only a bland, non-descript two-story stand-alone white building that could have been a small warehouse or a large garage. He pulled into a parking spot and killed the engine. He couldn't see her Mercedes anywhere. He got out of the car and locked it. Before he could call her he saw her approaching from across the parking lot. She had obviously been waiting and watching and she had seen him first. He took a few steps towards her. Then instinct kicked in and they both started running. They had been apart for less than 24 hours, but they came together in an embrace like that of lovers reuniting after being separated by years of war. "I missed you so much!" he hissed in her ear. Her frantic reply: "Me more! Come, quick, let's get inside!"

She took his hand and led him around a corner of the white building to the other side, where the only break in the siding was an unmarked blue door under a metal stairway. The 2006 he had looked for was painted in blue above the door so discreetly it had to be intentional. Whatever this place was, it was clearly invisible by design.

While it looked like maybe a dive from the outside, once they stepped through the door they found themselves in a dimly lit but very well appointed bar. A waitress carrying an iPad materialized next to Mahmoud and Taraneh told her they wanted to go upstairs. The waitress courteously asked if they were aware upstairs was bottle service only, and Taraneh nodded. Then she told the waitress something Mahmoud couldn't hear well enough to understand.

They were led to a curtained-off section at the far end of the second floor. Taraneh picked one of the high-back black leather couches and handed the waitress a credit card. Mahmoud liked what he saw, or rather, what he didn't. The place was so dark it was obviously somewhere patrons came not to see and be seen, but precisely not to be seen.

When the waitress left Mahmoud felt the wad of twenty $100 bills in his pocket and said: "I don't mind you running a tab on your card, but I'm paying when the check comes. How did you find this place?"

Taraneh had expected the question and was ready for it: "I've never been here before. One of my girlfriends told me about it."

Mahmoud believed her because he wanted to. The furniture was arranged so that they couldn't see anyone and nobody could see them, so when Taraneh leaned over and kissed Mahmoud, it was with free-spirited abandon. He reciprocated in kind. They took a break when the waitress returned with a bottle of Veuve Cliquot. She uncorked it, and for the first time in his life Mahmoud found an appreciation for the sound of the muffled pop. The waitress made herself scarce after pouring a measure of the champagne into each of two flutes. Before he knew it, Taraneh had picked up the two glasses and put one in his hand.

"To us!" she said, and raised the glass to her lips.

Mahmoud was shocked by his inability—or lack of desire—to control what he was doing. "To us," he crooned. He took the smallest of sips, barely more than a sniff, and for the first time in his life, his tongue was introduced to the astringent taste of alcohol.

**

Ten minutes into her review of the log of Mahmoud Massevadegh's calls that Noel had sent her, Dana found several calls that had been made to the same 713 number back in September and October of 2011. She noted that that would have been when Massevadegh had started his graduate studies at GMU, so when he had first arrived in the States. A quick check on Google showed 713 to be a Houston area code. Dana perked up. Houston was down to the southwest. She resisted the urge to dial the number and see how it was answered because she didn't want caller ID to reveal an incoming call from Northern Virginia, which would alert Massevadegh if he were to see it. She called Noel and gave him the number. He called her back within half an hour, his voice tremulous with excitement.

"Farzad Yazdi," he said. He spelled it out for her then added, "Google him then call me back."

Dana immediately ran the search and found the same articles Mahmoud Massevadegh had read when he googled his uncle's name on Monday night, and in the same order, the first on the Houston Chronicle's website, the second on the FBI's. Dana couldn't believe her eyes.

She called Noel, now sharing his excitement. "So this Yazdi guy was arrested for violating the sanctions against Iran, among other things, and there's some kind of connection between him and Massevadegh!"

"Coincidence?"

"No way! Not this! Not now!"

"I agree."

"Noel! We've got to get down there!"

"I thought about that."

"Let me restate what I just said. I'm going to Houston. I'd love for you to come too, but I'm as good as on the next flight."

He laughed. "Slow down, Dana! Do you think we should maybe tell the FBI guys about this?"

"Once we're down there, yes. But let's be sure the first visit paid to the Yazdi residence is not just the FBI. If Massevadegh is there, we'll need FBI and HPD, but do you want FBI to take the credit for nailing him?"

"Stay where you are. Let me see what I can do."

While she waited to hear back from Noel, Dana went back online and checked flights to Houston from the area's three main airports, Dulles, Reagan National and Baltimore. With the rush hour traffic in full tilt, there was no way she could get out of the D.C. area tonight. The last flight to Houston was Southwest Airlines out of Baltimore, 8:25 p.m. departure. No way. The earliest flight tomorrow was on Southwest out of Reagan National, 6:30 a.m. departure.

When Noel called back he was downbeat. "I couldn't get approval for a charter," he said. "We don't know for sure Massey's in Houston so we don't have enough to go on."

"What about commercial? There's a Southwest flight out of Reagan at six-thirty in the morning, puts us in Houston at 8:40."

"That I could probably do."

"Let's get on it. Flight 3451. I'm booking now."

"And the return?"

"I'm doing one-way. If Houston is a dead end I'll return whenever that becomes clear. We should know tomorrow, Friday at the latest."

"Okay. I'll alert the Houston office and see you at Reagan in the morning."

The Houston Field Office of the Secret Service is located on the second floor of 1801 Allen Parkway, on the south bank of Buffalo Bayou, just half a mile west of downtown. Special Agent

Tom Carlson was wrapping up for the day and getting ready to leave when he took the call from Noel Markovski from the D.C. headquarters. The two men had never met, but that was immaterial. Noel started filling Carlson in and was interrupted as soon as he mentioned a cyberattack against the power grid.

"Is this connected to the email from H Street yesterday?" Carlson said, referring to the Secret Service headquarters in Washington, D.C.

"Yeah."

"And on Infragard?"

"Yep. We think the guy might be in Houston. You know about the guy the FBI arrested in Houston last week for selling shit to Iran?"

"Yes. Micro-something."

"There's a connection. Not sure what. But keep that to yourself for now. FBI don't know."

"Okay…"

"I'm coming to Houston tomorrow. In the meantime, it might help if you got a warrant for—you got something to write with?"

"Go ahead."

"11520 Summerhill Lane. Yazdi residence."

"Got it."

"I'm flying into Hobby at 8:40 a.m. Southwest 3451. I'll have an ex-colleague of ours with me. Dana McLaughlan. She's pretty much been driving this."

"Ex-colleague?"

"Yeah. We'll explain tomorrow."

"Okay. If I can't meet you at Hobby I'll see you at the office and we go from there."

Noel called Dana and told her about his conversation with Carlson. "You think we should have him go over to the Yazdi's house now and scope it out?"

Dana thought about it. "I don't know. What's he going to do, knock on the door and say he's looking for Mike Massey? The Yazdis live on Summerhill Lane, a dead end street, I just mapped it. With only Carlson it wouldn't be hard for Massey to slip out the back door and get away. Tomorrow we'll have a warrant and there'll be three of us—at least—and we can secure Summerhill."

"Alright. I'll see you tomorrow."

"I'll be there!"

"Oh, and, Dana?"

"Yeah?"

"Regardless what happens in Houston, way to connect the dots."

"Thank you, Noel," Dana said, gratified by the recognition. "We can't just be sitting here waiting for the lights to go out."

***

When Taraneh ordered a bottle of champagne, it was because she knew that was the requirement to secure a private space on the second floor. It was never about drinking it. She also knew that both she and Mahmoud would be driving home—in separate cars— from the River Oaks area, so an elevated blood alcohol content was a no-no. When they stepped back out into the parking lot after what was for both of them an hour of unprecedented intimacy, they left behind a waitress who was surprised to find the bottle of Veuve still over half-full. Taraneh took Mahmoud by the hand and led him to his car. Once he had unlocked it, she fumbled with the seat controls until she had slid both front seats as far back as they would go. Then she climbed in to the driver's seat and told Mahmoud to get in next to her. Bemused, he did as she instructed. When they were both inside she took from him the keys and locked the doors. She checked and satisfied herself that there was no one else around. He reached over and kissed her. She let him, briefly, and then she pushed him back. He was confused, about to say something when she placed a finger on his lips and said: "Shhh."

Later that night, Mahmoud Massevadegh would reflect back on what followed next as the highlight of his life. Taraneh's touch was gentle but purposeful as she unbuckled his belt, undid his trousers, and eased his zipper down. He was in wondrous surrender as she exposed him. Her soft hand strokes produced an immediate erection, and time and space lost meaning as she took him in her mouth. His fingers caressed her hair and soft moans emanated from his heart. Her tongue weaved miraculous patterns, her suction calibrated to perfection. Everything that had ever meant anything to him was flushed away into oblivion, and he knew only a fierce, swelling pleasure. She was relentless; he was entranced. His release came with a spasmodic shudder that was prolonged by her insistence to consume every last drop of his deliverance.

Now there was no holding back. They professed boundless and eternal love for each other. She was surprised—delighted—when his hardness returned within minutes.

She felt his hand push her dress away as it explored the inside of her thigh. "I've never needed anyone like I need you," he gushed.

She grabbed his hand, held it in place, and whispered, "Mahmoud, please stop."

Taken aback and momentarily confused again, he could only implore her, *"Why?"*

"Not here, not now," she said softly.

"I don't understand," he protested.

She kissed his cheek and, with a smile, said: "I am a virgin."

Chapter Thirteen

Mahmoud's electric evening with Taraneh was followed by an uncomfortable, sleepless night alone in the guest apartment. The thought that she was so close, just yards away in her own room, yet so far away—they had agreed they couldn't risk Amir even suspecting, let alone discovering their romance—kept him wide awake and made every hour feel like ten. He endured a maelstrom of emotions. Two days ago he had arrived in Houston calm, calculating, at peace with himself and single-mindedly focused on his mission. The bad news of his uncle's arrest had only hardened his resolve. His original plan was to spend just a couple of days in Houston, long enough to warn his uncle about what was coming, perform the port scanning and build the target library, then skip over to Mexico and pull the plug on America and watch the misery unfold. Then...

Taraneh, the best thing that had ever happened to him. She was the most unpredictable, upending, disorienting, discombobulating, irresistible twist in the arc of his life.

He had long known love of family and love of country. But now he knew love of a woman, and its power surpassed all.

Before they had driven back to the house in separate cars last night, she asked him to stay in Houston longer than he had originally planned. He agreed because he wanted to be with her more than anything else, and because when she got teary-eyed at the mention of her father's bail being denied, he could not deny her anything she asked of him.

The thought of his uncle, and how his uncle might react if he knew what had happened last night, sobered him. He now felt less rudderless. There was a positive way to channel his energy instead of just tossing and turning in bed.

He would make use of the coming hours to set up how he would make the bastards pay. Should he tell Taraneh about it? He decided he would do so only after the fact. He would wait until after it worked well enough for him to be proud of himself.

He resumed his battle stance at his cyber-command post and started parsing through the targets database Metasploit was building for him. A smile soon softened his features. He had a plan. The federal prison where his uncle was being held was in downtown Houston. The courtroom where a federal magistrate judge had denied his uncle bail was in downtown Houston. Downtown Houston was where he would deliver his coupe de foudre, to be followed by the coup de grace a few days later from south of the border.

A fundamental characteristic of electric motors is that upon starting they draw six to eight times higher current than they do when running. That explains the momentary dimming of lights that can accompany the start of an air-conditioning unit. The higher current causes a voltage drop that dims the lights. It only lasts a fraction of a second, but it is inevitable. Mahmoud's plan was simplicity personified. The most common networked device on the planet may well be the ubiquitous thermostat, the wall-mounted gizmo that controls the temperature set points at which air-conditioning equipment starts and stops. Honeywell makes a large percentage—if not the majority—of thermostats in America's skyscrapers. This truth was borne out by Mahmoud's port scans. His database showed a preponderance of Honeywell devices in downtown Houston, all readily accessible from his perch overlooking Summerhill Lane. He set about writing a simple script that he would remotely load onto every single Honeywell thermostat in downtown. First the program would set all the thermostats to fail ON, meaning every time they lost power they would automatically start as soon as the power was restored. Next, the program would shut down all of the controlled air handlers at 8:00 p.m. and start them all, simultaneously, sixty seconds later. All those electric motors starting together would draw about seven times their normal running current from the grid supporting downtown Houston. That would cause an event; at least a brownout, but with luck, a blackout when protective devices opened to protect the grid from the overcurrent. The protective devices would cycle back on a few times, and each time they would trip again because the thermostats would start the motors, causing the same overcurrent. After a few cycles the switches would stay open, and it would require manual intervention to first diagnose, then remediate, the cause. That could take hours. The outage in the downtown area of the nation's fourth-largest city would make the national news.

Then he would tell Taraneh.

***

Southwest flight 3451 from Washington, D.C. nonstop to Houston departed on time, but had to circle around inclement weather en route, and arrived twenty minutes behind schedule. Special Agent Tom Carlson of the Secret Service's Houston field office had leveraged his badge in order to wait curbside at the arrivals pickup lanes, and he was on the phone with Noel until they made eye contact outside of baggage claim. After quick introductions, Dana and Noel put their luggage—both of them had limited themselves to carry-ons—in the trunk of Carlson's car and they were on their way.

"I assume you want to stop by the office and wait for the warrant?" Carlson said.

"What do you think, Dana?" Noel said.

Dana was eager to press on, but she decided they would be better positioned if armed with a warrant. "Yes."

"We haven't yet told the FBI about the connection between Massey and Yazdi," Noel said. "We don't even know what the connection is, other than they're both Iranian, and Massey called Yazdi when he first arrived in the country. And Yazdi's the guy who was arrested last week for violating the sanctions."

"Well I think we should tell the FBI," Carlson said. "They're the ones who arrested Yazdi."

"Agreed," Noel said. "We just wanted to wait till we got here."

"Shall I make the call now?"

"Let's do it from the office."

"The office it is." Carlson glanced at his watch. "9:32. We'll be there by ten."

***

Amir Yazdi had one hand on the stair railing to steady himself as he came down from his second-floor bedroom for a much-needed cup of coffee. He had had too much wine last night as he'd grappled with the bad news about his father. His head was throbbing, reminding him with every breath that he'd failed to stay hydrated. He washed two Advils down with a large glass of water and noticed that the coffee machine, a Nespresso, had not been turned on. That was unusual, as by now his mother would normally have had her first cup of Ristretto. "Mom?" he said.

Leticia came in from the laundry room. "Senora Laleh no wake yet."

That was very unusual.

Amir frowned as he walked past the family room to the master bedroom. The door was shut, so he knocked first. "Mom?"

There was no response. He tried the door. It wasn't locked, so he opened it and walked in. His mother was lying in bed apparently out cold. There was an empty vodka bottle on the carpet and two open pill containers on the side table.

"Mom!"

She didn't react.

"Mom!" Amir shouted.

She was breathing, but unresponsive.

"Fuck!"

Leticia appeared at the bedroom door. "Call Taraneh!" Amir said frantically. He grabbed the phone on the side table and dialed 911.

Ten minutes later, Mahmoud had just finished loading his script onto the target thermostats, unaware that anything was awry, when he first heard the siren. His heart skipped a beat and he looked up from his laptop. Concern turned to fear when the siren got louder, then panic as it became clear it was headed his way. In a flash he was at the window and peering down at Summerhill in time to see an ambulance pull up at the house. He watched with alarm and befuddlement as the EMTs jumped out.

Mahmoud ran downstairs into the house. There was no one in the kitchen, but he heard voices from beyond the den. When he reached the master bedroom he found Amir, Taraneh and Leticia watching as the EMTs checked Laleh's vital signs. He saw the empty vodka bottle and the pill containers. Taraneh was crying as she looked on in horror. Mahmoud wanted to run to her and hold her close and comfort her.

"Stay outside!" Amir said to him brusquely.

Mahmoud obliged him, understanding how personal this situation was and wanting to be respectful of Laleh's dignity.

One of the EMTs ran out and brought in a stretcher on wheels. It helped no end that the master bedroom was on the ground floor.

Amir ran out of his mother's bedroom and took the stairs to the second floor in twos, his hangover forgotten. He reappeared moments later in jeans, t-shirt and loafers. He didn't so much ignore Mahmoud as let his body language tell his cousin that he had overstayed his welcome.

As the EMTs wheeled Laleh out on the stretcher, an oxygen mask now covering her face, followed by Amir and Taraneh, Mahmoud could see Laleh was still unconscious. "Which hospital?" he asked.

"Memorial Hermann just down the road at I-10 and Gessner," one of the medics replied.

Mahmoud ran back to the guest apartment, grabbed his phone and his keys and watched through the window as Amir and Taraneh clambered into the ambulance with their mother. He ran downstairs and out to the Nissan parked at the curb. The ambulance was already on its way. Mahmoud took a moment to collect his thoughts. He decided not to chase the ambulance, as that risked being stopped by the police. Instead he located Memorial Hermann at I-10 and Gessner on Apple Maps and found it was indeed just down the road. The fastest way there was to go down Echo Lane, with which he was now very familiar, and take the freeway west. A couple of exits and he would be there. He dropped the phone onto the passenger seat, put his seatbelt on and waved at Leticia, who still standing at the front door, wiping away tears as she watched him go.

**

Tom Carlson made the call to one of his counterparts at the FBI's Houston resident agency on the speakerphone in his office with Noel and Dana listening in. The FBI agent didn't answer his desk line, but Carlson reached him on his cellphone.

"Stan, it's Tom Carlson. Am I calling at a bad time?"

"I'm in a high-speed car but I'm not driving. If you're calling about the port scans that hit Reliant Energy last night I already know about them."

"What port scans?"

"You got the advisory about the heightened risk of cyberattack against the grid?"

"Yeah."

"We just got a report of a large number of port scans hitting Reliant Energy overnight. Still in progress. One of the admins at Reliant saw the Infragard alert yesterday and reported the probes this morning. Source has been IDed. We're heading over there now."

Dana couldn't believe what she was hearing.

"Where?" Carlson said.

"Starbucks at I-10 and Echo Lane, outside the loop."

"On my way."

As Carlson hung up Dana was already on her phone. By the time they got out to the car she had what she was looking for. "That Starbucks is within half a mile of Summerhill Lane! It's got to be him!"

Carlson was already cranking the engine. "Let's go!" He turned right off Allen Parkway onto Studemont and raced north to merge onto the westbound lanes of the I-10 Freeway. From there he covered the seven miles to the Echo Lane exit in six minutes flat, in time to see two HPD cars pull off Echo Lane into the shopping center parking lot. Two of the black-and-white Memorial Villages

Police SUVs were already there, and distant sirens announced more were on the way. As the Secret Service trio arrived at the shopping center the scene was one of shock and pandemonium.

Two FBI agents were already inside the Starbucks, and HPD and Village police had taken up positions outside. No one was getting out unless they were allowed to. Other officers were already checking the cars parked around Starbucks, making sure nobody moved one way or the other. Dana let Carlson and Noel go first, then she followed them into Starbucks.

Staff and patrons had been told to freeze with their hands up. Two people who had been working on laptops were standing with their hands against the glass wall as the FBI men barked instructions at them about not touching their computers. Dana scanned the faces inside and her heart sank. She would have bet money they were going to catch Massevadegh red-handed, but he was nowhere to be seen. She told Carlson, and he in turn told an FBI agent who Dana assumed was Stan. IDs were demanded and presented. It was established that the laptop owners, a male and a female, were students from the high school across the street. One had been working on a PowerPoint presentation for a homework assignment, the other's web browser was running, but there was nothing there to hint of any port scanning activity. There was nobody working on a laptop in any of the cars in the parking spots within the WI-FI coverage area or even beyond. It took the best part of ten minutes for the lawmen to surmise they had responded to a false alarm. They put away their guns.

Tom Carlson introduced FBI Special-Agent-in-Charge Stan Toman to Noel and Dana, who he described as Secret Service from D.C. In the heat of the moment the liberty taken with the truth was neither intentional nor consequential.

Dana addressed Toman. "You said someone reported probes that were traced back to here, right?"

"Yeah. One of the IT people at Reliant Energy."

"Can you call him and find out if he's still seeing it?"

It was the obvious next step that only became obvious after Dana suggested it. Noel exchanged a chalk-one-up-to-the-Secret-Service look with Carlson that was not reciprocated by the FBI agents. Stan Toman got on his phone. As he waited for someone back at the agency to connect with Reliant Energy, one of his colleagues checked the restrooms and office area again. Dana knew the answer when Toman's eyes lit up. "He's still seeing it!" he said.

"What's next door?" Dana said, already on her way out.

Over the course of the next five minutes Starbucks' immediate neighbors, Baskin-Robbins, Campus Cuts, Dapper Dan Cleaners and Village Florist were subjected to the same level of scrutiny the coffee shop had endured, with the same outcome.

Dana was in the parking lot, looking around, scouring the parked cars.

"Still happening!" Stan reported, the phone at his ear.

Dana took in the office buildings across Echo Lane. If they say it's still happening then it's still happening, she thought, and right under our noses. We just can't see it. You're a crafty son of a bitch, Mahmoud Massevadegh. Are you sitting in one of those office buildings watching us? But the WI-FI won't go that far. Unless…

"The roof!" Dana shouted. "I need a ladder!"

As the men around her started looking around for a plumber's truck or an electrician's van, Dana ran to the nearest HPD officer. "Where's the closest fire station?"

A Village policeman overheard the question. "Collingdale Road," he said. He pointed east, at the office buildings. "Just behind them buildings. Five minutes."

"Let's get a ladder truck over here, now!" Dana said.

***

Some 1,300 miles northwest of where Dana was standing waiting impatiently for a fire truck, the Secretary of State was munching on a bowl of pineapple slices at his desk in the Harry S. Truman Building in Washington, D.C., when his secretary told him the foreign minister of Iran was on his secure line. He swallowed his mouthful of fruit, pushed the bowl aside and picked up the handset.

"Good afternoon, Javad." He always accounted for time zones when speaking with his counterparts around the globe.

"Good morning, John. I hope this is not too early."

"Not at all. I'm finishing breakfast."

"Very good. I just wanted to follow up on our last discussion."

"Yes."

"There is no official knowledge of what you made me aware of."

"I see. Any pointers?"

"There is also no unofficial knowledge of it. I dug deep. Only one thing that may or may not help."

"What is it?"

"He has only one relative in the U.S., an uncle in Houston. You may have heard there was an arrest last week in Houston, a man by the name of Farzad Yazdi, for violating the sanctions. I don't know the merits of the case, but that is the uncle."

Kerry scribbled notes on a pad. "Thank you," he said. "That might be helpful."

232

"And John, looking at this fellow's family history, it's not difficult to imagine he is in the hardliner's camp, meaning probably against any deal."

"Enough to do something so drastic it would kill it?"

"Perhaps, yes."

"Okay. Hopefully I will see you in a few weeks."

John Kerry stabbed another slice of pineapple with his fork and told his secretary to place a call to the director of the FBI.

***

Mahmoud eschewed the parking garage at Memorial Hermann Medical Center, well aware that parking structures like that frequently have CCTV cameras recording all traffic around the clock. He parked instead across Gessner Road in the surface lot of the Memorial City Mall complex. He crossed Gessner on foot and followed the signs to the emergency room. His progress was momentarily interrupted by a text message alerting him that port scans he had initiated were now complete. He asked at the control desk for information about Laleh Yazdi. The nurse checked and told him there was nothing in the system yet that she could report, and told him where the waiting room was. Mahmoud found it, took one look around, and decided he wouldn't stay. The place was too depressing. Amir and Taraneh were nowhere to be seen. He didn't know how long he'd have to wait to find out what Laleh's status was, let alone to see her. And while he was itching to talk to Taraneh and try to comfort her, that was not on the cards with Amir around. He could call from the house for status updates, and he would always be able to say, truthfully, that he had come to the hospital and tried to check on her. He went back outside, crossed over to the mall parking lot and climbed back into the Nissan.

His heart was with Taraneh, but this was not the place, and now not the time, to be doing anything about that.

He got back on I-10 eastbound and stayed in the right lane. He took the Echo Lane exit and coasted to a stop at a red light where the feeder meets Echo Lane. The road was clear, so he turned right. Within a hundred yards he found himself alongside an orgy of law enforcement vehicles, HPD cars and Village Police SUVs, even a fire truck, its ladder extended to the roof above Starbucks! He slowed down, mesmerized as he watched a fireman climb up the ladder towards the roof.

Could the drone have somehow sparked this crazy scene? He was of a mind to stop and watch to see if he could find out, but the resounding answer shocked him into bolting when he saw Dana.

What the fuck?

He drove on, flabbergasted. *What the hell is that bitch doing here?*

They had figured him out! There was no other explanation! He had let his guard down and allowed himself to slip into a false sense of security. There was only one thing to do, and that was get out now!

He was shaking as he drove past the high school, suddenly overcome by a sense of panicked vulnerability like he had never felt before.

***

"There's a drone!" the fireman said.

"That's it!" Dana shouted. "Don't touch it! I'm coming up!"

No one tried to stop her, and she made it up to the roof faster than the fireman had. She took one look at the drone and realized what she was looking at. She snapped several photographs with her

234

phone, all different angles, including close-ups of the electronics strapped to the underbelly. When she got back down to the ground she announced that the mystery of the invisible IP traffic had been solved: "He set up a 4G bridge to throw us off. He's somewhere doing his thing and routing it through Starbucks' WiFi. It's natting. Network address translation. Son of a bitch!"

Stan Toman's phone rang and he answered it.

"So," one of the FBI men started, "when you say he's somewhere doing his thing—"

"He's running the scans, penetration testing for vulnerabilities on the power grid, making it look like he's doing it here. But it's definitely him, and he's somewhere in Houston, or he was, because he flew that drone onto that roof. He flew another one just like it into a power line in Virginia last week." Dana suddenly remembered what had brought her to Houston in the first place. "And I bet I know where he is."

Stan Toman put his phone back in his pocket, his face flushed with excitement. "You know that guy we arrested last week, Farzad Yazdi? Lives less than half a mile away on Summerhill? He's this joker's uncle!"

"11520 Summerhill Lane!" Dana said. "Let's go! No sirens!"

The posse started getting in each other's way as they exited the shopping center parking lot, but the pecking order quickly sorted itself out. First out were the two FBI cars, then the Secret Service, then local police.

"Good call on no sirens," Noel said. "If he hears us coming he'll be gone by the time we get there."

Tom Carlson was frowning as he drove. "So, we didn't tell Stan and the FBI guys about a connection between Massey and the Yazdi guy, and you guys found out from the NSA records. How'd the FBI find out?"

Dana and Noel were stumped.

"I'll ask Toman later," Carlson said.

South on Echo Lane, a right turn through the stop sign at Taylorcrest, a hundred yards to Blalock. Left, two blocks, then left again on Summerhill. It was a dead end street, so an easy matter for the cops behind the feds to secure it. Summerhill Lane suddenly went from having no cars on it to being clogged. 11520 Was a grand mansion, stately and tranquil, and Dana could barely wait for what she hoped would unfold in the next few minutes. She noted there was no white Nissan parked in the street.

They took a moment to organize and set up a perimeter around the property before the FBI knocked on the front door of the main house. A housekeeper opened it. Leticia's field of vision included several police vehicles down the street and she was clearly horrified.

"Is there anybody home?" Toman asked.

Leticia recoiled in fear.

"Do you speak English?" Dana said.

Leticia shook her head.

Tom Carlson stepped forward. "I speak Spanish," he said. He held out a photograph of Mahmoud and had a quick exchange of words with Leticia, who pointed to the side of the house.

"He's staying in the guest apartment over the garage," Carlson said.

Leticia led them through the house to the kitchen and pointed at the stairs to the landing that connected to the space above the garage. The door at the far side was closed.

Guns were drawn. Apart from Leticia, only Dana was unarmed. She was ex-Secret Service, but civilian, so no longer able to carry a weapon through the TSA checkpoints and onto a civilian aircraft. Her SIG Sauer had remained behind in Reston. She gestured to Leticia to stay in the kitchen, out of harm's way.

A shout went out: "FBI! We've got you surrounded! Come out with your hands up!"

Not a sound from behind the door.

Louder now: "FBI! Game's up! Come out with your hands up and you won't get hurt!"

Not a rustle.

One of the agents tried the door. It was unlocked. They went in leading with their guns.

They found all the signs that a guest was in residence, but currently absent. Toiletries, a suitcase, clothes, an unmade bed. Agents checked the bathroom and the closet, to no avail. Dana walked around the small apartment imagining the Mike Massey she knew sleeping in the bed, sitting at the desk.

Desk. No computer. No backpack.

Dana stormed back out of the apartment to the kitchen. "Let's check the garage!" she said.

Again it was armed agents who went through the door first, followed by Noel and Dana. They found a Range Rover, a seven series BMW, and space for a third vehicle. One of the agents opened the garage door. There was a Mercedes SLK outside. No white Nissan.

"Find out if the Reliant guy's still seeing the traffic!" Dana shouted.

Now Toman had a direct number, so he didn't have to ask anyone at the agency to connect him.

"I'm betting it's stopped," Dana said dejectedly. "I'm betting he's outta hear."

They had the answer in thirty seconds. Toman pursed his lips and said, "The traffic has stopped."

237

"Ask the housekeeper when she last saw him!" Dana said.

Carlson stepped back into the kitchen and exchanged more words with Leticia. He turned to face his colleagues. "We just missed him," he said. "He drove off in a hurry right before we arrived."

Chapter Fourteen

Desperate to retain some clarity of thought despite the maelstrom in his mind, Mahmoud Reza Massevadegh made some crucial decisions as he hightailed it out of Houston. First was what to take with him, which he limited to the stark essentials: his laptop, his backpack, his passport, his wallet, which contained credit cards and both his Virginia and British driver licenses, and the wad of cash, still close to twenty thousand dollars. The last thing he grabbed before he scrambled out of the guest apartment was his uncle's gun. It promised to be a very long time before his uncle might need it, if ever again.

He turned left off Summerhill Lane onto Blalock road, away from Taylorcrest, Echo Lane and the shopping center with the constabulary congregation, and he immediately saw them in his rearview mirror as they careened off Blalock onto Summerhill. He had escaped with mere seconds to spare.

How could things have deteriorated so drastically so fast? In the blink of an eye he had gone from being in control to panicking like a fox fleeing for his life as the scent hounds closed in. Now, in hindsight, it had been a terrible call to lash out at eRock. Were it not for that misguided schoolyard fit of pique, the Dana bitch wouldn't be in Houston, and the cops wouldn't know who they were looking for, let alone where. He should have waited to leave his calling card until after the deed was done, not before. Such an amateurish mistake! How could *Khoda* not have guided him and steered him clear of such a miscalculation?

Oh my God, Khoda!

Just as he began to drown in despondency, an epiphany reset his bearings. Everything suddenly snapped into focus. Today was payback for yesterday! The real blunder wasn't last Friday, the drone, Dominion Power and eRock, it was last night, the total collapse of discipline with Taraneh. *That* is what angered *Khoda* and precipitated this. There was no question; it was crystal clear. Last night he had failed himself by violating his lifelong credo of abstinence from alcohol and from the temptations of the flesh. What happened today was *Khoda's* punishment, and it was deserved. He was overcome by self-loathing for having been so egregiously weak. He had jeopardized everything he had worked for by losing his focus on the one thing that mattered most to him. Throughout history men have been compromised by their weaknesses and vices, and yesterday he had let his guard down and fallen into the same trap. His love for Taraneh was real and powerful, but not as much as his for *Khoda*. Now he knew what he had to do. Through his anguish, it became clear his sin had not been fatal, otherwise they would already have had him in custody. *Khoda* had issued the sternest of warnings, not a condemnation.

The situation was salvageable, but it required the most poignant sacrifice. He solemnly pledged to *Khoda* a new vow of abstinence from alcohol, and a commitment to celibacy for the rest of his days. The effect was immediate, a familiar cleansing of the spirit and nourishment of the soul, only more profound than ever before.

His mood swung back to optimism, hope and tranquil resolve.

He decided to stay off the freeways and stick instead to by-roads. The freeways were potentially faster, although they could be shut down for hours on end by accidents, or slowed down by construction, but they were too well patrolled by lawmen, city cops, highway patrol, county sheriffs and the like, all to be avoided.

It was a conscious decision, sacrificing speed for the lower likelihood of encountering the law. He focused on staying calm, avoiding speed, obeying all traffic laws, and maintaining westward momentum. Within minutes he made a right turn on FM 1093, signposted in the city as Westheimer Road, and knew he no longer had to consult the map on his iPhone. FM1093 would take him all the way to Eagle Lake, thirty miles away, where he would be well and truly out of the big city. From there the iPhone in his pocket, communicating with satellites in the sky, would again be his virtual beacon, keeping him on the route he had already mapped out as he followed the sun.

He thought about fate, about the sacrifices men he revered had made throughout the history of the Shias, starting way back when Hussein, the prophet's grandson, and his supporters had been massacred in Karbala some thirteen hundred years ago. He thought about the heroism of hundreds of thousands of Iranians, one of them his father, who in the eighties marched into a no man's land booby-trapped by Saddam Hussein with mustard gas acquired under the aegis of the United States, and he repeated the mantra to banish fear.

He thought about Taraneh, and forced himself not to.

They police had been within touching distance of him, and they obviously knew he had been at his uncle's house. How? Right now, that didn't matter. Getting caught meant prison. Top priority was to get out of the country, get beyond their reach. He suddenly heard a siren and could barely suppress the onset of panic. He slowed down as a red fire department ambulance approached from behind him and raced past. It was as undeniable and acute a signal as he had ever received from *Khoda*.

Clarity restored and perspective regained, he pushed on.

At the same time that Mahmoud's escape route took him past the southern edge of George Bush Park in west Houston, an intense brainstorming session got underway curbside at 11520 Summerhill Lane.

"Okay, so we don't know where he is or where he's going," Stan Toman said.

"He could be anywhere," Dana said. "Right after we found the 4G bridge the traffic stopped. That's either a hell of a coincidence or he knew we were on to him, and I don't believe in coincidences. He could have been in his car in the parking lot connected to the bridge through a personal hotspot and watching us as we're going after people in Starbucks. He could have been in one of those office buildings next door. He could have been anywhere."

"So if he came to Houston because his uncle's here, it would make sense he'd see him, right?" Noel said. "His uncle's at the federal detention center downtown, right? Let's find out if he's had any visitors."

"And what about the family here?" Carslon said. "The uncle's in prison, but we know Massey's been staying here. Who else lives here?"

One of the other FBI men spoke up: "Uncle's wife, son and daughter. We questioned them after we arrested Yazdi. The boy's at Rice, the girl works."

"Let's get someone over to Rice, talk to the kid again, see if he knows where his cousin is."

"They could be on his side," Dana pointed out. "His cousins, his uncle's wife. For all we know they could be in on what he's up to."

"Could be," Toman said. "We have to question them regardless. I'll send someone to Rice and we'll have someone wait here, wait for the old lady or the daughter to come home and see what she knows."

"Let's get the police cars out of here. They come home now and see this, if they're on his side they keep going."

"Right. One unmarked car, two agents," Toman said. The rest move out now. Let's meet back at the office and make sure everybody knows what everybody else knows."

"And we need a nationwide APB on the white Nissan," Dana said. "It's a rental from National, but the guy's a fox, so regardless of plates, let's get them all stopped and checked."

***

Leticia was watching as the lawmen huddled at the curb, and she watched them disburse. It was all getting too much for her, what with the arrest of Senor Yazdi last week, the medical emergency with Senora Yazdi this morning, now the police again, all terrible. At least the police were leaving. She was worried about Senora Yazdi. Now she noticed that not all of the police were leaving. Two of them stayed behind in one car, and it wasn't one of the cars with police markings on it, just a plain brown sedan. It moved down the street and parked in front of the neighbor's house. Sneaky, as if trying to hide who and what they were. This was all very frightening. It was now several hours since the ambulance had left. Maybe she should call Senora Yazdi and see if she was awake? Better still, she should call Senor Amir or Senora Taraneh and tell him what was going on and find out about Senora Yazdi. Yes, that was the best thing to do.

She went to the kitchen and used the house phone to dial Amir's cell number. He would see it was the house calling and he would answer.

"Hello?"

"Senor Amir, es Leticia."

"Si, Leticia."

"Senor, hay policias afuera."

When he heard there were policemen outside the house, Amir thought maybe things were moving with his father, maybe he was being freed.

"Gracias."

Before Leticia could ask about Taraneh, the line went dead.

Amir called Ken Leach's office and was connected to Leach's secretary. "Mr. Leach is in court today," she told him. "I will let him know you called. Is there anything I can do?"

"I wanted to know if anything had changed with my father's status. I'm told there are policemen outside our house. I just wondered if my father's being released, I thought the cops might be there in case the media vans show up."

"I haven't heard anything. I'll send Mr. Leach a text message and let you know when I hear back. What number can I reach you at?"

Amir dictated his number and hung up. What a great turn of events it would be if his father were being released. That would do more to bring his mother out of her vicious cycle of anxiety and depression than any drugs or alcohol. Maybe today wasn't all bad news after all.

***

Mahmoud didn't know if radar detectors were legal in Texas, but he had turned on the one in the car anyway and was glad he had done so because it worked. It chirped twice on his way out of Houston, and sure enough, on both occasions he passed police officers, one in a car, the other on a motorcycle, both parked on the side of the road pointing handheld radar guns at oncoming traffic. He was within the posted speed limit, so he passed unhindered. Most of the time the limit was 55 mph, and he knew he could do 70 on the freeway, but he stayed disciplined and stuck to his strategy of by-roads only.

Under different circumstances it might have been a therapeutic drive. The flat rural landscape was a collage of fields and trees, cattle, farms and ranches. But Mahmoud couldn't stop reflecting on what had happened today. It was no coincidence that everything had gone haywire after what he did with Taraneh yesterday. He hoped this was the extent of his punishment—the cops on his tail and the end of anything more to do with Taraneh—or was there more to come? Only *Khoda* knew.

What a fool he had been. Without *Khoda* on his side he would be on his own against the wolves.

He stayed on FM 1093, through Wallis to where it ended in Eagle Lake. He pulled over and checked the map rather than risk trouble by looking at his phone while driving. From Eagle Lake he took Route 90 through the towns of Altair, Rock Island, Sheridan, Sublime and Hallettsville to Shiner, where he made his first stop for gas. He paid with cash, careful to use only the high-octane variety, and not bothering to go back inside to collect his change from the three twenty-dollar bills he gave the cashier. He stopped again at the next town, Gonzales, this time for food. He used the drive-thru at McDonald's and ate in the car in the parking lot. He wanted to avoid San Antonio, and after consulting the map, he made a southerly swing to Nixon, where he caught SH97 to Pleasanton. Now, four hours after leaving Houston, he was due south of San Antonio. The by-roads had cost him an hour, but the drive had been uneventful, so his strategy had thus far been vindicated. He planned to arc back up to the northwest to Hondo, which was west of San Antonio, and where he could once again link up with Rte. 90 and run west parallel to I-10. He figured another four hours would bring him to Del Rio, right on the border, but not where he wanted to cross. It would take a further four hours to reach his crossing point, so he still had eight hours to go. Allowing for another couple of stops for gas and food, he estimated he would make it by midnight.

It was just after 3 p.m. Sunset and the added security of darkness would come in about four hours, somewhere in the vicinity of Del Rio.

He again made a silent and solemn pledge to *Khoda* that he was repentant and that he would never again sin.

***

When Dana returned to the Secret Service office with Noel and Tom Carlson she was beset by what ifs and unknowns. What if they had spread out more, divided resources between Summerhill Lane and Starbucks? Would they have caught him? What if she had caught a flight to Houston the night before instead of this morning? Might that have made a difference? What if she had thought about pulling Massevadegh's phone records from the NSA earlier? She would probably have caught a flight last night. What if the damn NSA had cooperated from the get go instead of stalling until they received the presidential order?

She had been right to zero in on Houston, and she knew that but for a tiny slice of luck, with better timing they might have had the son of a bitch in custody by now. Instead here they were hoping for a break again, and where was one going to come from this time? The best bet was the Nissan. One of the multitude of lawmen spread out across the roadways of Texas had to see it. But that was lame, wishful thinking. He had somehow stayed ahead of them from Virginia to Texas, what was to say he didn't have more evasive strings to pull?

The word came back from the FBI: Farzad Yazdi had only received one visitor since he was locked up at the federal jail, Kenneth Leach, his attorney of record. No Mahmoud Massevadegh, no Mike Massey. Not even his wife or son. Speaking of the son, he had missed his two morning classes at Rice that day and hadn't been seen on campus. Dana wondered whether he was in on whatever scheme Massevadegh had hatched. She decided she'd had enough sitting around waiting for something to happen. With every passing minute Massevadegh could be getting closer to trumping them.

"Let's to go back to Summerhill and talk to the housekeeper again," she said. "I think we can trust her. She looks like she has the love of Jesus in her. Maybe she knows more. Maybe she knows where the son is."

Carlson was inwardly skeptical, but he obliged her. He drove Dana and Noel back to the Yazdi's house. The two FBI men were still there in their car. Too passive, Dana thought. To avoid any hard feelings she had Carlson tell them what was going on, and everyone agreed that Dana would approach the housekeeper with Just tom Carlson to translate for them.

Leticia answered after the first few knocks. Dana tried to make her smile look heartfelt. Help me out, you dear, sweet good lady, her eyes said.

Tom Carlson spoke softly but firmly. After a couple of minutes of question and answer, they had the information they needed.

Dana decided she not only believed this woman, she liked her. In any case, it wouldn't take more than a few minutes to find out if what they had just heard was the truth. "Gracias," she said.

Noel was waiting expectantly, and she aw noticeable purpose in Dana's stride as she and Carlson returned to the cars on the street.

"Yazdi's wife was taken ill this morning," Dana said. "She was taken by ambulance to a hospital. Someone call the emergency response center and find out which hospital the ambulance that responded to the call from this address took its patient to."

Dana's pep was back. It might not lead anywhere, but at least they were getting out of neutral again. One of the FBI agents got on his phone and had the answer within minutes. "Memorial Hermann Memorial City, I-10 and Gessner, a couple of miles from here."

"We'll go check them out," Carlson said. "You guys might best stay here in case Massey shows up."

The FBI agents didn't argue. They took their marching orders from Special-Agent-in-Charge Stan Toman, and they weren't going to leave their post without a nod from him. One of them called Toman and brought him up to speed. Toman's instructions for them were to stay put.

Once at the hospital the Secret Service men split up. Dana went with Noel to the ER, while Carlson headed for the information desk at the main entrance. They found out near simultaneously that Mrs. Yazdi had been admitted, and what room she was in. Shortly thereafter the team assembled at the nurses' station nearest Laleh's room, identified themselves and requested to speak to the patient and/or her children. A nurse checked and informed them Mrs. Yazdi and her daughter were asleep, and the son was not with them in the room. The nurse confirmed that he had been there earlier. Dana asked her to accompany them to the visitor lounge so she could point him out to them if he was there. There was only one visitor lounge in the wing and he wasn't in it.

"What now?" Noel said.

"He could be in the cafeteria," Dana said. "Or maybe outside puffing on one if he's a smoker."

"Or he could have left," Carlson said.

"Can you come with us to the cafeteria and see if he's there?" Dana asked the nurse.

"I can't leave the wing, let alone the floor. There's two of us on duty at our station and we both have to be here."

"What does he look like?"

"Black hair cut short. Darkish complexion. Handsome."

"What's he wearing?"

"Jeans. Plain grey t-shirt."

Noel handed the nurse a card. "Thanks for your help. If he shows up please call my cell phone."

They took the elevator down to the first floor and tried the cafeteria first. It wasn't crowded, which made it easy for them to spot the black-haired dark-skinned man in a grey tee sitting alone with a half-finished smoothie, his hands and attention on his phone. He didn't look up from the screen as the trio approached him.

"Amir Yazdi?" Carlson said.

Now Amir looked up. "Yes?"

Two badges were displayed. "Secret Service. We'd like to ask you a few questions about your cousin."

"My cousin?" Amir said in surprise. "Mahmoud?"

"Mahmoud Massevadegh," Dana said.

Amir glanced at the badges. "Secret Service? What's he done, shot the president?"

"We're here to ask you what you know about what he's planning to do, and where he is." It was Dana again, and it didn't occur to Amir that she was the only one of the three that hadn't shown him a badge.

"What he's planning to do? He's here to see my father, his uncle, then he's leaving the country."

"When?"

"Well, it was supposed to be after he sees my father. But that doesn't look like happening anytime soon."

"Do you know where he is?"

"He was at home—at my parent's house—this morning."

"He's not there now. Do you know where he might be?"

Amir shook his head. "No idea."

"You said he was leaving the country," Dana said. "Do you know how?"

"What do you mean, how?"

"Is he flying out?"

"I don't know."

"Do you know where he's going when he leaves?"

"He mentioned Mexico and Venezuela."

"Why Mexico and Venezuela?"

"He said he was going to visit friends. Friends he met at college. George Mason University."

Dana nodded. "How did he get to Houston?"

"He drove."

Dana nodded again. Her gut told her Amir was telling them truthfully what he knew. "How's your mother?"

"She's going to be okay. What does that have to do with Mahmoud?"

"It has nothing to do with him. I was just asking."

"Did he tell you if he was going to drive or fly to Mexico?" Noel said.

"He didn't say."

Tom Carlson handed him a business card. "Your cousin is wanted for questioning in relation to a number of crimes. If you see him or find out where he is, please call my cell phone."

Amir was taken aback. "What crimes?"

"Never mind that now. Just…please call us if you see or hear from him."

"Okay."

"I hope your mother recovers fully and quickly," Dana said.

"Thank you."

"Amir," Carlson said. "Withholding information from us would get you in trouble. Serious trouble."

"I'm not withholding information from you. I've told you what I know. He's my cousin, but that doesn't mean I like him."

"Right. Call us if anything comes up."

Amir watched them go and wondered what the hell was happening to his family. First his father, then his mother, now Mahmoud. He hoped whoever said shit happens in threes was right, and that he or Taraneh wouldn't be next.

Chapter Fifteen

Tom Carlson knew and accepted that standard protocol for a multi-agency investigation and pursuit dictates the FBI take the lead. He called Stan Toman from the car and told him about the conversation with Amir Yazdi at the hospital. Moments later a blanket notification was sent to all of the official crossing points along the U.S. – Mexico border, instructing heightened vigilance for wanted fugitive Mahmoud Reza Massevadegh, a.k.a. Michael Massey, last known to be driving a White Nissan Pulsar. He was not known to be armed, but should be considered dangerous and was to be apprehended. Two photographs were included, headshots, one from his GMU master's program application, the other from the security access badge records at eRock.

Back at the Secret Service office on Allen Parkway, Dana was her usual antsy self. "He's not just going to approach a border crossing out in the open," she said. "He's too calculating for that."

"You think he'll disguise himself?" Carlson said.

"I don't know what he'll do. I just know he's managed to stay a step ahead of us at every turn, and that he's a sly one."

"We don't even know he really is headed for Mexico," Noel said. "He could have told his cousin that to hide his real intentions."

"True," Dana said. "But I don't think he drove all the way down to Houston to then turn around and drive up to Canada. If he knows we're onto him, it makes sense that he'll want to get out of the country as quickly as possible. He's not going to try getting past TSA at an airport. Mexico is his best bet. Plus, our border patrol is there to keep people from crossing *into* the U.S. There's not much attention paid to people going in the other direction. I think Mexico is real. We just don't know where and when."

Carlson tended to agree with her. "If that's right, it's going to take him at least ten, maybe twelve hours to drive to the border from here. Let's say he left at eleven, he'll be somewhere west of San Antonio by now. It's going to be dark by the time he gets to the border. Does he cross tonight or wait for daybreak?"

"I need to use a computer," Dana said.

Carlson pointed to a cubicle next to the one across from his office. "That a floater. If you just need the browser there's no password. Anything else, I'll unlock it for you."

"The browser's all I need." She left Carlson's office.

"Smart and relentless," Carlson said to Noel when they were alone. "You go back a long time with her?"

"We were first teamed together almost twenty years ago, here in Texas. Austin. We beat the FBI on a case involving hackers, and it was mainly down to her. She's the one who linked Massey to Yazdi from NSA phone records and decided we should come down here. Very sharp, and when she sets her mind to something either get on board or get out of the way."

"Married?"

Noel shook his head. He realized that he didn't know of anyone Dana had been romantically involved with, but decided against commenting on that.

Dana searched U.S. Mexico border crossings and discovered from Wikipedia that there are 47 active places where one can cross legally. It was depressing to think of how many more illegal spots dotted the border, but there was not going to be a listing of those to be found on Google, so she dismissed the thought. Of the 47 legal ones, six were in California, nine in Arizona, three in New Mexico and the rest in Texas. The 29 in Texas were grouped in four categories based on the state on the Mexican side of the border; seven for Chihuahua, five for Coahuila, one for Nuevo-Leon and sixteen for Tamaulipas. She leaned back and contemplated the array of choices available. Some had limitations, like no trucks. Others had limits on hours of operation, like Falcon Dam, 7 a.m. to 9 p.m. But it looked like most were open around the clock.

She tried to put herself in Massevadegh's mind. Definitely cross as soon as you get to the border, at the closest spot that was a 24-hour operation. She drew a straight line west from Houston through San Antonio to the border. Anywhere south of that point to the Gulf of Mexico would meet the least distance criterion. That ruled out the seven in Chihuahua. It occurred to her he could go to the southernmost spot in Texas, near Brownsville, and if he had access to a boat, make a crossing via the Gulf. But that was probably an area well patrolled by the U.S. Coast Guard, and he would know that. Working up from Brownsville, she starting compiling a list of the crossing points that stayed open around the clock.

The Brownsville Veteran International Bridge at Los Tomates came first, and she couldn't find any indication of operating hours, so she assumed the worst and put it on the list. Next was Brownsville Gateway, 24 hours. Brownsville & Matamoros International Bridge, 24 hours. Los Indios Free Trade International Bridge closed at midnight, ignore. Progresso, 24 hours. Donna-Rio Bravo International Bridge closed at 8 p.m. Pharr closed at midnight, Hidalgo stayed open. Anzalduas closed at ten. Los Ebanos, no. Rio Grande City, no. Roma, yes, Falcon Dam, no. Laredo Juarez-Lincoln, wide open. Laredo Bridge, ditto that. Laredo World Trade, out.

It was disheartening how many options there were, but she pressed on, unable to just sit back and wait to hear something.

Laredo Columbia Solidarity, quits at midnight. On to Coahuila. Eagle Pass II, yes; Eagle Pass, no. Del Rio, 24 hours. Amistad Dam shuttered at six p.m. Finally, there was Boquillas, 9 a.m. to 6 p.m.

That last one looked like a joke. Wikipedia informed that there was no bridge, that crossing of the Rio Grande was by one of three options, rowboat, burro or on foot, wading across the river. There was a photograph that showed the rowboat and the Mexican man who steered it across what looked like no more than thirty yards of water. But what jumped out at Dana was the fact that of all the crossing ports of entry she had just read about, this one, Boquillas, was the only one that was unmanned.

Unmanned!

She took the time to learn more from Wikipedia:

"The Boquillas Port of Entry is a port of entry into the United States from the Mexican town of Boquillas del Carmen to Big Bend National Park. Having opened in April 2013, it is a port of entry that is unstaffed by Customs and Border Protection agents, but at least one National Park Service employee is present while the port of entry is open."

Dana paused, read the sentence over again, and couldn't believe what it said. An official crossing point with no Customs and Border Protection agents, staffed only by a National Park Service employee, and then only while the port of entry is open. And it was open from nine till six, meaning that for fifteen out of twenty-four hours, there was no one—on the U.S. side at least—watching. And that was for Wednesday through Sunday! She learned that persons entering from Mexico must report to the video inspection kiosks and connect via telephone to a U.S. Customs and Border Protection agent in El Paso. On the Mexican side there is a customs checkpoint in the town of Boquillas del Carmen, a mile upstream from the crossing point. Locals offer transportation on horses or in trucks from the river to the town for $5 to $10 per passenger. Crossing on foot was possible at times, a short thigh-deep wade when the water was low, a swim when it was high.

Dana again put herself in the shoes of Mahmoud Massevadegh, or for that matter any fugitive wanting to flee from the U.S. The criteria she had previously used for prioritizing the border crossing point now changed. First priority became a crossing point that was unmanned, unbelievable as it was that one even existed. First by far! Boquillas was not quite on the stretch of border between the Gulf of Mexico and the line she had drawn west from Houston to Mexico, but it was close, just an additional three, maybe four hour's drive from Del Rio into Big Bend National Park via the town of Marathon. She Google-mapped Boquillas border Crossing. There it was, secluded as you want, dirt tracks on either side of the river, on the U.S. side the Rio Grande Village Store and the Rio Grande Village campground the only signs of civilization; on the Mexico side, Jose Falcon's Restaurant at Boquillas del Carmen. If she were trying to flee the U.S., she would pick a time outside of Wednesday through Sunday, nine to six, and wade across or swim across, depending on the depth of the water. She would pay one of the Mexicans on the other side to give her a ride, not just to Boquillas del Carmen, but to the nearest city where she could take a train or buy another truck ride to Mexico City, or wherever else would get her to her ultimate destination.

She went back to Wikipedia for one last look.

"Finally, a somewhat self-deprecating statement told about the village by persons who live there. 'Boquillas del

257

Carmen has 200 people, 400 dogs and one million scorpions.'"

She hated scorpions. But she hated Mahmoud Massevadegh more.

"Noel!"

The way she called him suggested she was on to something, and both Noel and Tom Carlson responded.

"What's the good word?" Carlson said.

She swiveled the chair around to face them. "Not good. Bad."

"How's that?" Noel said.

"If I told you that in this day and age there's a formal border crossing point on the Rio Grande where you can wade or swim across thirty yards of river from the U.S. into Mexico, and that it is unmanned by U.S. Customs and Border Protection, and the nearest Mexican border checkpoint is a shack one mile away, what would you say?"

"I'd say that's pretty bad," Carlson said.

Dana swiveled around again and faced the screen. "Boquillas Crossing Port of Entry. Check it out." She showed them the Wikipedia page. "If I wanted to get out of the U.S. and I couldn't go through a manned checkpoint because I know the feds had my name and photograph, this is where I'd do it. I'd get there tonight, stay in my car so I don't get stung by a scorpion, wait until daylight and be across before the nearest National Parks Service ranger left his home. By nine a.m., when he gets to his post, I'm a hundred miles into Mexico. Adios amigos."

Carlson let out a long, slow whistle.

Noel took a deep breath and exhaled slowly. "My problem with it is, we don't know for sure he's heading for Mexico. He mentioned Mexico to his cousin, but we don't know that it's true, and if it is, we don't know that it's now."

"So we just sit here and hope and wait?" Dana said.

"There's a nationwide APB out for his Nissan. How come he hasn't been spotted on the roads?" Carlson said, siding with Noel.

"So he's either in a different car or he's laying low somewhere in Houston," Dana said. "If he's in Houston, us sitting back and waiting for him to come out of his hole is fine. But if he's on the road…" She raised her eyebrows and tilted her head.

"So what do you propose?" Carlson said. "We tell the FBI?"

"Tell them what?" Dana said indignantly. "That Dana McLaughlan thinks he might be planning to cross at Boquillas? No. We've told the FBI what the cousin said about Mexico. I'm just speculating. I'm saying if I were him and I wanted out ASAP, that's how I'd go about doing it."

"So what do you want to do?" Noel said.

"If he's there, we don't want a hoard of sirens descending on the spot, he'll hear them coming and bolt across the river whether it is dark or light. If he's there, we need to act with stealth. Let him show his face and then we move in. Of course he might not be there, so we don't want to embarrass ourselves. This is me speculating." She paused, took a deep breath, and channeled her conviction. "I want to be in Boquillas at sunrise tomorrow. If he doesn't show, no sweat, I come back to Houston."

"And if he shows you confront him?" Noel said. "What if he's armed?"

Dana looked him straight in the eye. "If you're concerned about that, come with me. You've got your gun and you can carry it on a plane. We fly to San Antonio, rent a car, we're there before sunrise."

259

Noel wanted to tell her this was one speculation too far, but he held back. After all, she had been right at every turn so far. "It's a real long shot," he said.

"But the alternative is sitting here doing nothing. And if I'm wrong, what do we lose? Tom stays in Houston, if the action ends up being here, the agency's still in the midst of it."

"I need to think about this, Dana."

"That's fine, Noel. No pressure." She pulled the Black Madonna out of her purse and held it up at him. "If I go alone, your faith will protect me."

Emotional blackmail, Noel thought as he went back to Carlson's office.

"I have to give it to you, Dana," Carlson said. "You make a case." He followed Noel.

Dana checked flights from Houston to San Antonio. Southwest 1938 was scheduled to depart from Hobby Airport at 8:50 p.m., ETA San Antonio at 9:40 p.m. It was now pushing six, rush hour still rocking. She pushed the chair back and stuck her head into Carlson's office. "Don't think too long," she told Noel. "If we're going to make the last flight to San Antonio we'll need to get going soon. Like, very soon."

Noel nodded.

"In the meantime," Dana added, "let's put out an alert to all the border crossings. Make sure all agents are watching for a white Nissan."

***

With Taraneh by her mother's side in the patient room, Amir was in the visitor waiting room, leafing through a National Geographic magazine, when Ken Leach returned his call. The attorney was shocked to learn Laleh had been admitted. "I'm so sorry, Amir. I've been in court all day. How is she?"

"She's stable. They're keeping her overnight. I'm still at the hospital with her."

"I'm so sorry. I can only imagine the stress she's been under."

"I called you earlier because our housekeeper told me the cops were at our house."

"Why?"

"I thought maybe the judge had reversed the decision on my father, that dad was coming home."

"No. There'd have to be another hearing for us to get a reversal."

"I know that now. They spoke to her and she told them my mother and I were here and they came and spoke with me."

"About Farzad?"

"No. About Mahmoud, my cousin."

"What about him?"

"The Secret Service are looking for him."

"The Secret Service? What the hell's that about?"

"I don't know. He's in some kind of trouble."

"Why are they talking to you?"

"He's staying with us."

"What did you tell them?"

"I told them what I know. He showed up on Monday, says he's going to Mexico, wants to see Dad so he hangs around hoping the bail hearing goes our way."

"Okay, listen Amir. I don't know anything about this cousin of yours, but please do me a favor. Don't talk to the cops, Secret Service, FBI, whoever it is, without me present, okay?"

"I called you before they talked to me but I couldn't reach you."

"Yeah, I know, I know. Next time tell them you want your attorney present. Can you do that for me?"

Amir rolled his eyes. "Yes."

"And one more thing. Tell your housekeeper not to talk to anyone either."

"Okay."

"Let me know if anything else happens. And please update me on Laleh's status."

"Okay. Bye."

"Bye."

Amir hated people telling him what to do, but he also hated not having had the presence of mind to tell the Secret Service agents he wanted his attorney present before he answered their questions. That was his bad.

He looked in on his mother and found her sound asleep. Taraneh was dozing on a chair. One of the nurses on duty told him they expected Laleh to sleep through the night. He decided there was no longer any point in him being there. It wouldn't take him but fifteen minutes to return to the hospital if the need arose. He asked the nurse to tell his sister he would be at home if she needed him. He requested an Uber car and found it waiting when he got downstairs.

**

Mahmoud adjusted the sun visor to block out the glare from the setting sun. A sense of relief at the impending darkness mitigated his low spirits as he approached Laughlin Air Force Base on the eastern outskirts of Del Rio. As the light faded he would become harder to spot, and with hours still to go, he felt that the riskiest part of today's drive was now behind him. He had meticulously researched his exit route before he had left Virginia, and he knew exactly where he was going and why he was going there. It had not escaped his attention that after Laughlin AFB, the Border Patrol was the city of Del Rio's second-largest employer, housing two large stations and the headquarters of the Del Rio sector. That same research had informed him that the mission of the U.S. Border Patrol, a sub-agency of the U.S. Customs and Border Protection, itself a component of the U.S. Department of Homeland Security, is first and foremost to prevent the infiltration of illegal aliens and terrorists into the United States, and to prevent the illegal trafficking of contraband and humans into the United States. Keyword: *Into*. The 20,000-plus Border Patrol agents were far less concerned with the traffic of people and drugs out of the United States, because there simply was so little of it, and what trickle existed didn't concern them. That fact was the cornerstone of his exit plan.

He took care to stay on Hwy 90 as it veered to the right after Laughlin AFB, taking him away from Del Rio proper. From here on it would be a few small towns, Comstock, Dryden and Sanderson, before Marathon, where he would turn south for the final stretch down towards the border. Discipline was still the order of the day. No speeding, no recklessness, no dropping of his guard. His backpack was on the front passenger seat next to him, the gun just inside it and within direct reach if needed. The biggest threat—apart from the lawmen—was fatigue, and he was mindful of the fact that he hadn't slept the night before. But so far the adrenaline had trumped the weariness. He popped the tab off another can of Coke and replenished the caffeine coursing through his veins.

***

Of all the calls Dana had fielded since the start of the Mike Massey affair last Friday, none caused her as much anguish as the one she received at 5:56 p.m. while still at the Secret Service office in Houston. She knew it would be so even before she answered, when she saw that the caller was her mother.

"Oh, God, Mom, I am *sooo* sorry!" Dana said when she answered.

"Are you coming to Hampstead?" her mother said. "We're all here, waiting for you to bring out the cake and sing happy birthday."

"Oh, Mom. Oh, God. I—"

"Kate and Mark and Allie are here, and I figured you're on the way but it's almost seven. Where are you?"

Dana's head dropped, and she brought her free hand to her forehead as she realized what she had done. Or what she hadn't done. Blinded by her zeal to find and stop Mahmoud Massevadegh, she hadn't called her parents' house to tell them she couldn't be there for her father's birthday. This, of all years…

"Where are you, Dana?" her mother said again.

"Mom, I'm so sorry, I had to leave town—"

"Leave town? So you're not coming?"

"Mom, I want to…I so desperately want to, but I can't."

"Why? Where are you? What's going on?"

Dana's eyes started tearing up. She got up and walked out of the office to be alone. "I can't tell you, Mom."

"Why? What do you want me to tell your father?"

"Tell him…" Dana succumbed to her emotions, a powerful cocktail of love, guilt and frustration that came through in audible sobs. "Tell Dad…I love him…and…I'll stop in first thing…" She swiped her hand across moist cheeks. "When I get back."

"I don't understand, Dana, I really don't. You didn't even call to tell us. All those years in the secret service, at least we always knew where you were!"

"I know, Mom," Dana said as she choked up again. "I'm so sorry...I'm not...I can't say anything now."

"Well, I'll go tell Dad, but...really, instead of making up you've made things worse."

"It's beyond my control, Mom." Dana paused as her voice quavered. "But I promise...I'll make it up when I get back."

"Are you safe? Can you at least tell me that?"

What an angelic soul, Dana thought. After everything, she just wants to know I'm safe. Best mother ever. "Yes," she said. "Yes, I'm safe."

"Well, alright. Sorry you're not here, but I hope you know what you're doing. You always did your own thing anyway, regardless what anyone thought."

"It's not... I love you, Mom. I'm so sorry. I love you and Dad more than you can know."

"I love you too. And so does your father. We'll try to fix things when you get home. Now I'll let you go, the others are waiting."

"Bye, Mom. Love you."

"Bye, Dear."

With the conversation over, Dana let go. She cried with abandon, a release of pent-up angst over the trident of vexation she had been parrying for the past week: her estrangement from her father, her disgruntlement with eRock, and the overarching threat posed by Mahmoud Massevadegh. They had intertwined to where the whole exceeded the sum of the parts. Cause and effect was moot; what was unambiguous, though, was that her obsession with stopping Massevadegh had accelerated her separation from eRock—not necessarily a bad thing—and had exacerbated the situation with her father, leaving her in torment. How could she have forgotten to call them and say she couldn't be there for his birthday? Even if she had remembered, how would she have explained it? Right now it was all more than she could bear, and she couldn't deal with it.

"Dana, you OK?"

Noel's voice jarred her. She hadn't noticed that he'd come outside to look for her, and to her lowest emotional ebb in memory she could now add the chagrin she felt because he'd seen her so distraught. Her response was to push past him back to the building entrance, into the lobby, then the women's restroom, where she locked herself in a toilet stall, this last haven of solitude an apt reflection of the bottomless pit her spirits had sunk to.

When she re-emerged ten minutes later, tears dried but eyes red and tired, Noel was waiting in the lobby, his face charged with concern.

"What is it that has so distressed you, Dana?" Noel said.

Dana shook her head dismissively. "Nothing," she said.

"Yeah, right. Come on. You want to talk about it?"

"No."

They stood a few yards apart, an awkward, unstable equilibrium between them.

"Do me a favor," Dana said.

"Anything."

"Call home right now. Talk to Linda and Amy and tell them how much you love them, and never, ever, ever take them for granted."

That told Noel the issue was one with her family. He knew well enough not to pry further. He nodded and said, "I will."

As the two of them were buzzed back into the office, Dana's phone chirped. It was a text message from her sister, Kate: *Really, Dana?*

Chapter Sixteen

The Federal Air Marshall Service (FAMS), easily confused with the United States Air Marshall Service (the latter a U.S. Department of Justice agency) is a Department of Homeland Security agency supervised by the Transportation Security Administration (TSA). Part of FAMS's remit is to oversee the Law Enforcement Officers Flying Armed program. Federal law enforcement officers are considered to be on duty anywhere in the United States. As such, they may carry guns on civilian aircraft by meeting four requirements: They must be able to prove current status as a federal law enforcement officer, be sworn and commissioned to enforce criminal or immigration statutes, be authorized by the employing agency to have the weapon in connection with a need to travel armed or for duty at the destination, and they must have successfully completed the TSA's Law Enforcement Officers Flying Armed training program. There was a time when Dana met the requirements, but that was no longer the case. Noel still met them, and he decided to accompany Dana to the border because he knew she would go with him or without him, and he didn't want her out there possibly confronting Mahmoud Massevadegh while she was unarmed. He simply cared for her too much to allow that to happen. Which is how the two of them ended up being driven to Hobby Airport by Tom Carlson in the middle of the Thursday evening rush hour.

Dana opted for the back seat and let Noel sit next to Carlson. She tried to switch her mind off but there was no escape from the brooding. Once again she was indebted to Noel, for they were heading to west Texas on a whim, her whim, and while she would have gone anyway, it was comforting to have him accompany her. The conversation with her mother had left her emotionally drained, and a solo drive from San Antonio to the Mexican border was not her idea of therapy. She knew Noel well enough that if she didn't feel like talking, she could tell him so and he wouldn't take it personally, wouldn't be offended. She certainly didn't want to talk in front of Tom Carlson, who she barely knew, so she decided it was OK to stay withdrawn until he dropped them off at the airport.

"First game of the opening series of the NBA finals tonight," Carlson said as they skirted downtown on the elevated section of the freeway. "Houston's up against Dallas at the Toyota Center, to our left. The so-called I-45 rivalry, because Dallas is north on 45."

"Houston's favored, right?" Noel said.

"Yeah, the Rockets had the second-best regular season record after Golden State, and I expect they should see off the Mavs without too much fuss."

Dana rolled her eyes. An attack on the national power grid was on the cards and the guys were talking basketball. All she had thought about for the past thirty minutes was *Really Dana?* Now it felt refreshing to redirect that into, *Really guys?*

Her initial reaction to Kate's text was borderline fury. Her first thought had been to reply with: *Kate, you have no right to judge me, you have no idea what's going on in my life...*but the more she thought about it the longer the text would be, the more potential for added hurt and misunderstanding. In the end she let it be. She would have to deal with the family later, straighten everything out after this Massevadegh affair was over, because right now she didn't have enough energy to deal with both, and she had to prioritize one over the other.

Going through airport security was a breeze. There was over an hour to kill before boarding, and Noel suggested they grab some dinner. Dana went along, a nicely chilled white wine sounding just what she needed to snap out of her funk.

They opted for Cajun-style at Pappadeaux Seafood Kitchen and sat at the bar. They shared fried calamari with spicy marinara sauce for appetizer. Dana ordered the blackened Mississippi catfish Opelousas while Noel succumbed to the shrimp and scallop orrechiette pasta. She asked for a glass of sauvignon blanc, he a draft beer.

"So how long do you want to stay at the border?" Noel said once their order had been taken.

She appreciated that he had given her the time and space to internalize what had made her cry earlier, and this was the right time to show him she was not only back in the saddle, but ready, willing and able to ride. "If we're not too late already, and if he doesn't show up to cross the river in the morning, then we're in the wrong place at the wrong time," she said.

"And then what? We come back to Houston?"

"Let's play it by ear. It's no coincidence that the port scanning stopped right after we discovered the drone on the Starbucks roof. He figured out we were onto him and disappeared. He's either heading to Mexico, or he's holed up in some motel in Houston. He told his cousin Mexico, but he didn't say when. But knowing we're onto him, it makes sense he would try to get across ASAP. If he doesn't try to cross at Boquillas, then I have no idea where or how." Dana paused, as if something else had just come to mind. "At least we're going to see firsthand whether Boquillas really is what the web says it is, an official port of entry that is unmanned. Hard to believe, right? I mean you have Customs and Border Protection, the largest federal law enforcement agency, with over sixty-five thousand employees, forty-five thousand agents and officers manning three hundred ports of entry, their prime mission to prevent terrorists from entering the country, and in a two thousand mile border with Mexico we have one port of entry where a terrorist can wade across thirty yards of river—or catch a ride on a rowboat, for God's sake—then stroll into the U.S. without talking to a single customs or border patrol agent? Hello? We might as well erect a billboard saying Welcome Islamic State!"

"I know. Crazy, right?"

"Obscene."

"And how did you find it?"

"Boquillas? I just googled U.S. Mexico border crossings and went through the list on Wikipedia, and there it was, the only one on the list with the word 'unmanned'. There's even a photograph of the Mexican dude with his rowboat!"

The bartender brought their drinks.

"Cheers."

"Cheers."

Wine had never tasted better to Dana. She followed up the first sip with a larger gulp, eager to feel the relaxant effect run up and down her spine. She was hungry, but with the wine in hand she didn't care how long it took for them to prepare the food.

"So, what are you going to do for work after this is over?" Noel asked, glad to see her tongue had finally loosened again.

"I'll figure something out. But it's not going to be writing and implementing access security protocols in a corporate environment. That shit suffocates me."

"Well, what do you *want* to do?"

She shrugged. "I need to do what we're doing now. Investigative work, stuff that matters, you know?"

"Maybe you should start an investigative agency." Noel suddenly chuckled. "Just don't call it MIA!"

"MIA?"

272

"McLaughlan Investigative Agency."

Dana laughed. "How about MMIA?"

Now it was Noel who didn't get it.

"McLaughlan Markovski Investigative Agency," she said wryly.

"Oh, that's good," he said with a smile. "Of course, to respect alphabetical rules it would be Markovski McLaughlan."

"Alphabet has nothing to do with it. First come, first served. Seriously, though, you're going to leave the Service at some point. Now that Amy's two, maybe time to think about it?"

Noel took a sip of his beer. He held Dana's gaze and he realized she was serious. "You never know," he said.

When their food came Dana checked her watch and saw it was 7:52. "Still half an hour to boarding time," she said. "No rush. Another round?"

"Sure," Noel said.

Dana signaled to the bartender, who winked and nodded.

***

Tom Carlson cursed out loud when he encountered gridlock on Broadway Street between Hobby Airport and the I-45 freeway. He was eager to get home so he could watch the game between the Rockets and the Mavericks on TV. He ended up stuck in neutral for the best part of half an hour due to a three-car accident with injuries at the intersection of Broadway and the feeder. His only recourse was to listen to the buildup commentary and the start of the game on the radio. By the time he finally got past the wreck and accelerated onto the freeway, the dashboard clock indicated it was 7:54. The first quarter was drawing to a close with the Rockets having built up a double-digit lead. He resigned himself to missing the whole of first half and thought he should have let Noel and Dana catch a cab to Hobby.

***

Inside Houston's Toyota Center the home crowd was rocking. Even with their star forward on the bench in foul trouble, the Rockets closed out the first quarter up on the Mavericks by thirteen points, a dream start to the first playoff game of the season. The game had started at 7:30 as scheduled, and although regulation time per quarter is only twelve minutes, with stoppages and breaks for TV commercials the first quarter ended at 7:59. While some fans made for the restrooms and concessions stands, most stayed in their seats for the start of the second quarter. Jokes were cracked about the billionaire owner of the Mavericks, who had alienated Rockets fans with disparaging words about their team. High fives and daps abound. The strains of Queen's *We Will Rock You* blared through the overhead speakers. Clutch, the team's bear mascot, strutted his stuff.

Suddenly, without warning, the music died and the lights went out.

The crowd's initial reaction was raucous, cheers and applause, as if the next item on the agenda was fireworks. But as the arena stayed unlit, people began to realize this was not part of the program.

***

Tom Carlson was back on the elevated section of I-45, downtown to his front-right, when it happened. But if the crowd at the game got a micro-view of the outage, Carlson's view was on the macro level. He watched with astonishment as the whole of the city's central business district, all 1,200 acres of downtown Houston went inexplicably, eerily, dark. The traffic on the freeway slowed down as motorists rubbernecked in amazement. Some of the older and more long-time residents among them could remember the day in April 1986 when French musician Jean Michel Jarre's open-air concert *Rendez-Vous Houston* had transformed downtown by using its skyscrapers as giant projection screens and fireworks launchpads, and they wondered if perhaps something similar was afoot that had somehow escaped their attention. But it soon became clear there were no images projected onto the buildings, and there were no fireworks to be seen streaking into the sky.

It took mere minutes for the local news helicopters to arrive and start beaming live video of the black hole bounded by I-45, I-59 and I-10. By then Tom Carlson had reached his freeway exit for Memorial Drive, and he pulled off into a parking lot and dialed Noel Markovsky's cell phone.

Noel and Dana were still at the bar at Pappadeaux when the local Fox affiliate interrupted its regular programming for breaking news about a power outage in downtown Houston. As they watched mid-meal on the overhead television screen, Noel's phone vibrated and he saw it was Carlson.

"You calling about downtown?"

"Yes. How'd you hear?"

"Watching it on TV."

"You guys still flying out?"

"Just a second." Noel looked at Dana, who was transfixed on the television. "Are we still flying out?"

She nodded without taking her eyes off the screen.

"Yeah," Noel said. "I'll call you if anything changes."

"You think it's him?" Carlson asked.

Again Noel looked at Dana. "You think this is him?"

This time she turned and looked at him with the most stoic expression he had ever seen on her face. "Two days ago his uncle was denied bail at a hearing in downtown Houston," she said calmly. "I don't believe in coincidences,"

"Yes," Noel said into the phone. "We think it's him. I'll call you."

Dana turned back to the TV and pushed her plate away.

"You don't think he's still in Houston?" Noel said.

"It's cyberspace, Noel. He could be anywhere in the world where there's a good Internet connection, and he could make something happen on the other side of the planet."

"How come not a single cop has seen him on the roads? There's been a nationwide APB out since noon, and nothing."

"I don't know. But I don't think he's in Houston. This is a great way for him to distract us while he makes his getaway, don't you think?"

"You've been right about him all along, Dana. For everyone's sake, I hope you're right again this one more time."

***

Amir Yazdi took a long shower with his phone in a waterproof Mophie case so he could hear it and answer if it rang. It was weird being alone at home with his father in a jail cell and his mother and sister in a hospital room, an unwelcome first. Leticia, bless her heart, had still been there when he arrived at the house, insisting she would spend the night to make sure he had what he needed, but he had in turn insisted she go home, and she had eventually relented.

He dried off and got dressed and thought of going out for a bite, then decided against it. The solitude felt strangely soothing. He ordered a pizza for delivery, and with the memory of this morning's hangover still fresh, he resisted the impulse to uncork a bottle of wine. He ate in quiet at the island counter in the kitchen. He considered throwing out all of the vodka in the house and expunging his mother's space of all prescription medicine containers. But it was readily replaceable, so that wasn't the answer. He had to talk to her when she came home tomorrow, try to get her to see how self-destructive her resort to numbness had been, and how close she had come to far more serious consequences.

Halfway through his meal he remembered tonight was Game 1 of the Rockets vs. Mavericks playoff series, and he turned on the television. That's when he learned that downtown Houston was without power. He had lived through two hurricanes, Katrina and Ike. A partial power outage in the city was no big deal.

He turned the TV off. Tomorrow had to be better than today. He walked upstairs to his bedroom, got in bed, and fell asleep.

***

Dryden, Texas, is still on the map more for historical reasons than anything to do with its present-day status of virtual ghost town. What was in its heyday a community of 100 residents in the Chihuahuan desert of southwest Texas, Dryden's population has since dwindled to a dozen people. Which, Mahmoud thought, suited him just fine. He had figured he would get there around nine, figured it would be a good time and place to pull over, get out of the car, stretch his legs and find out how his plan for downtown Houston had panned out. He was tired and sleepy when he finally got there, but the good news was he was still undetected by the law, and ever closer to the border. The bad news was his cellphone showed no service. The next community was Sanderson, twenty miles down the road. Weary though he was, he didn't even bother getting out of the car to stretch in Dryden. He decided instead that would have to wait another twenty minutes.

Four miles before he reached Sanderson the inevitable happened. The combination of lack of sleep and driver fatigue caught up with him. He nodded off at the wheel, only for a second before he jerked his head back up, but it scared him witless. The realization of how close he had come to disaster was shocking. He would have stopped right then and there, but he pushed on for two reasons: First, the shock had given him second wind and revived him. Equally important, he knew Sanderson was now just a couple of minutes away. He rolled down his windows, turned the radio on, cranked up the volume and started drumming to the beat of the music on the steering wheel. Up ahead the welcome sight of lights flickered into view.

Sanderson was no Dryden, no ghost town. As he drove into town he passed a Budget Inn on his right, an RV park on his left, several eateries and a Baptist church. 1st through 5th streets on his right suggested a residential area several blocks deep. He drove past the Pecos County State Bank and wondered if they had an ATM machine. Next up on his left was Stripes. He pulled in for gas. He put the nozzle in the tank filler neck, pulled the handle valve to start the flow, and lowered the catch for auto-fill. With both hands free he checked his phone and found the signal was strong. He accessed chron.com, the Houston Chronicle's website, and what he read delighted him. The downtown area had suffered a power outage that was still in effect. Water systems had lost pressure, the playoff game at the Toyota Center had been

278

abandoned, cellular service was interrupted as mobile networks were overloaded, the METRO rail service between downtown and the Medical Center had shut down, there were several reported failures of backup generator systems. Traffic lights had been knocked out, and regular operations at hotels and restaurants had been disrupted. The fire department was now reporting that all stalled elevators in downtown's high-rise buildings had been cleared of trapped passengers, and the area was teeming with police officers to maintain law and order.

It was all unbelievably thrilling. The confirmation of his ability to wreak havoc from a remote location was nothing short of exhilarating.

He paid for the gas and some snacks and pulled away from the well-lit area immediately around Stripes. There were two motels across the street, Outback Oasis and Desert Air, but he had long decided against motels. His options were drive on right now, as he had originally intended when he fled from Houston, or call it a day, get a good night's sleep in Sanderson, then complete the journey in the morning. That was the safer option. He was still several hours' drive from where he would cross the border into Mexico, too big a risk considering how tired he was. He had made great progress towards the border today, but he was spent. This was no time to tempt fate. He drove around Sanderson some more, passed Slim's Auto Sales & Wrecker Service on his left, then turned right off 90 onto Cam Al Arroyo. He came upon a few roads to his left that were dead ends with no homes or businesses on them. He picked Piedras Street, two blocks removed from I-90. He parked at the end of Piedras, killed the engine and the lights, locked the doors and set his phone alarm to 5 a.m. He slid the seat back all the way and pushed the seatback down as far as it would go. He placed his

279

backpack on his lap, put his hand on the gun inside it, and closed his eyes.

In the distance, a dog barked. He tried to ignore it but it persisted. He opened his eyes and sat up, suddenly spooked. What if they were closing in on him right now, without him being aware of it? He cracked the window open and listened. Everything was still; only the dog's barking pierced the night. Why doesn't someone shut it up? Was it a stray, perhaps? What if it sensed there was a new car in the neighborhood and came and barked up a storm right here? He could shoot it, but people would hear the gunshot. No, he would move, it was that simple. It was the darkness and the stillness that spooked him. And the mind plays games. They were not closing in on him because they didn't know where he was. He dropped the window all the way and stuck his head out. Nothing. He was alone. The westerners had this expression: So close and yet so far. Tomorrow he would cross into Mexico, and in the days to come, he would serve America its comeuppance.

He should never have touched Taraneh or allowed her to touch him. Just as abstinence nourishes the soul, so does indulgence corrupt it. The way of purity for both of them would have been to first get her parents' blessings, then allow their mutual attraction to blossom and, at the right time, to be consummated. But now it was too late for any of that.

He closed his eyes again and for the hundredth time since leaving Houston made a solemn vow to his Almighty Creator that he had learned from his sins and would never again stray from the path of righteousness.

The dog stopped barking. Another sign from *Khoda*.

***

250 Miles east-southeast of where Mahmoud succumbed to tiredness, Southwest Airlines flight 1938's pilot eased his Boeing 737 down with practiced precision and taxied to the gate with characteristic brio for yet another on-time arrival. The passengers that streamed off the aircraft looked typically sapped, but two in particular had expressions that portrayed a resolve to resume a mission as yet unfinished. Not that Dana and Noel cared if anyone noticed, for their minds were singularly tuned to the task at hand.

Noel called Tom Carlson. There had been no reported sightings of the white Nissan at any of the border crossings.

With no baggage to claim they made straight for the rental car shuttle bus curb. On the way to picking up a Chevy Sonic at Budget, Dana checked the driving directions on her iPhone. They could either take I-10 west to Fort Stockton, then Rte. 385 south via Marathon to Boquillas, or take what looked like a more direct route on Rte. 90 to Marathon, then 385 to the border. The I-10 option was 457 miles but would take around seven hours, whereas going on Rte. 90 would be 418 miles but take closer to eight hours. It was going to be a slog either way. When she bounced it off Noel they both agreed driving time trumped distance. I-10 was more miles but higher speeds and less time, so it was the easy winner. They agreed on a two-hour rotation, the hope being that each would be able to grab some shuteye when the other was driving. Dana was the more wired of the two, so she would drive first. On the bus to Budget she went online for an update on downtown Houston, and what she read made her ever more determined to wrap her hands around Mahmoud Massevadegh's neck and wring it for all she was worth. Limp and lifeless was the only way that lowlife deserved to be.

It quickly became clear to Noel that he wasn't going to be able to sleep, at least not on this first rotation. He adjusted the seatback

281

to upright and turned on the radio. Dana suppressed a yawn. It was too early for that. The realization set in that they would have to drive through the night to get to Boquillas before sunrise, and it struck Dana how far out on a limb she was taking them. Self-doubt brought a fear of futility and, worse, ridicule. She believed in visualizing success, always had, but now she found herself visualizing tomorrow morning with no Mahmoud Massevadegh anywhere to be seen. It was a depressing thought, an outcome that threatened to rankle her for the rest of her days if it materialized. This was a battle of wits, and the notion of failure was unthinkable.

"What are you thinking?" Noel asked.

"I'm thinking I am never going to forget you doing this for me, Noel. Jumping in blind with me, going on this…what might be the quintessential wild goose chase through the deserts of west Texas. I'm thinking I'm glad we didn't tell the FBI guys what we're doing because they might have laughed us out of the room. I'm thinking about how I'm going to feel if they catch him in Houston while you and I are out here. Will I be more happy or angry? I don't know, Noel, I really don't know. Damn, that's bad, isn't it?"

"Don't be too hard on yourself, Dana. Truth be told, I think there's less than a five percent chance we're going to find him out here, but even with those odds, I feel good about not just sitting back in Houston waiting for him to make the next move. Besides, we've been down blind alleys before, it goes with the territory, right?"

The fading lights of San Antonio began in the distance behind them added to the sense that they were chasing a shadow they couldn't see. Noel pinpointed their location on his iPhone map and scrolled ahead, looking at the names of the towns they'd be passing on their odyssey out west. He suddenly laughed out loud. "Wouldn't you know it!" he said. "Way up ahead, before we hit

Fort Stockton, there's a town off to the north of the freeway called Iraan. Two A's."

"You're kidding me!"

"Wouldn't it be something if he were hunkered down there for the night? Maybe he believes in karma."

"Oh, I think he believes in karma," Dana said. "I just hope he's on a bad karma trip that catches up with him and takes him to another world where he gets whupped and skewered."

"I'm hoping he's going to get whupped and skewered right here in this world, and it's going to be us doing it."

"Amen!"

They took turns driving as planned, and eventually tiredness came into play and they traded fitful bouts of sleep. The miles rolled by; Thursday lost out to Friday. At Fort Stockton they turned south onto 385, and a newfound solitude made the freeway they had left behind seem riotous in comparison. At one point, when Dana was driving, she noticed that Noel was looking at her intently. "What?" she said.

"If it really is none of my business," he replied, "tell me and I'll back off. But I can't stop wondering what it was that made you so upset back there in Houston."

There was something about the mood—just the two of them in a little car out in the middle of nowhere, total darkness but for the light from the headlamps—that drove Dana to open up. She sighed and told him. She started with the fact she'd missed her father's birthday without even calling him, and it unraveled from there in reverse chronological order all the way back to her childhood and her sense that she could never seem to do anything to garner her father's approval, and that with time it had become ever clearer that he favored her sister. Noel was a great listener, smart enough to realize she was probably pouring her heart out like she might never have done before—on this subject, at least—and letting her get it all off her chest. When she had said it all she resisted the inclination to repeat herself and just stopped talking.

"For what it's worth, Dana," Noel said, "I think you being here doing what you're doing is the right thing. But when we get back to D.C.—"

"When we get back to D.C. I'm going straight to my parents' house and I'm staying there as long as it takes to mend things with him," she interjected.

Noel nodded and said: "Good. I'm sure everything will be all right. Your heart is in the right place. If he knew what you're doing down here, he would understand."

"Yeah, I'm of a mind to tell him. If that's what it takes, I'll tell him. Hopefully we'll have the right ending to talk about."

They reached Marathon at 3:40 a.m. with Dana still at the wheel, and she thought the town was aptly named but for the fact they still had forty miles to go before making Big Bend National Park, then even farther than that to the border and Boquillas. But now it felt like they were within touching distance of the finish line.

Dana knew they had finally made it when she drove by the Rio Grande Village Visitor Center, then the Rio Grande Village Store, both moribund for the night. She woke Noel, who sat up, rubbed his eyes and peered through the windshield like a child at an aquarium.

"I'm half expecting John Wayne to appear on a horse with a Winchester and demand to know where we're going," Dana said, excitement in her voice now.

Noel laughed. "Or maybe the ghost of John Wayne!" he said. He checked his cell phone. "No signal down here."

"I had a signal like, just fifteen minutes ago," Dana said. She checked her phone. "Yeah, my signal's gone too."

The came upon the Rio Grande Village Campground right where Noel's map said it would be. "Shall we drive through it and see if there's a White Nissan anywhere?"

"Of course."

Dana drove slow and kept the engine noise at a purr so as not to wake anyone up. There was a smattering of tents, a few cars, but no Nissan.

"Let's go to the actual border crossing point," Dana said. "It's only a mile down the road."

The road gave way to a dirt track, and Dana was now more than ever grateful she had Noel with her. He navigated them around to where the track suddenly turned right toward the river, and they were there, at the farthest point they could go toward the water in a car. The rest of the way was a hundred yards or so of footpath between the trees. The Port of Entry building was on their right, a dozen or so parking spaces on their left. No sign of a Nissan anywhere.

"Okay," Dana said, "I say we park here where we can see anyone approaching the crossing point from our side, and we call it a night. Come break of day, we can either stay here or walk down to the river or maybe spread out, do both."

"Agreed," Noel said. There was not much else they could do in the darkness.

Dana backed the car into a space, turned off the lights and killed the engine. The quiet was eerie, the total darkness foreboding. They yawned in succession.

"Shall I set the alarm?" Noel said.

"The light will wake me," Dana replied, "but let's not take any chances. Let's both set alarms for six."

"Here's to a successful hunt tomorrow."

"Yes."

Dana could have gone to the restroom; she assumed there was one in the Port of Entry building, but she wasn't about to fumble around in the darkness looking for it, and she wasn't about to ask Noel to come with her, so she decided to wait for daylight. It was manageable. Besides, who knows what might be out there? Maybe Mahmoud Massevadegh. *Hopefully* Mahmoud Massevadegh. For sure, scorpions, lots of them. Of course she could wait till daylight!

Chapter Seventeen

The crowing of a distant rooster nudged Mahmoud's mind into consciousness before his phone alarm could jar him awake. He sat up, propped himself on one arm and looked around. It was still dark, but a faint reddish hue on the eastern horizon told him the rooster had timed it to perfection. He wondered how roosters did that. It occurred to him this was the first rooster he had heard in America. It was ironic that it should happen on his last day in the country. He took it as an omen, a message from above that all was well, that he was being watched after, that he should get going while the going was good. Pity the infidels. They do not receive God's messages because they do not open their hearts and minds to them.

He adjusted the seatback to driving position and sipped water from the bottle on the passenger seat. He reached into a side pocket on his backpack and retrieved his toothbrush and a tube of toothpaste. He stepped out of the car, taking the now half-full bottle of water. He brushed his teeth, and used the last of the water to splash his face and wash the sleep out of his eyes. He had taken a handful of paper towels from the supply next to the gas pump at Stripes yesterday, and he used two to dry his hands and face. A large serving of coffee would be good, a couple of doughnuts would go down well too. Stripes was open 24 hours, they would certainly have coffee. The doughnuts might have to wait until he reached the next town down the road.

As the light spread he could make out the silhouettes of the houses behind him. He had slept well, free of the angst that eaten at him yesterday after witnessing God's retribution for his sins.

That was a good sign. His faith was unshakeable, for the cause and effect of the past two days was beyond question. He was now wide-awake and there was no reason to dally. He felt like an Olympic marathoner who had completed twenty-six miles in the city and had made it back to the stadium for the final lap around the track before crossing the finish line. He got back in the car and cranked the engine. Halfway through making a three-point turn he frowned. Something felt amiss. Either one of the steering components had broken, or...

He stepped of the car again and turned on his phone's flashlight and used it to check out the car. To his dismay, he saw he had a flat tire. It was front left, and as he looked closer he found the nail. Screw actually, for the Philips head was clearly visible.

He added a wince to the frown. He sighed and decided he must not let this rattle him. It was *Khoda* again, another little test. No big deal. He would reaffirm his faith by smiling and taking it in stride.

He found the owner's manual in the glove compartment and searched the index for the section that would tell him where the jack was stored and how it worked. He was surprised to learn there was no jack and there was no spare tire. The owner's manual said the car was fitted with run flat tires that could be driven for up to 50 miles at speeds not exceeding 50-mph, more than enough in most cases to allow the driver to reach a service station and have the flat repaired. Mahmoud thought this was ridiculous. Whatever happened to the traditional spare tire one could mount in fifteen minutes and resume the journey? He smiled. *Khoda* worked in mysterious ways indeed!

Decision time.

Given the circumstances, this was not the day to be testing new technology and discovering it had flaws that left him stranded on a highway in west Texas needing a tow and inviting interest from the police. He would have to get the puncture fixed here in Sanderson–Slim's Auto was just down the road, closer in fact than Stripes–before pushing on to the border. But that meant waiting until Slim's opened for the day, which was probably not before eight or nine.

Maybe he'd get his doughnuts in Sanderson after all.

He got back into the car. It was less than a mile to Slim's and the drive was surprisingly smooth, but then again he didn't go over 30-mph. The sign at Slim's said they opened at 8:00 A.M., so this was going to cost him at least two hours, almost as long as it would take him to reach the border from here. No matter.

He drove on to Stripes, bought a large cup of coffee and two doughnuts left over from yesterday's batch, and then drove back to Slim's. Technology was a double-edged sword, but all in all, considering the bigger picture of how he was going to exploit it in the days to come, it was something he could live with. He parked, stayed in the car, rolled down the windows and resigned himself to an unavoidable delay. The only predictable thing about *Khoda* was that He was so unpredictable.

***

Sitting next to each other in the car while one of them was driving was normal. But both Dana and Noel found it awkward being in such close proximity in a parked car in total darkness, seemingly in the middle of nowhere with nothing to do but wait for the sun to rise. Noel busied his mind with thoughts of home, ABC's *Good Morning America* and his morning routine around breakfast with Linda and Amy. Dana's head was filled only with visions of what might lie in store in the coming hours. She fantasized about confronting and overwhelming Mahmoud Massevadegh. Neither of them slept a wink, adrenaline trumping their fatigue.

At first light Dana announced that there had to be a ladies restroom somewhere in the Port of Entry structure, and she was going to find it. Noel needed to go too, but he told her he would wait until she got back so one set of eyes stayed peeled on the approach to the river. Sunrise was officially at 6:51, and by that time they were both back in the car, quietly anticipating what they hoped would happen.

"Say," Noel said. "If he's here, we don't want him seeing you and bolting one way or the other."

"If he sees me he'll die of a heart attack," Dana quipped.

"We don't know if he's armed, so let's assume he is."

"You want to drive back to the campground and see if he's there?"

"I think one of us needs to stay right here. He'll likely pass through here to get to the river. How about I walk down to the river while you drive back to the campground and we'll meet back here in fifteen minutes?" He checked his phone. "Still no signal down here. Damn."

Dana glanced at her phone. "Same here. Nothing we can do about that. OK. Just mind the scorpions."

Dana watched Noel walk down the dirt path towards the river for a few moments, then drove off in the opposite direction. It felt good to be on the move again. She wanted action.

When they met back at the same spot they learned they had both drawn blanks. Dana had driven around the campground and had backtracked as far as the Rio Grande Village Store and the Visitor Center before returning to the crossing point. Noel had walked down to the edge of the water and back. Neither had seen any sign of Massevadegh or his White Nissan.

"The official hours of the port of entry are nine to six," Noel said.

"What I don't get is, what's to stop someone just coming across the river and walking right past the building and disappearing into the U.S?" Dana said. "Nothing that I can see! I mean, this is effectively an honor system for entry into the country. I've never seen anything like it! All the mindless blather we hear from both sides of the immigration debate in Washington, D.C., all the money we spend on the TSA, and here it is, wide open, Welcome to America, drugs, weapons, and whatever else you'd like to bring with you."

Noel agreed. "If I hadn't seen it with my own eyes I wouldn't have believed it."

"Is the river shallow enough to wade across?"

"I don't know. I couldn't tell and I wasn't about to get in and find out."

"Well, this is disappointing," Dana said. "I really thought..." She sighed and shook her head.

"It was always a long shot," Noel said. "But it's early. He could still show up."

Again Dana shook her head. "If he planned to cross here he would be here by now. It would make sense for him to be the first one on the boat."

"It could still happen. The boat doesn't start until eight."

Dana frowned despondently. "We've come all this way, let's wait till noon. If he's not here by then..." She grimaced. She didn't want to think about being wrong.

Noel was of like mind. He had never held much hope that Massevadegh would be there in the first place. There wouldn't be much point staying past noon. "Your call," he said.

***

A pickup truck rolled up outside Slim's a few minutes after eight, and Mahmoud was disappointed to see it was driven by a woman. Slightly plump, she looked to be in her forties and wore jeans, a flannel shirt and heavy-duty leather mechanic work boots. She was unlocking the front door when Mahmoud approached her.

"Morning," she said with a grating voice.

He guessed she smoked a lot, or had had a long night, or maybe both.

"How can I help you?" Her smiled suggested Sanderson was short on dentists, but she nonetheless exuded confidence.

"Flat tire," he said.

"Let's take a look."

He had already positioned the car so that the screw in the tire was visible. She crouched down, took a look and ran a rough thumb over the screw head. "I'll have that baby outta there in no time," she said, her drawl pronounced.

He waited by the car as she disappeared into the store. The roll-up metal door next to the storefront went up, and she pushed out a jack on wheels.

"Do you need me to move the car?" he said.

"Don't need you to do a thing."

She located the jacking point and raised the front left side of the car like she was just warming up, which she probably was. She walked into the garage and brought out a pneumatic wrench attached to an air hose. The lug nuts came off effortlessly, and before Mahmoud had a chance to ask her if she needed help removing the wheel, she had yanked it off the hub and onto the ground.

Mahmoud stiffened when he noticed a police vehicle coming their way down 90. He stepped back and slipped into the store, backed in to where he could see out of the window without being seen. It was a black and white extended-cab Ford pickup truck with the words STATE TROOPER emblazoned across the front. It slowed down and pulled into the Slim's lot. Mahmoud realized his backpack was in the front seat and tried to remember if the gun was still concealed inside it.

"Whatcha workin' on there, Marcy?" the cop said, taking an interest in the car she had lifted on the jack.

"Hey, Don. Just fixin' a flat."

"How's Bud?"

"Be here in a few minutes if you want to hang around."

"Gotta do something. I'll be back."

"We'll be here."

Mahmoud watched the cop pull away and realized how hard his heart was beating.

Marcy took a pair of pliers out of a back pocket and pulled the screw out on the first try. She covered the spot on the tire with an index finger and retrieved a rasp tool from another pocket with her free hand. She inserted it in the hole and massaged it with short, quick strokes. A pre-cemented fill plug materialized out of her breast pocket and she pushed it into the hole with an insertion tool like it was something she could do in her sleep. She used a razor blade to slice off the inch of plug she'd left exposed, and Mahmoud was sure if he'd asked her to she could have shaved his face blindfolded with matching aplomb. He couldn't hide his bemusement as she lifted the wheel back onto the hub and torqued the lug nuts. She eased the car back down and wheeled the jack back into the garage, her swagger telling him she knew he was impressed.

"That'll be fifteen ninety-nine," she said, wiping her hands on a blue rag.

293

Mahmoud handed her a twenty. "If that was an Olympic sport you'd be a gold medalist."

She grabbed the bill between her index and middle fingers. "I'll get some change."

"Keep it, ma'am. You've earned it."

"Much appreciated. Don't you be speeding out there. Place is crawlin' with cops."

***

A few minutes after nine a Subaru Outback pulled into one of the parking spaces next to Dana and Noel. A thirty-something couple dressed in light khakis, safari hats and hiking boots got out, locked the car and headed towards the footpath leading to the river.

"They were at the campground," Dana said. "I remember the car."

"I'll follow them down to the water," Noel said.

He returned after ten minutes. "They're from Austin, hiking Big Bend, going across to Boquillas del Carmen for the day. As soon as they got to the river the rowboat came across and took them. I spoke to the operator, Miguel. No one crossed in either direction yesterday, and those two are the first customers today."

"Figures," Dana said with a frown. "This doesn't look good, Noel."

He didn't disagree.

***

Mahmoud passed a Big Bend Pizza and turned left off Highway 90 onto Highway 385. His planned route would bring him to the north entrance of Big Bend National Park, forty miles away, and after a further thirty miles he would reach Panther Junction, where he would turn left for the final run to the border. It seemed like he had the road to himself, other vehicles few and far between. That suited him perfectly, and he was buoyed by the knowledge that he was almost there. He wasn't taking anything for granted just yet, but he had a growing sense that he was now as good as out of the country.

He wondered how Laleh was doing and if she was back home by now. He glanced at his phone. The signal strength was good, three bars, but he could not risk using the phone to check. Besides, he didn't want to risk either Amir or Taraneh answering the house phone.

Cruise control maintained the preset speed of precisely sixty miles per hour. It was tempting to drive faster, but discipline was still key.

It was just north of Panther Junction when he first noticed what looked like a roadblock up ahead. His right foot instinctively touched the brake pedal. "What the fuck is this?" he murmured under his breath. It quickly became clear that it was indeed a roadblock, and it was manned by law-enforcement. Worst of all, there were no other cars on the road, so he was so obvious that it was too late for him to make a U-turn because they would see him and give chase. Visions of martyrdom flashed through his mind. He reached into his backpack, felt the gun and brought it out onto his lap. He reduced his speed as he approached. He could see two vehicles and four men, maybe more. This was the most serious challenge he had faced, and he quickly decided that his first shots would have to take out at least one tire on each of the cars so they couldn't pursue him. After that, he'd shoot any of them who drew weapons. From thirty yards he noticed they hadn't yet given him any indication they wanted him to stop. He kept slowing down until he was crawling along at school zone speeds. He could see his side of the street was open, and they had a barricade for the northbound traffic. Then he was close enough to see the words BORDER PATROL. Still they didn't motion for him to stop. As he drew level with them he raised his left hand in a wave and got blank stares in return. He thanked the Almighty for the tinted windows on the car. They probably hadn't even seen him waving. He kept going, passed them, and slowly accelerated away with his eyes on the rear view mirror. Their primary mission was to check northbound vehicles for illegal aliens. They watched him go. Within a quarter of a mile he knew he was in the clear. If they were going to come after him it would have already happened. He breathed easier and put the gun in his backpack.

They soon faded from view behind him. More than ever before, he wallowed in the glow of knowing that *Khoda* had his back. He lapped up the soothing scenery and anticipated with relish a quick noontime bite of lunch in Mexico.

***

Amir Yazdi awoke late on Friday morning and immediately called Taraneh. She reported that Laleh had slept well and they expected she would be discharged after her doctor saw her at 11:00 am. Amir decided to skip his classes so he could be there when the doctor came, after which he would hopefully bring his mother home. He showered and shaved and went downstairs. Leticia had already brewed a pot of coffee and had busied herself cleaning and dusting an already spotless house. Her relief when Amir told her that his mother might be coming home in a few hours was genuine.

After breakfast, Amir went online and caught up with what was happening in the world. By 10:30 he was ready to head to the hospital. He told Leticia he was leaving. He noticed his car key was missing from the key rack on the wall next to the door from the kitchen to the garage. He ran upstairs to his room and checked there.

"Leticia," he shouted as he came back down the secondary staircase to the kitchen. *"Save donde esta el llave de mi carro?"*

Leticia checked the key rack. "No, Senor," she replied.

"Shit," Amir muttered. "Never mind, I'll look for it later." He went back upstairs, found his spare key, and again told Leticia he was leaving. He entered the garage and froze. His father's car and his mother's car were there, but his was not. He opened the garage door. Taraneh's Mercedes was parked outside in its usual spot. The street in front of the house was clear, but then he didn't expect to see his car out on the street because he had parked it in the garage, like he always did. It had to have been there when they rode to the hospital in the ambulance, and he hadn't driven it since. He walked around the side of the garage past the trash containers to the space between the garage and the summer kitchen and pool house. He couldn't believe his eyes when he saw the white Nissan Pulsar with Louisiana license plates. Disbelief turned to rage when he realized he was looking at the car Mahmoud had driven to Houston in!

He spat the words out with venom: "You fucking psycho, Mahmoud! Fuck you, fuck you, *fuck you!"*

He went back into the kitchen and confronted Leticia. "Where's my car?" he shouted. "Did my cousin take my car?"

The poor woman was at a loss. "I don't know, Senor!"

Amir whipped his phone out of his pocket and called Mahmoud's mobile. The phone rang and rang and went to voicemail. He hung up and took the stairs to the guest apartment in twos. Mahmoud's suitcase and clothes were there, but of course, not Mahmoud. He ran back to his bedroom and found the Secret

Service agent's business card on his dresser. This time the phone he called was answered on the second ring. Amir irately informed Tom Carlson that his cousin, whom they had asked him about at the hospital, had apparently stolen his red BMW M3.

***

The drive was so monotonous, so peaceful, that Mahmoud was startled when his phone rang. He picked it up and saw it was Amir calling. He promptly dropped it back on the passenger seat. Sorry, dear cousin, he thought to himself, but we all have to do what we have to do.

Chapter Eighteen

Tom Carlson's first reaction was to call Noel Markovski. He tried him twice and both times went straight to voicemail, a sign Markovski must be somewhere with no signal. He left an urgent voice message and followed it up with a text message describing the car Massevadegh was now believed to be driving, and asking for a call back to confirm the message had been received and understood. Then he called Stan Toman of the FBI. Moments later, the national All Points Bulletin that had been issued previously in relation to a white Nissan Pulsar was updated to reflect an automobile held in considerably higher esteem by driving aficionados the world over.

***

By the time the rowboat ferry started its third crossing from the U.S. to Mexico, Dana had decided enough was enough. After she and Noel had observed the first couple pull up in their Subaru and make their way down to the river, an hour had gone by before the second group showed up, three young men who had also spent the night at the campground. The third party was like the first, an outdoorsy couple in a Jeep Grand Cherokee with two mountain bikes locked to a rear-mounted rack. In between, no one had crossed in the other direction, at least not anyone Dana and Noel had seen.

Really, Dana? Dana thought to herself. *Really?*

Suddenly something occurred to Dana and she said, *"Oh shit!"*

Alarmed, Noel said: "What?"

"I just realized it's April 17th! I've been so wrapped up with all of this I forgot to file my tax return on the 15th!"

"Oops!" Noel said.

"Did you file yours?"

"Last month. I've already received my refund check."

Dana let out a sigh of utter frustration. She fell silent for a few moments, uncharacteristically consumed by self-pity. "I don't know what's happening to me," she said despondently. "I'm sorry I dragged you down here, Noel. Next time talk me out of my grandiose ideas."

"Hey," Noel replied. "It was your idea to go to Houston, and you were right on. If I wanted to cross into Mexico without being seen by Border Patrol, this is where I'd do it. Maybe Massey doesn't know about Boquillas."

"Whatever. He's not here. Let's go."

Noel checked his watch. "It's almost eleven. You said we'd wait till noon."

"This is futile. For all we know he could be at the Canadian border. Let's go."

Noel started the car. "So much for the park ranger that's supposed to man this joint!"

"Right? That must be the world's most boring job. He probably doesn't have to be here full time."

They took the dirt track back to the road and didn't see another car until they passed the campground. "Shall we check it one more time?" Noel said.

"No," Dana said abjectly. "Let's not waste any more time." Her morale was at a nadir. The son of a bitch had outsmarted her, and on top of that she would now have to answer to the IRS about missing the tax return filing deadline. Could it get any worse?

Noel's presence was the only thing that kept her from venting with a good scream and cry.

They stopped at the Rio Grande Village store and bought snacks and sodas for the road. They were the only customers and found the sales clerk only too happy to chat when they went to pay. "Y'all headed across the river?" she asked.

"No, going north," Noel said. "Is it always this slow?"

"It picks up a little at times, but yeah, mostly a trickle. I like it that way, you know?"

"How far before there's a cell signal?" Noel said.

"Mile marker 16. We're at four here, so ten, fifteen minutes up the road. Whose your carrier?"

"AT&T."

"Yep, mile marker 16. Where y'all from?"

"We're headed to San Antonio."

"Well drive safe now, and come back and visit us, y'hear?"

With the store receding in the rearview mirror, Noel started looking for the next mile marker. The clerk was right about the store being at four, because the first one he saw was five. Just past marker seven he saw a car coming in the opposite direction, the first he'd seen on the road since leaving the crossing point. He instinctively edged to the right, away from the dividing line. It was an SUV, and when they passed each other the markings identified it.

"There goes the park ranger," Noel said. "It's about time!"

There was no response from Dana. Not even a shrug.

A few minutes later, after they'd passed the marker for mile twelve, he saw another car coming south, a red one. As it got closer he made out the kidney-shaped grille of a BMW, one of the smaller ones. When it flashed past he heard the distinctive growl of the exhaust note and figured it was a souped-up M model. "Now there's a set of wheels for a road like this," he said.

Dana chewed a Tostitos chip and gave him a sideways "Whatever" glance.

Noel sensed how down she was and thought he had never seen her like this. She was more than inconsolable; she was unapproachable. He had to try to cheer her up. "A few more miles we'll have cellular coverage, I'll call Tom in Houston. Maybe there's been a sighting at one of the other crossings."

Dana didn't respond.

A few more minutes, a few more miles, and the three-tone chime of his phone told him he had voicemail. He hadn't noticed they'd passed mile marker sixteen, but then he'd stopped looking. He picked the phone up and held it at the steering wheel so he could look at it and still see the road. The screen told him he had a missed call, voicemail and a text message, all from Tom Carlson. His thumbprint unlocked the phone, and he listened to the voicemail.

"Noel, Tom Carlson, 10:38 Saturday morning. Massey's not in the Nissan, he's in a red BMW M3. He took his cousin's car while the guy was at the hospital with his mother. Repeat, red BMW M3. Call me when you get this."

"*Fuck!*" Noel yelled. He hit the brakes hard, thrusting himself and Dana against the seatbelts shoulder straps.

"What?" Dana said with alarm.

"Massey's in his cousin's car. Red BMW, like the one that just passed us a few minutes ago!"

"*No way! Son of a bitch!*"

"*You were right, Dana! You were fucking right!*"

302

They both cut loose with profanities as Noel used both dirt shoulders to make a U-turn and accelerated hard back towards the border.

***

Mahmoud had studied the map so well it was etched into his brain. First up was the Visitor Center, then the store. The campground was also exactly where he expected it to be, and soon the asphalt ended and he was on a dirt track, just like Google Earth's close-up satellite view had shown. There were three cars in the spaces to the left at the end of the track, opposite the Port of Entry building. He pulled into the space between a Subaru and a Jeep Grand Cherokee. He saw the Parks & Wildlife truck on the other side of the track. He grabbed his backpack and got out of the car. With the door still open he pushed the lock button on the key FOB and tossed it onto the driver's seat. When he closed the door the car doors locked. He chuckled as he thought that Amir politics sucked, but the asshole sure had impeccable taste in cars.

Mahmoud maintained a casual pace as he ambled towards the footpath that would lead to the river. The American authorities were interested in people traffic into the U.S., they didn't care about traffic into Mexico, but he still needed to act normal and not attract attention. Moments later he was beyond the tree line and the river came into view. He saw the rowboat on the Mexico side, but there was nobody in it. Attempting to wade across was out of the question. He couldn't swim, he didn't know deep it was, and he couldn't get his backpack wet, not with its precious cargo of computer and cash. Twenty or thirty yards up the Mexican riverbank there were a couple of trucks, horses and several men sitting under a tarp, out of the sun. He waved. One of the men emerged from the shadows, put on a wide-brimmed hat and started towards the river.

Mahmoud glanced over his shoulder. All was still. No park ranger, no movement. An eerie serenity descended upon him as he realized that after all the scheming and conniving and running from the law, he was finally as good as home and dry.

***

Dana was beside herself, jockeying the elation of knowing she had guessed right with the dread that he could still elude them. High-speed driving was part of Secret Service agents' training, and Noel, a veteran, was pushing it to the limit like never before. "He can't have more than ten, fifteen minutes on us," he said.

"That's enough time for him to get across the river," Dana said.

"He can't get far. I'll go after him."

"We'll both go."

"They've got trucks and horses. If he just goes into the town, we'll catch up with him. If he gets one of the trucks to just drive him the hell into Mexico, we're screwed!"

"Which is what I'd do in his shoes. Go, Noel, go!"

The Visitor Center flashed past, then the store. They had to slow down for the corners, which Noel slid around expertly. They flew onto the dirt track and kicked up a contrail of dust behind them. When they saw the red BMW parked between the other cars Noel slammed on the brakes and came to a stop where the dirt track ended. They jumped out of the car.

"Stay in the trees, stay behind me!" Noel implored, mindful that Dana was not armed.

They tore down the footpath.

When he came through the riverside tree line Noel saw the boat, halfway across the river. Miguel, the Mexican operator, was facing the U.S. and rowing with both oars towards Mexico. His passenger was sitting in front of him, facing Mexico. Noel couldn't see that the passenger's hand was inside the backpack on his lap.

"Stop!" Noel shouted as he brought his gun up and took aim at the boat. "Massey! Stop or I'll shoot!"

Dana stood watching from the relative safety of inside the tree line. The first thing she noticed was that the bastard had shaved his goatee, but there was not a shadow of a doubt that it was Massevadegh. The next few seconds were a blur.

In one swift motion Mahmoud ducked and turned as he brought the gun up and started firing at the figure behind him on the riverbank.

Miguel saw guns and heard shots, panicked, dropped the oars and threw himself into the river.

Noel waited a split second out of fear of hitting Miguel, then squeezed the trigger when he realized Massevadegh was shooting at him.

Dana heard the shots, saw the boat rock and a body hit the water, saw Massevadegh fall backwards, and only then registered that Noel was down. She ran out from behind the trees, crouched down at his side and realized he had been hit in the right shoulder, his shooting arm. Another shot rang out and a bullet kicked up the sand two feet to her left. In a flash she had Noel's gun in her hand and swiveled as she brought it up to face Massevadegh. He was sitting in the boat now, unsteady, propped up on his left arm. A bizarre expression broke on his face when he recognized her, and his right hand came up again, his gun pointing at her. She was the last thing he saw. One more bullet discharged, this from the SIG Sauer in Dana's hand, and it put a clean hole in the middle of

Mahmoud's forehead. He slumped backwards again and moved no more.

"Did you get him?" Noel rasped.

Dana knew the park ranger would appear at any moment, the cavalry, always too late. She slipped the gun back into Noel's hand. "*We* got him, Noel," she said. "*We* got him."

She reached one hand up behind her back and pinched the clasp of her bra from over her shirt, unhooking it. She pulled the straps out of her sleeves, past her elbows and slipped her hands out of them. Then she pulled the bra down and out of the front of her shirt, and tied it tight around Noel's arm just above the wound.

"You're a real piece of work," Noel said with a grimace.

Before Dana could answer a frenzied shout rang out from behind her: *"Freeze! Drop the gun and freeze!"*

Chapter Nineteen

The official report filed by Texas Parks and Wildlife Ranger Winston Beal stated that he arrived at the scene at the Boquillas crossing to find one male adult on the west bank of the Rio Grande with a gunshot wound to the right shoulder, and one male adult on a rowboat on the river expired from two gunshot wounds, one to the chest and one to the forehead. The wounded male dropped his gun upon being told to do so. An unarmed female attending to the wounded male heeded the instructions to lie on the ground and not move. A verbal exchange with the female and the wounded male indicated that the wounded male was Noel Markovski, an agent of the United States Secret Service, a fact confirmed by the man's identification badge, and the expired man was a wanted fugitive attempting to escape to Mexico. The female identified herself as Dana McLaughlan, ex-Secret Service agent and friend of Markovski. Beal immediately returned to the Port of Entry building and requested emergency medical service teams, then together with McLaughlan administered first aid to Markovski in the form of gauze pads applied to the wound to stanch the flow of blood.

The first EMS response arrived in twenty minutes, a Frazier ambulance of the Terlingua Fire and EMS service staffed by a licensed paramedic and an EMT Intermediate. They were joined ten minutes later by a Pecos County AeroCare Medical Transport System Bell 407 helicopter certified as a mobile intensive care unit and based at the Pecos County-Fort Stockton Airport. Markovski was airlifted to the trauma center at Pecos County Memorial Hospital in Fort Stockton. The deceased man's body was returned to the U.S. A passport in his backpack identified him as Mahmoud

Reza Massevadegh, date of birth March 4, 1987, citizen of the Islamic Republic of Iran.

Chapter Twenty

More than a few times during her eighteen years with the Secret Service, Dana McLaughlan thought to herself that if she could only tell her father what she was doing to serve her country, he might see her in a different, more appreciative light, one that would change their relationship for the better. She never did because of the Service's longstanding tradition of sworn secrecy, and her determination always to remain *worthy of trust and confidence*. But on Saturday, April 18th, 2015, as she drove to her parents' home from Baltimore-Washington International Airport after arriving back from Texas, she decided she needed to—and would—buck that trend. She needed to because she believed that if the truth behind her repeat no-shows of the past few days didn't justify her behavior, nothing ever could. And she would, because she was no longer with the Secret Service, and now she was desperate to mend things with Dad.

Her strategy proved sound. Her father heard her out, understood, and forgave. He called her his prodigal daughter, and she bent with the wind and let the biblical analogy pass. She thanked him when he told her that his prayers for her had put God on her side. She consciously left Cain's wife and Lott's daughters out of the conversation. She stayed the whole weekend, and when she headed home to Reston on Sunday evening, it was with a mind at peace.

The tranquil mindset lasted all of a couple of days. The immense satisfaction she felt from having thwarted Mahmoud Reza Massevadegh's plan to unleash a widespread attack against the U.S. power grid was less than whole because Dana found herself beset by the awareness that there were still unanswered questions. Massevadegh had shrewdly trumped all of the law-enforcement agencies searching for him on Texas roads by stealing his cousin's car for his final push to the border. Were it not for Amir Yazdi's decision to cooperate with the Secret Service, Massevadegh would have disappeared into Mexico. But how was it that the son of a bitch changed his National rental car so soon after the APB was issued for the Volkswagen Jetta he had originally rented at Dulles Airport? And how was it that the Nissan Pulsar that was eventually retrieved from the Yazdi's house in Houston had Louisiana license plates, instead of the North Carolina plates that were on it when National delivered it to Massevadegh in Raleigh? Dana couldn't suppress the nagging suspicion that the answers to those questions lay behind Massevadegh's ability to evade capture as he drove from Northern Virginia to Texas.

A brief Gaussian episode of out-of-the-box staring at the ceiling didn't help, so she resorted to meditation. Twenty minutes on her *zafu* cushion rid her of the incessant mental churn, and when she emerged from the oblivion she sat down at the dining room table and drew up a timeline of events, starting with the drone attack against the Dominion power line.

- Friday 10th: Drone attack. Visit with Sheriff Hart, call to 3D Robotics, FBI involved, call to Noel, learned MM rented VW from National. ATM jackpotting attack in N.C.
- Saturday 11th: First meeting with Noel. Noel visits with professors at GMU. Meeting with Hart & FBI in Manassas. MM switches rental cars in Raleigh (as reported by National).
- Sunday 12th: Second meeting with Noel. Report typed for presidential briefing. Drive to National Car Rental at

Dulles. Meeting with Vergas at GMU re MM's *Rating the Grid* paper.

- Monday 13th: Quit at eRock. Read MM *Grading the Grid* paper.
- Tuesday 14th: NSA request put in. Infragard notification.
- Wednesday 15th: NSA call log from Noel. Decision to go to Houston.
- Thursday 16th: Arrive in Houston. Starbucks. Hospital with Yazdi kid. Learn about Mexico. Fly to San Antonio.
- Friday 17th: Shootout at Boquillas.

Dana zeroed in on when Massevadegh switched from the VW to the Nissan. According to National, that happened on Saturday the 11th. Next she figured it would make sense that Massevadegh switched the Nissan's plates from North Carolina to Louisiana plates while he was in Louisiana, either Sunday or Monday because he must have arrived in Houston on Monday or Tuesday.

She poured herself a glass of wine and had the first few sips while staring blankly out of the kitchen window. She came back to the dining table and looked again at her timeline. There was only one possible common denominator between the two events. Now was the time to bounce this off Noel. She picked up her phone and called him.

"How's that shoulder feeling?" She said when he answered.

"Hey, Dana. Still a bit sore, but coming along nicely. How are you?"

"Good, good. I need to pick your brain. Is this a good time?"

"Go ahead."

"You remember that Sunday when we went to National at Dulles, and as we're driving back you get that call from Vergas at

GMU and we go and see him and he gives you that paper Massevadegh wrote?"

It was all still fresh in Noel's mind. "Yes."

"And while we're talking with Vergas you get the call from the manager at National, and he tells you Massevadegh switched cars in Raleigh."

"Yes."

"And then you told me about it."

"I must have, yes."

"And Vergas heard you telling me about it."

"I... I don't know that, but I guess if I told you and he was there he would have heard."

"You did tell me, and he was standing right there, so he heard what you said."

"Okay."

"And you had met Vergas the day before, right?"

"Let me think..."

"That was Saturday, right after the first time we met for breakfast at the diner."

"Uh...yeah. I think that's right."

"That first time you met him, when you were there at GMU, we had already learned he'd rented a VW from National, right?"

"I don't remember, Dana."

"Yes, we had. We found out about the rental car on Friday, and on the next day, Saturday, you and I met for breakfast then you went to GMU."

"Okay..."

"When you met with Vergas at GMU on Saturday, did you say anything about the VW?"

"I don't remember. Why?"

"You must have. Because Massevadegh switched rental cars in Raleigh after that meeting. And sometime after we met with Vergas the next day, on Saturday, Massevadegh switched the license plates on the Nissan from North Carolina plates to Louisiana plates."

"What are you getting at?"

"I think Vergas must have warned Massevadegh. That's how the son of a bitch stayed one step ahead of the APBs."

"Are you kidding me?"

"How else did he time it so perfectly? Both times we put out an APB he changed either car or plates and stayed invisible to the cops."

"God damn! Where'd you come up with this shit, Dana?"

"Think about it, Noel! The guy makes it all the way to Houston without being stopped despite all the cops looking for him! Same thing from Houston to Boquillas, we were looking for the wrong car! If it hadn't been for his cousin calling Carlson and telling him, we wouldn't have known Massevadegh was in that red BMW, and he would have got away."

Noel was silent as he thought about it. The one thing he knew for certain was that he didn't want to be second-guessing Dana McLaughlan.

"Say something," she said.

"You want me to get Vergas' phone call log from the NSA?"

"He wouldn't have used his phone. We're not dealing with dummies."

"What, then?"

"I say it's time for another visit with professor Vergas."

"And do what? We can't just casually ask him if he aided and abetted Massevadegh. If it's true he's not going to admit it."

Noel was right and Dana knew it. "We could bring him in for formal questioning," she said. "Or…"

313

"Or what?"

"I'm thinking."

"Uh-oh!"

"I'd love to be able to take a peek at Vergas' computer."

"What are you looking for?"

"I don't know. Just a hunch."

"The first time I went to GMU, on that Saturday after breakfast with you, I met Vergas and the chairman of the electrical engineering department. I found him on their website. I have his card somewhere. Mitchell. I could call him and see if he'll let us look at Vergas' computer."

"Noel, I know when we were in Boquillas I told you next time talk me out of my grandiose plans, but I promise you this time you won't get shot."

"I'll call Mitchell and call you back."

Dana poured another glass of wine while she waited. Once again she was high on the thrill of the hunt. Once again she could be wrong, but she knew she had earned the benefit of the doubt, and she knew Noel thought so too.

Noel called back within minutes, and what he said gave Dana goose bumps. "I got a hold of Brandon Mitchell. Daniel Vergas resigned his position at GMU last Monday, two days ago!"

"No way!" Dana said. "Did he give a reason?"

"He told Mitchell it was an urgent personal situation. Family. Mitchell hasn't seen him since."

"Unbelievable!"

"Mitchell's going to give you access to Vergas' computer whenever you can get over there. I told him you're a colleague."

"I can go now!"

"I'll call him again and make sure he's expecting you. I'm going to give him your phone number and ask him to call you so he can tell you where to go."

Dana sipped the last of the wine in her cup. She'd had two glasses. With the new burst of adrenaline she was not close to being too impaired to drive. "I'm leaving now," she said.

Brandon Mitchell told Dana where to park and greeted her at the entrance to the Long & Kimmy Nguyen Engineering Building. He took her directly to what had been Daniel Vergas' office, now still vacant pending the position being backfilled. He logged into the desktop machine, an Apple iMac, and watched as Dana searched for one particular document. It took a few tries, but eventually she found the *Grading the Grid* paper Vergas had given Noel a copy of. Dana held her breath as she right-clicked on the file. A window opened with multiple options, and she clicked on the fourth from the top, *Get Info*. A new window popped up, also with options. Dana clicked on *General*. Now she had the information she was looking for:

Kind: Office Open XML word processing document
Size: 87,346 bytes (90KB on disk)
Where: Macintosh HD > Users > danielvergas > Documents
Created: Saturday April 11, 2015 at 4:39 PM

The date was what Dana had wanted to see, and it confirmed her hunch. But there was one more thing she could do to eliminate all doubt. She was high on expectation when she opened the file and the top of the first page appeared.

Grading the Grid

Presented by   : Michael Massey
Advisor   : Professor Daniel Vergas
Attending Faculty : Professor Keith Braithwaite

Dana pointed at the name after *Attending Faculty.* "Is Professor Braithwaite here?"

Brandon Mitchell looked surprised. "He should be. Let me try him."

Mitchell succeeded on the first attempt. "Keith, Brandon here," he said into his phone. "Are you in your office?"

A pause.

"Good. Can you come down to Daniel Vergas' office? Someone here wants to speak with you."

Mitchell nodded to Dana as he hung up the phone. "He'll be here momentarily," he said.

When Keith Braithwaite appeared a few minutes later Brandon Mitchell made the introductions. Dana pointed at the document on the computer screen.

"Professor Braithwaite, do you recall attending the presentation of this paper by Mike Massey on October 23rd, 2012?" she said.

Braithwaite looked at the screen. "October 2012. That was two and a half years ago."

"Yes."

"I don't know. Let me see." He took over the mouse and slowly scrolled down through the document." Eventually he straightened up, stepped back and shook his head. "I can't say I remember that one."

"Do you think you would have remembered if you had attended it?"

"Yes, I think so. It's the topic, you know? I'd expect that I would have remembered it."

"Thank you," Dana said, her fears confirmed. "Thank you both."

She waited until Braithwaite had left before turning again to Mitchell. "Help me get this straight, professor. I read this paper, and I want to be sure I understand what it says. If you wanted to take down large sections of the power grid for a long time, you'd target the large transformers, right?"

"That's exactly right. Disable enough of the very high voltage transformers and you'd paralyze the country for a long time. It would be catastrophic."

"And that's because it would take a long time to replace them and there aren't any spares lying around, right?"

"Yes, it takes many months to build a transformer of that size. There are a few spares at some of the utility companies, but only a small number."

"So I understand you could attack transformers physically, like with bombs, but how would a hacker destroy transformers?"

"Well, the surest way would be to disable the protection system, relays and surge protectors and the like. They are there to protect the transformers from damage due to system faults, over-currents, power surges, that kind of thing. With no protection, the transformers' key components become vulnerable, the windings, the core, insulation, bushings and the cooling system. The transformers are filled with oil. If the cooling system fails the temperature inside a transformer will rise, gas pressure builds up and the whole thing can explode."

"So, given all of the billions we spend on defense, why doesn't the government maintain an inventory of spare transformers to reduce the length of an outage?"

"Great question. Mainly because we've never had a situation where they've been needed. If it happens once, that will all change. Of course the grid and all the transformers out there are not owned by the government, and we don't run budget surpluses, but, yeah, all it will take is one serious incident and the politicians will wake up."

"It's hard to believe. And we're always going to be beholden to this power grid of ours?"

"It's not just our grid, it's the same everywhere. The national grids are the product of the way the generation and distribution of electricity evolved from scratch."

Dana couldn't hide her concern with what Mitchell was saying.

"There are new technologies that show long-term potential to change that," Mitchell continued. "But not on a wide scale in the foreseeable future, so the grid isn't going anywhere."

"What new technologies?" Dana said.

"So, the grid is a hub-and-spoke model," Mitchell explained. Centralized generation, distribution outward to the consumers, then interconnection between networks. We're seeing some innovative alternatives being developed...a distributed generation model in which electricity is produced at the points where it is consumed. Google Bloom Energy, you'll see an example of what I'm talking about."

Dana made a mental note to do so later. "Do you have an address on file for Daniel Vergas?" she said.

"Yes, of course." Mitchell used Vergas' computer to access a database and jotted the address down on a Post-it note that he handed to Dana.

"Thanks again," she said. "You've been most helpful."

She called Noel as soon as she stepped outside the building. "That's a bogus paper," she said. "It was created on Saturday April 11th, after you met with Vergas. He created it. We know Massevadegh didn't because he was already on the run. Vergas created it so he could call you and give it to you and hope you'd see that Massevadegh had downloaded tools like Shodan and HAVEX because they were relevant to a scholarly paper he wrote. It was icing on the cake when you got the call from National and told me he'd switched cars. Vergas called him as soon as we left and warned him that we knew, so Massevadegh knew to switch plates. Vergas was on his side."

"Son of a bitch! Dana, you're fucking brilliant!"

"Here, take down Vergas' address and have it checked out. I'm betting he's cleared out of there. I'm betting he's gone."

She dictated the address and hung up.

When Noel called Dana back he confirmed that once again, her hunch had proven true. Daniel Vergas was nowhere to be found. "And for good reason," Noel added. "I got a warrant and had a search done on airline passenger manifests. On Tuesday, April 21st, the day after he resigned his position at GMU, Daniel Vergas caught a Copa Airlines flight to Caracas via Panama."

"Caracas?"

"Venezuela."

"That's Hugo Chavez, right?"

"It was, until he died in 2013. But get this, just a few months ago, in March, Obama declared Venezuela a national security threat."

"Oh, shit,"

"Declaring a country a national security threat is the first step before starting a sanctions program. We did that with Iran."

"Shit!"

"Shit is right!"

"Is Vergas Venezuelan?"

"He must be. And the scary part, it looks like he was mentoring Massevadegh. A Venezuelan and an Iranian, both experts on the power grid and its vulnerabilities."

"You know what this means," Dana said. "It means we've taken Massevadegh out of the picture, but the picture itself is still intact. The threat is still there, and the specific threat we know about, Daniel Vergas, is offshore."

"I'm afraid you're right."

"So what do we do now?"

"I don't know that there's much we can do other than make sure the president knows what we know. We spend billions on defense, it's time we spent millions building up an inventory of transformers and generators, because I think it's not a matter of if, it's a matter of when."

"Damn it, Noel. Just when I thought I could get on with my life."

"You can, Dana. What was that you said about MMIA? You remember, when we were at the airport in Houston."

"Oh, yeah. McLaughlan Markovski Investigative Agency."

"Markovski McLaughlan. Alphabetical order, remember?

Dana smiled to herself. "I remember I never agreed to that."

"But no, seriously, Dana."

Dana tingled at the thought. "Seriously, Noel? Fifty-fifty."

"Deal," Noel said.

Dana could barely conceal her delight: "Hot damn! Deal!" she squealed.

"Done!"

"And Noel," Dana added, "I say we arm-wrestle tomorrow for naming rights. We'll use right arms, and the winner calls it."

Together on the phone and separately off it, they laughed long and hard into the night.

Epilogue

Under orders from the Commander in Chief, the few U.S. law enforcement personnel who were aware of what transpired at the Boquillas del Carmen Border Crossing on April 17th, 2015, kept that information strictly to themselves.

***

While the Yazdi family in Houston would eventually celebrate the release, and subsequently, court-determined innocence, of Farzad Yazdi, Taraneh remains haunted by Mahmoud's sudden disappearance, and by how neither she nor any of the family in America or in Iran ever heard from him again. Her broken heart has yet to heal.

***

In June 2015, Iranian and P5+1 negotiation teams met in Vienna in a final push for an accord that would recognize Iran's right to civil nuclear power while preventing it from producing a nuclear weapon. As was the case in prior rounds of negotiations, the key interlocutors were American Secretary of State John Kerry and his Iranian counterpart, Mohammad Javad Zarif. At the start of their meetings Mr. Kerry told the international press corps covering the event that important differences still remained to be resolved. In his own press briefing, Mr. Zarif commented that hard work was still required to make progress and move the talks forward. But forward the talks moved, the differences were resolved, and a few weeks later the negotiations culminated in the signing of the historic agreement that came to be known as the Joint Comprehensive Plan of Action.

Neither John Kerry nor Mohammad Javad Zarif gave the rapt international audience the slightest hint of how perilously close it had all come to unraveling, just how narrowly an incident had been averted that would have caused prolonged catastrophic hardship in the United States, torpedoed the negotiations, and most likely led to a major punitive war in the Persian Gulf.

Acknowledgments

While writing this book, I leaned on to two men you never want to have to hire. I am privileged that Andy Bennett let me pick his brain. His official title at the time, Director, Center of Excellence in Digital Forensics at Sam Houston State University, could not be more apt. And I am lucky to have a friend in David Gerger, who graciously gave of his valuable time to ensure I got legal details right. Criminal defense attorney par excellence, his professional expertise far surpasses his squash prowess, which is not to belittle the latter.

While the narrative was still a work in progress, Carma Abboushi enthusiastically reviewed it and gave me excellent feedback that was integrated into the first draft. Thereafter, three sets of discerning eyes wired to scalpel-sharp minds parsed the manuscript. I am indebted to Daria Daniel, Sima Ladjevardian and Thomas Pritchard for the refinement that their efforts wrought.

Underpinning everything is the enduring love, patience and understanding that has been so foundational to my serenity for the past thirty-eight years, embodied, of course, by Rana.

33913158R00186

Printed in Poland
by Amazon Fulfillment
Poland Sp. z o.o., Wrocław